The Scandalous Summerfields

Disgrace is their middle name!

Left destitute by their philandering parents,
the three Summerfield sisters—
Tess, Lorene, and Genna—and their
half-brother, Edmund, are the talk of the *ton*…
for all the wrong reasons!

They are at the mercy of the marriage mart
to transport their family from the fringes of
society to the dizzy heights of respectability.

But with no dowries, and a damaged
reputation, only some very special matches
can survive the scandalous Summerfields!

Read where it all started with tempestuous
Tess's story
Bound by Duty

Read Edmund's story in
Bound by One Scandalous Night

Read Genna's story in
Bound by a Scandalous Secret

All available now!

And look for Lorene's story,
coming soon!

Author Note

In my Author Notes for *Bound by Duty* and *Bound by One Scandalous Night* I explain that The Scandalous Summerfields series was inspired by my mother, her two sisters and their brother. Their actual life stories are nothing like those in my books, but without intending it I realise there are similarities.

Like Genna, my Aunt Gerry was the youngest in the family. Their parents died when Gerry was still a teenager and my Aunt Loraine became her legal guardian. The three sisters lived together and took care of each other. Their sisterly bond continued all their lives. Although we never lived near Aunt Gerry, we visited her and her family every year. My mother and Aunt Loraine talked to her on the phone at least once a week, even when long-distance phone calls could be expensive.

Also like Genna, Aunt Gerry was strong, resourceful and creative. Gerry's creativity showed itself in her sewing and needlework. Several of her handmade Christmas ornaments still decorate our Christmas trees. Aunt Gerry had her share of adversity in her life, but she met adversity with strength. She could sew anything, grow any kind of flower and she knew the name of every one of them.

Like the Summerfield family, Aunt Gerry had three daughters and a son—who died tragically in his thirties. I can see parts of her in my cousins Gail, Marge and Marty, so it is a little like not losing her at all.

BOUND BY A
SCANDALOUS
SECRET

Diane Gaston

MILLS &
BOON

Published in Great Britain 2016
by Mills & Boon, an imprint of HarperCollins*Publishers*
1 London Bridge Street, London, SE1 9GF

© 2016 Diane Perkins

ISBN: 978-0-263-91738-3

Our policy is to use papers that are natural, renewable and
recyclable products and made from wood grown in sustainable
forests. The logging and manufacturing processes conform to the
legal environmental regulations of the country of origin.

Diane Gaston always said that if she were not a mental health social worker she'd want to be a romance novelist, writing the historical romances she loved to read. When this dream came true she discovered a whole new world of friends and happy endings. Diane lives in Virginia, near Washington DC, with her husband and three very ordinary house cats. She loves to hear from readers! Contact her at dianegaston.com or on Facebook or Twitter.

Books by Diane Gaston

Mills & Boon Historical Romance

The Scandalous Summerfields

Bound by Duty
Bound by One Scandalous Night
Bound by a Scandalous Secret

The Masquerade Club

A Reputation for Notoriety
A Marriage of Notoriety
A Lady of Notoriety

Three Soldiers

Gallant Officer, Forbidden Lady
Chivalrous Captain, Rebel Mistress
Valiant Soldier, Beautiful Enemy

Linked by Character

Regency Summer Scandals
'Justine and the Noble Viscount'
A Not So Respectable Gentleman?

Mills & Boon Historical *Undone!* eBooks

The Unlacing of Miss Leigh
The Liberation of Miss Finch

Visit the Author Profile page
at millsandboon.co.uk for more titles.

To the memory of my Aunt Gerry,
who was endlessly energetic, efficient and,
it seemed to me, could do just about anything.

Chapter One

Lincolnshire—December 1815

Genna Summerfield first glimpsed him out of the corner of her eye, a distant horseman galloping across the land, all power and grace and heedless abandon. A thrilling sight. Beautiful grey steed, its rider in a topcoat of matching grey billowing behind him. Horse and rider looked as if they had been created from the clouds that were now covering the sky. Could she capture it on paper? She grabbed her sketchpad and charcoal and quickly drew.

It was no use. He disappeared in a dip in the hill.

She put down the sketchpad and charcoal and turned back to painting the scene in the valley below, her reason for sitting upon this hill in this cold December air. How she wished she could also paint the galloping horse and rider. What a challenge it would be to paint all those shades of grey, at the same time conveying all the power and movement.

The roar of galloping startled her. She turned. Man and horse thundered towards her.

Drat! Was he coming to oust her from the property? To chase her from this perfect vantage point?

Not now! She was almost finished. She needed but a few minutes more. Besides, she had to return soon before someone questioned her absence—

The image of the horse and rider interrupted her thoughts. Her brush rose in the air as she tried to memorise the sight, the movement, the lights and darks—

Goodness! He galloped straight for her. Genna backed away, knocking over her stool.

The rider pulled the horse to a halt mere inches away.

'I did not mean to alarm you,' the rider said.

'I thought you would run me down!' She threw her paintbrush into her jug of water and wiped her hands on the apron she wore over her dress.

He was a gentleman judging by the sheer fineness of his topcoat and tall hat and the way he sat in the saddle, as if it were his due to be above everyone else.

Please do not let this gentleman be her distant cousin, the man who'd inherited this land that she once—and still—called home.

'My apologies.' He dismounted. 'I came to see if you needed assistance, but now I see you intended to be seated on this hill.'

'Yes.' She shaded her eyes with her hand. 'As you can see I am painting the scene below.'

'It is near freezing out,' he said. 'This cold cannot be good for you.'

She showed him her hands. 'I am wearing gloves.' Of course, her gloves were fingerless. 'And my cloak is warm enough.'

She looked into his face. A strong face, long, but not thin, with a straight nose that perfectly suited him, and thick dark brows. His hair, just visible beneath his hat was also dark. His eyes were a spellbinding caramel, flecked with darker brown. She would love to paint such a memorable face.

He extended his hand. 'Allow me to introduce myself. I am Rossdale.'

Not her cousin, then. She breathed a sigh of relief. Some other aristocrat.

She placed her hand in his. 'Miss Summerfield.'

'Summerfield?' His brows rose. 'My host, Lord Penford, is Dell Summerfield. A relation, perhaps?'

She knew Lord Penford was her cousin, but that was about all she knew of him. Just her luck. This man was his guest.

'A distant relation.' She lifted her chin. 'I'm one of the scandalous Summerfields. You've heard of us, no doubt.'

The smile on his face froze and she had her answer. Of course he'd heard of her family. Of her late father, Sir Hollis Summerfield of Yardney, who'd lost his fortune in a series of foolish investments. And her mother, who was legendary for having many lovers, including the one with whom she'd eloped when

Genna was almost too little to remember her. Who in society had not heard of the scandalous Summerfields?

'Then you used to live at Summerfield House.' He gestured to the house down below.

'That is why I am painting it,' she responded. 'And I would be obliged if you would not mention to Lord Penford that I trespassed on his land. I have disturbed nothing and only wished to come here this one time to paint this view.'

He waved a dismissive hand. 'I am certain he would not mind.'

Genna was not so certain. After her father's death, Lord Penford had been eager for Genna and her two sisters to leave the house.

She stood and started to pack up her paints. 'In any event, I will leave now.'

He put his hand on her easel. 'No need. Please continue.'

She shook her head. The magic was gone; the spell broken. She'd been reminded the house was no longer her home. 'I must be getting back. It is a bit of a walk.'

'Where are you bound?' he asked.

Surely he knew *all* the scandals. 'To Tinmore Hall.' She gave him a defiant look. 'Or did you forget that my sister Lorene married Lord Tinmore?'

He glanced away and dipped his head. 'I did forget.'

Genna's oldest sister married the ancient Lord Tinmore for his money so Genna and her sister Tess and half-brother Edmund would not be plunged into poverty. So they, unlike Lorene, could make respectable marriages and marry for love.

Genna had not forgiven Lorene for doing such a thing—sacrificing her own happiness like that, chaining herself to that old, disagreeable man. And for what? Genna did not believe in her sister's romantic notions of love and happily ever after. Did not love ultimately wind up hurting oneself and others?

The wind picked up, rippling her painting.

Rossdale put his fingers on the edge of it to keep it from blowing away. His brow furrowed. 'You have captured the house, certainly, but the rest of it looks nothing like this day...'

She unfastened the paper from the easel and carefully placed a sheet of tissue over it. She slipped it in a leather envelope. 'I painted a memory, you might say.' Or the emotion of a memory.

The wind gusted again. She turned away from it and packed up hurriedly, folding the easel and her stool, closing her paints, pouring out her jug of water and wrapping her brushes in a rag. She placed them all in a huge canvas satchel.

'How far to your home?' Rossdale asked.

Her *home* was right below them, she wanted to say. 'To Tinmore Hall, you mean? No more than five miles.'

'Five miles!' He looked surprised. 'Are you here alone?'

She pinched her lips together. 'I require no chaperon on the land where I was born.'

He nodded in a conciliatory manner. 'I thought perhaps you had a companion, maybe someone with a carriage visiting the house. May I convey you to Tinmore Hall, then?' He glanced towards the clouds. 'The sky looks ominous and you have quite a walk ahead of you.'

She almost laughed. Did he not know what could happen if a Summerfield sister was caught in a storm with a man?

Although Genna would never let matters go so far, not like her sister Tess who'd wound up married to a man after being caught in a storm. Why not risk a ride with Rossdale?

She widened her smile. 'How kind of you. A ride would be most appreciated.'

Ross secured her satchel behind the saddle and mounted Spirit, his favourite gelding, raised from a pony at his father's breeding stables. He reached down for Miss Summerfield and pulled her up to sit side-saddle in front of him.

She turned and looked him full in the face. 'Thank you.'

She was lovely enough. Pale, flawless skin, eyes as blue as sea water, full pink lips, a peek of blonde hair from beneath her bonnet. Her only flaw was a nose slightly too large for her face. It made her face more interesting, though, a cut above merely being beautiful. She was not bold; neither was she bashful or flirtatious.

Unafraid described her better.

She spoke without apology about being one of the scandalous Summerfields. And certainly was not contrite about trespassing. He liked that she was comfortable with herself and took him as he was.

Possibly because she did not know who he was. People behaved differently when they knew. How refreshing to meet a young woman who had not memorised Debrett's.

'Which way?' he asked.

She pointed and they started off.

'How long have you been a guest of Lord Penford?' she asked.

'Two days. I'm to stay through Twelfth Night.' Which did not please his father overmuch.

'Is Lord Penford having guests for Christmas?' She sounded disapproving.

He laughed. 'One guest.'

'You?'

'Only me,' he responded.

She was quiet and still for a long time. 'How—how do you find the house?' she finally asked.

He did not know what she meant. 'It is comfortable,' he ventured.

She turned to look at him. 'I mean, has Lord Penford made many changes?'

Ah, it had been her home. She was curious about it, naturally.

'I cannot say,' he responded. 'I do know he plans repairs.'

She turned away again. 'Goodness knows it needed plenty of repairs.'

'Have you not seen the house since leaving it?' he asked.

She glanced back at him and shook her head.

The grey clouds rolled in quickly. He quickened Spirit's pace. 'I think it will snow.'

As if his words brought it on, the flakes began to fall, here and there, then faster and thicker until they could not see more than two feet ahead of them.

'Turn here,' she said. 'We can take shelter.'

Through a path overgrown with shrubbery they came to a folly built in the Classical style, though half covered with vines. Its floor was strewn with twigs and leaves.

'I see Lord Penford did not tend to all of the gardens,' Miss Summerfield said.

'Perhaps he did not know it was here.' Ross dismounted. 'It is well hidden.'

'Hidden now,' she said. 'It was not always so.'

He helped her down and led Spirit up the stairs into the shelter. There was plenty of room. She sat on a bench at the folly's centre and wrapped her cloak around her.

He sat next to her. 'Are you cold?'

Her cheeks were tinged a delightful shade of pink and her lashes glistened from melted snowflakes. 'Not very.'

He liked that she did not complain. He glanced around. 'This folly has seen better days?'

She nodded, a nostalgic look on her face. 'It was once one of our favourite places to play.'

'You have two sisters. Am I correct?'

She swung her feet below the bench, much like she must have done when a girl. 'And a half-brother.' She slid him a glance. 'My bastard brother, you know.'

Did she enjoy speaking aloud what others preferred to hide?

'He was raised with you, I think?' It was said Sir Hollis tried to flaunt his love child in front of his wife.

'Yes. We all got on famously.'

She seemed to anticipate unspoken questions and answered them defiantly.

'Where is your brother now?' he asked.

'Would you believe he is a sheep farmer in the Lake District?' she scoffed.

'Why would I not believe it?' Almost everyone he knew could be considered a farmer when you got right down to it.

'Well, if you knew him you'd be shocked that he wound up raising sheep. He was an officer in the Twenty-Eighth Regiment. He was wounded at Waterloo.' She waved a hand. 'Oh, I am making him sound too grand. He was a mere lieutenant, but he *was* wounded.'

'He must have recovered?' Or he would not be raising sheep.

'Oh, yes.'

'And your other sister?' He might as well get the whole family story, since she seemed inclined to tell it.

'Tess?' She giggled but tried to stop herself.

'What amuses you?'

'Tess is married.' She strained not to laugh. 'But wait until I tell you how it was she came to be married! She and Marc Glenville were caught together in a storm. A rainstorm. Lord Tinmore forced them to marry.'

How ghastly. Nothing funny about a forced marriage. 'I am somehow missing the joke.'

She rolled her eyes. '*We* are caught in a storm. *You* could be trapped into marrying me.' She wagged a finger at him. 'So you had better hope we are not discovered.' Then an idea seemed to dawn on her face. 'Unless you are already married. In that case, only I suffer the scandal.' She made it sound as if suffering scandal was part of the joke.

'I am not married.'

She grinned. 'We had better hope Lord Tinmore or his minions do not come riding by, then.'

No one would find this place unless they already knew its location, even if they were foolish enough to venture out in a snowstorm. If they did find them, though, Ross had no worries about Lord Tinmore. Tinmore's power would be a trifle compared to what Ross could bring to bear.

She took a breath and sighed and seemed to have conquered her fit of giggles.

'I am acquainted with Glenville,' he remarked. 'A good man.'

'Glenville *is* a good man,' she agreed.

He could not speak of why he knew Glenville, though.

He'd sailed Glenville across the Channel in the family yacht several times during the war when Glenville pursued clandestine activities for the Crown. Braving the Channel's waters was about the only danger Ross could allow himself during the war, even if he made himself available to sail whenever needed. This service had been meagre in his eyes, certainly a trifle compared to what his friend Dell had accomplished. And what others had suffered. He'd seen what the war cost some of the soldiers. Limbs. Eyes. Sanity. Why should those worthy men have had to pay the price rather than he?

He forced his mind away from painful thoughts. 'I had not heard Glenville's marriage had been forced.'

'Had you not?' She glanced at him in surprise. 'Goodness. I thought everyone knew. I should say they seem very happy about it now, so it has all worked out. For the time being, that is.'

'For the time being?'

She shrugged. 'One never knows, does one?'

'You sound a bit cynical.' Indeed, she seemed to cycle emotions across her face with great rapidity.

Her expression sobered. 'Of course I am cynical.

Marriage can bring terrible unhappiness. My parents' marriage certainly did.'

'One out of many,' he countered, although he knew several friends who were miserable and making their spouses even more so. His parents' marriage had been happy—until his mother died. In his father's present marriage happiness was not an issue. That marriage was a political partnership.

'My sister Lorene's marriage to Lord Tinmore is another example.' She glanced away and lowered her voice as if speaking to herself and not to him. 'She is wasting herself with him.'

'Has it been so bad? She brought him out of his hermitage, they say. He'd been a recluse, they say.'

'I am sure *he* thinks it a grand union.' She huffed. 'He now has people he can order about.'

'You?' Clearly she resented Tinmore. 'Does he order you about?'

'He tries. He thinks he can force me to—' She stopped herself. 'Never mind. My tongue runs away with me sometimes.'

She fell silent and stilled her legs and became lost in her own thoughts, which excluded him. He'd been enjoying their conversation. They'd been talking like equals, neither of them trying to impress or avoid.

He wanted more of it. 'Tell me about your painting.'

She looked at him suspiciously. 'What about it?'

'I did not understand it.'

She sat up straighter. 'You mean because the sky

was purple and pink and the grassy hills, blue, and it looked nothing like December in Lincolnshire?'

'Obviously you were not painting the landscape as it was today. You said you painted a memory, but surely you never saw the scene that way.' The painting was a riot of colour, an exaggeration of reality.

She turned away. 'It was a memory of those bright childhood days, when things could be what you imagined them to be, when you could create your own world in play and your world could be anything you wanted.'

'The sky and the grass could be anything you wanted, as well. I quite comprehend.' He smiled at her. 'I once spent an entire summer as a virtuous knight. You should have seen all the dragons I slew and all the damsels in distress I rescued.'

Her blue eyes sparkled. 'I was always Boadicea fighting the Romans.' She stood and raised an arm. *'"When the British Warrior queen, Bleeding from the Roman rods..."'* She sat down again. 'I was much influenced by Cowper.'

'My father had an old copy of Spencer's *The Faerie Queene.*' It had been over two hundred years old. 'I read it over and over. I sought to recreate it in my imagination.'

She sighed. 'Life seemed so simple then.'

They fell silent again.

'Do you miss this place?' he asked. 'I don't mean this folly. Do you miss Summerfield House where you grew up?'

Her expression turned wistful. 'I do miss it. All the familiar rooms. The familiar paintings and furniture. We could not take much with us.' Her chin set and her eyes hardened. 'I do not want you to think we blame Lord Penford. He was under no obligation to us. We knew he inherited many problems my father created.' She stood again and walked to the edge of the folly. Placing her hand on one of the columns, she leaned out. 'The snow seems to be abating.'

He was not happy to see the flakes stop. 'Shall we venture out in it again?'

'I think we must,' she said. 'I do not want to return late and cause any questions about where I've been.'

'Is that what happens?' he asked.

'Yes.' Her eyes changed from resentment to amusement. 'Although I do not always answer such questions truthfully.'

'I would wager you do not.'

Rossdale again pulled Genna up to sit in front of him on his beautiful horse. How ironic. It was the most intimate she had ever been with a man.

She liked him. She could not think of any other gentleman of her acquaintance who she liked so well and with whom she wanted to spend more time. Usually she was eager to leave a man's company, especially when the flattery started. Especially when she suspected they were more enamoured of the generous sum Lord Tinmore would provide for her dowry than they were of her. No such avaricious gleam reached Rossdale's eyes. She had the impression the subject of her dowry had not once crossed Rossdale's mind.

They rode without talking, except for Genna's directions. She led him through the fields, the shortest way to Tinmore Hall and also the way they were least likely to encounter any other person. The snow had turned the landscape a lovely white, as if it had been scrubbed clean. There was no sound but the crunch of the horse's hooves on the snow and the huff of the animal's breathing.

They came to the stream. The only way to cross was at the bridge, the bridge that had been flooded that fateful night Tess had been caught in the storm.

'Leave me at the bridge,' she said. No one was in sight, but if anyone would happen by, it would be on the road to the bridge. 'I'll walk the rest of the way.'

'So we are not seen together?' he correctly guessed.

She could not help but giggle. 'Unless you want a forced marriage.'

He raised his hands in mock horror. 'Anything but that.'

'Here is fine.' She slid from the saddle.

He unfastened her satchel and handed it to her. 'It has been a pleasure, Miss Summerfield.'

'I am indebted to you, sir,' she countered. 'But if you dare say so to anyone, I'll have to unfurl my wrath.'

He smiled down at her and again she had the sense that she liked him.

'It will be our secret,' he murmured.

She nodded a farewell and hurried across the bridge. When she reached the other side, she turned.

He was still there watching her.

She waved to him and turned away, and walked quickly. She was later than she'd planned to be.

She approached the house through the formal garden behind the Hall and entered through the garden door, removing her half-boots which were soaked through and caked with snow. One of the servants would take care of them. She did not dare clean them herself as she'd been accustomed to do at Summerfield. If Lord Tinmore heard of it, she'd have to endure yet another lecture on the proper behaviour of a lady, which did not include cleaning boots.

What an ungrateful wretch she was. Most young ladies would love having a servant clean her boots. Genna simply was used to doing for herself, since her father had cut back on the number of servants at Summerfield House.

She hung her damp cloak on a hook and carried her satchel up to her room. The maid assigned to her helped her change her clothes, but Genna waited until the girl left before unpacking her satchel. She left her painting on a table, unsure whether to work on it more or not.

She covered it with tissue again and put it in a drawer. She would not work on it now. Of that she was certain. Instead she hurried down to the library, opening the door cautiously and peeking in. No one was there, thank goodness, although it would have been quite easy to come up with a plausible excuse for coming to the library.

She searched the shelves until she found the volume she sought—*Debrett's Peerage & Baronetage*. She pulled it out and turned first to the title names, riffling the pages until she came to the Rs.

'Rossdale. Rossdale. Rossdale,' she murmured as she scanned the pages.

The title name was not there.

She turned to the front of the book again and found the pages listing second titles usually borne by the eldest sons of peers. She ran her finger down the list.

Rossdale.

There it was! And next to the name Rossdale was *Kessington d.* D for Duke.

She had been in the company of the eldest son of the Duke of Kessington. The heir of the Duke of Kessington. And she had been chatting with him as if he were a mere friend of her brother's. Worse, she had hung all the family's dirty laundry out to dry in front of him, her defiant defence over anticipated censure or sympathy. He'd seen her wild painting and witnessed her nonsense about Boadicea.

She turned back to the listing of the Duke of Kessington. There were two pages of accolades and honours bestowed upon the Dukes of Kessington since the sixteen hundreds. She read that Rossdale's mother was deceased. Rossdale's given name was

John and he had no brothers or sisters. He bore his father's second title by courtesy—the Marquess of Rossdale.

She groaned.

The heir of the Duke of Kessington.

Chapter Two

Ross sipped claret as he waited for Dell in the drawing room. The dinner hour had passed forty minutes ago, not that he'd worked up any great appetite or even that he was in any great need of company. He was quite content to contemplate his meeting with Miss Summerfield. He'd been charmed by her.

How long had it been since a young woman simply conversed with him, about herself and her family skeletons, no less? Whenever he attended a society entertainment these days all he saw was calculation in marriageable young ladies' eyes and those of their mamas. All he'd seen in Miss Summerfield's eyes was friendliness.

Would that change? Obviously she'd not known the name Rossdale or its significance, but he'd guess she'd soon learn it. Would she join the ranks of calculating females then?

He was curious to know.

The door opened.

'So sorry, Ross.' Dell came charging in. 'I had

no idea this estate business would take so long. I've alerted the kitchen. Dinner should be ready in minutes.'

Ross lifted the decanter of claret. 'Do you care for some?'

Dell nodded. 'I've a great thirst.'

Ross poured him a glass and handed it to him.

'First there is the problem of dry rot. Next the cow barn, which seems to be crumbling, but the worst is the condition of the tenant cottages. One after the other have leaking roofs, damaged masonry, broken windows. I could go on.' He took a swig of his wine.

'Sounds expensive,' Ross remarked with genuine sympathy.

How many estates did Ross's family own? Five, at least, not counting the hunting lodges and the town house in Bath. There were problems enough simply maintaining them. Think of how it would be if any were allowed to go into disrepair. This was all new to Dell, as well. He'd just arrived in Brussels with his regiment when he'd been called back to claim the title. His parents, older brother and younger sister had been killed in a horrific fire. Ross had delivered the news to him and brought him home.

A few weeks later Dell's regiment fought at Waterloo.

'A drain on the finances, for certain,' Dell said. 'Curse Sir Hollis for neglecting his property.'

'Do you have sufficient funds?' Ross asked.

His friends never asked, but when Ross knew they were in need he was happy to offer a loan or a gift.

Dell lifted a hand. 'I can manage. It simply rankles to see how little has been maintained.' He shook his head. 'The poor tenants. They have put up with a great deal and more now with this nasty weather.'

The butler appeared at the door. 'Dinner is served, sir.'

Dell stood. 'At least food is plentiful. And I've no doubt Cook has made us a feast.'

They walked to the dining room, its long table set for two adjacent to each other to make it easier for conversing and passing food dishes. The cook indeed had not disappointed. There were partridges, squash and parsnips. Ross's appetite made a resurgence.

'I hope your day was not a bore,' Dell said. 'Did you find some way to amuse yourself?'

'I did remarkably well,' Ross answered, spearing a piece of buttered parsnips with his fork. 'I rode into the village and explored your property.'

'And that amused you?' Dell looked sceptical.

'The villagers were talkative.' He pointed his fork at Dell. 'You are considered a prime catch, you know.'

Dell laughed. 'I take it you did not say who *you* were.'

Not in the village, he hadn't. 'I introduced myself simply as John Gordon.'

'That explains why there are no matchmaking mamas parked on the entry stairs.'

Ross smiled. 'I do believe tactics were being discussed to contrive an introduction to you.'

Dell shrugged. 'They waste their time. How can I marry? These properties of mine are taking up all my time.'

How many did he have? Three?

'I'm not certain your actual presence was considered important.' To so many young women, marrying a title was more important than actually being a peer's wife. 'In any event, it would not hurt to socialise with some of your more important neighbours, you know.'

'Who?' he asked unenthusiastically.

Ross took a bite of food, chewed and swallowed it before he answered. 'They said in the village that Lord Tinmore was in the country.'

'That prosy old fellow?' Dell cried.

'He's influential in Parliament,' Ross reminded him. 'It won't hurt at all to entertain him a bit. He might be a help to you when you take your seat.'

'Your father will help me.'

'My father certainly will help you, but it will not hurt to be acquainted with Tinmore, as well.' Ross tore off some meat from his partridge. 'You are related to Tinmore's wife and her sisters, I was told.'

'They are my distant cousins, I believe,' Dell said. 'The ones who grew up in this house.'

'Perhaps they would like to visit the house again.' Ross knew Genna would desire it, at least.

Dell frowned. 'More likely they would resent the

invitation. I learned today that, not only was the estate left in near shambles, but the daughters were left with virtually nothing. My father turned them out within months of their father's death. That is why the eldest daughter married Tinmore. For his money.'

'Seems you learned a great deal.' No wonder Genna Summerfield sounded bitter.

Dell gave a dry laugh. 'The estate manager was talkative, as well.'

'Perhaps it would be a good idea to make amends.' And it would not hurt for Dell to be in company a little.

Dell expelled a long breath. 'I suppose I must try.'

Ross swirled the wine in his glass. 'I would not recommend risking offending Lord Tinmore.'

Dell peered at him. 'For someone with an aversion to politics, you certainly are cognizant of its workings.'

'How could I not be? My father talks of nothing else.' Ross refilled Dell's glass. 'I would not say I have an aversion, though. I simply know it will eventually consume my life and I am in no hurry for that to happen.'

Dell gulped down his wine and spoke beneath his breath. 'I never wanted this title.'

Ross reached over and placed his hand on Dell's shoulder. 'I know.'

They finished the course in silence and were served small cakes for dessert.

When that too was taken away and the decanter of

brandy set on the table, Dell filled both their glasses. 'Oh, very well,' he said. 'I will invite them to dinner.'

Ross lifted his glass and nodded approvingly.

Dell looked him in the eye. 'Be warned, though. The youngest sister is not yet married.'

Ross grinned. 'I am so warned.'

Two days later, Genna joined her sister and Lord Tinmore at breakfast. Sometimes if she showed up early enough to share the morning meal and acted cheerful, she could count on being left to her own devices until almost dinner time. Besides, she liked to see if Lorene needed her company. There were often houseguests or callers who came out of obligation to the Earl of Tinmore. Most were polite to Lorene, but Genna knew everyone thought her a fortune hunter. Genna often sat through these tedious meetings so Lorene would not be alone, even though it was entirely Lorene's fault she was in this predicament.

A footman entered the breakfast room with a folded piece of paper on a silver tray. 'A message arrived for you, sir.'

Tinmore acknowledged the servant with a nod. The footman bowed and left the room again.

Tinmore opened the folded paper and read. 'An invitation,' he said, although neither Lorene nor Genna had asked. He tossed the paper to Lorene. 'From your cousin.'

'My cousin?' Lorene picked up the paper. 'It is

from Lord Penford, inviting us to dinner tomorrow night at Summerfield House.'

Genna's heart beat faster. Was she included?

'We must attend, of course,' Tinmore said officiously. 'He peered over his spectacles at Genna. 'You, too, young lady.' He never called her by her name.

'I would love a chance to see Summerfield House again!' she cried.

Lorene did not look as eager. 'I suppose we must attend.'

The next day Genna was determined not to agonise over what to wear to this dinner. After all, it would be more in the nature of a family meal than a formal dinner party. There would not be other guests, apparently, save his houseguest, perhaps. A small dinner party, the invitation said, to extend his hospitality to his neighbour and his cousins.

Genna chose her pale blue dress because it had the fewest embellishments. She allowed her maid to add only a matching blue ribbon to her hair, pulled up into a simple chignon. She wore tiny pearl earrings in her ears and a simple pearl necklace around her neck. She draped her paisley shawl over her arm, the one with shades of blue in it.

She met Lorene coming out of her bedchamber.

Lorene stopped and gazed at her. 'You look lovely, Genna. That dress does wonders for your eyes.'

Genna blinked. Truly? She'd aimed to show little fuss.

'Do I look all right?' Lorene asked. 'I was uncertain how to dress.'

Lorene also chose a plain gown, but one in deep green. Her earrings were emeralds, though, and her necklace, an emerald pendant. The dark hue made Lorene's complexion glow.

Lorene looked like a creature of the forest. If Lorene were the forest, then Genna must be—what? The sky? Genna was taller. Lorene, small. Genna had blonde hair and blue eyes; Lorene, mahogany-brown hair with eyes to match. No wonder people whispered that they must have been born of different fathers. They were opposites. One earthbound. The other…flighty.

Genna put her arm around Lorene and squeezed her. 'You look beautiful as always. Together we shall present such a pretty picture for our cousin he will wish he had been nicer to us.'

Lorene smiled wanly. 'You are speaking nonsense.'

Genna grinned. 'Perhaps. Not about you looking beautiful, though.' They walked through the corridor and started down the long staircase. 'What is he, anyway? Our fourth cousin?'

Lorene sighed. 'I can never puzzle it out. He shares a great-great-grandfather or a great-great-great one with our father. I can never keep it straight.'

Genna laughed. 'He got the fortunate side of the family, obviously.'

They walked arm in arm to the drawing room next

to the hall where Lord Tinmore would, no doubt, be waiting for them. Before they crossed the threshold, though, they separated and Lorene walked into the room first, Genna a few steps behind her. Tinmore insisted on such formalities.

Lord Tinmore was seated in a chair, his neckcloth loosened. His valet, almost as ancient as the Earl himself, patted his forehead with a cloth. Tinmore motioned the ladies in, even though they were already approaching him.

Lorene frowned. 'What is amiss, sir? Are you unwell?'

He gestured to his throat. 'Damned throat is sore and I am feverish. Came upon me an hour ago.'

Lorene put her cloak and reticule on the sofa and pulled off a glove. She bent down and felt her husband's wrinkled, brown-spotted forehead. 'You are feverish. Has the doctor been summoned?'

'He has indeed, ma'am,' the valet said.

She straightened. 'We must send Lord Penford a message. We cannot attend this dinner.'

Not attend the dinner? Genna's spirits sank. She yearned to see her home again.

'I cannot,' Tinmore stated. 'But you and your sister must.'

Genna brightened.

'No,' Lorene protested. 'I will stay with you. I'll see you get proper care.'

He waved her away. 'Wicky will tend me. I dare say he knows better than you how to give me care.'

So typical of Tinmore. True, his valet had decades more experience in caring for his lordship than Lorene, but it was unkind to say so to her face.

'I think I should stay,' Lorene tried again in a more forceful tone.

Tinmore raised his voice. 'You and your sister *will* attend this dinner and make my excuses. I do not wish to insult this man. I may need his good opinion some day.' He ended with a fit of coughing.

A footman came to the door. 'The carriage is ready, my lord.'

'Go.' Tinmore flicked his fingers, brushing them away like gnats buzzing around his rheumy head. 'You mustn't keep the horses waiting. It is not good for them to stand still so long.'

Typical of Tinmore. Caring more for his horses' comfort than his wife's feelings.

Genna picked up Lorene's cloak and reticule and started for the door. Lorene caught up with her and draped the cloak around herself.

At least Lord Tinmore was too sick to admonish Lorene for not waiting for the footman to help her with her cloak.

'I really do not want to go,' Lorene whispered to Genna.

'Lord Tinmore will be well cared for. Do not fret.' Genna was more than glad Tinmore would not accompany them.

'It is not that,' Lorene said. 'I do not wish to go.'

'Why not?' Genna was eager to see their home

again, no matter the elevated company they would be in.

Lorene murmured, 'It will make me feel sad.'

Goodness. Was not Lorene already sad? Could she not simply look forward to a visit home, free of Tinmore's talons? Sometimes Genna had no patience for her.

But she took her sister's hand and squeezed it in sympathy.

They spoke little on the carriage ride to Summerfield House. Who knew what Lorene's thoughts must be, but Genna was surprised to feel her own bout of nerves at the thought of seeing Rossdale again.

The Marquess of Rossdale.

If he expected her to be impressed by his title, he'd be well mistaken. *She* would not be one of those encroaching young ladies she'd seen during her Season in London, so eager to be pleasing to the highest-ranking bachelor in the room.

Heedless of the cold, she and Lorene nearly leaned out the windows as they entered the gate to Summerfield House, its honey-coloured stone so familiar, so beautiful. She'd seen the house only from afar. Up close it looked unchanged, except that the grounds seemed well tended. At least what she could see of them. A thin dusting of snow still blanketed the land.

When the carriage pulled up to the house, Genna saw a familiar face waiting to assist them from the carriage.

'Becker!' she cried, waving from the window.

Their old footman opened the door and put down the stairs.

'My lady,' he said to Lorene, somewhat reservedly. He helped her out.

'So good to see you, Becker,' Lorene said. 'How are you? In good health?'

'Good health, ma'am,' he replied.

He reached for Genna's hand next and grinned. 'Miss Genna.'

She jumped out and gave him a quick hug. Who cared if it was improper to hug a servant? She'd known him all her life.

'I have missed you!' she cried.

His eyes glistened with tears. 'The house is not the same without you.'

He collected himself and led Lorene and Genna through one of the archways and up the stairs to the main entrance. A guidebook had once described the house:

> *Summerfield House was built by John Carr, a contemporary of Robert Adam, in the Italianate style, with the entrance to the house on the first floor.*

Genna loved that word. *Italianate.*

The door opened as they reached it.

'Jeffers!' Genna ran into the hall and hugged their old butler, a man who had been more present in her life than her own father.

'Miss Genna, a treat to see you.' He hugged her back, but quickly released her and bowed to Lorene. 'My lady, how good to have you back.'

Lorene extended her hand and clasped Mr Jeffers's hand in a warm gesture. 'I am happy to see you, Jeffers. How are matters here? Is all well? Are you well?'

He nodded. 'The new master has had much needed work done, but it is quiet here without you girls.'

Genna supposed Jeffers still saw them in their pinafores. She touched his arm. 'We were never going to be able to stay, you know.'

Jeffers smiled sadly. 'That is true, but, still...' He blinked and turned towards the door. 'Are we not expecting Lord Tinmore?'

'He sends his regrets,' Lorene explained. 'He is ill.'

'I am sorry to hear it. Nothing serious, I hope?' he asked.

'Not serious.' Lorene glanced away. 'You should announce us to Lord Penford, I think.'

How very sad. Lorene acted as if Lord Tinmore was looking over her shoulder, ready to chastise her for performing below her station with servants. These were servants they'd known their whole lives, the people who had truly looked out for their welfare, and, even though Tinmore was nowhere near, Lorene could not feel free to converse with them.

Jeffers looked abashed. 'Certainly. They are in the octagon drawing room.'

He and Lorene started to cross the hall.

'Wait!' Genna cried.

She stood in the centre of the hall and gazed up at the plasterwork ceiling. There was the familiar pattern, the rosettes, the gold gilt, the griffins that hearkened back to her grandfather's days in India. Why had she never drawn the ceiling's design? Why had she not copied its pale cream, green and white?

'Come,' Lorene said impatiently. 'They are waiting for us.'

Genna took one more look, then joined her sister. As they walked to the drawing room, though, she fell back, memorising each detail. The matching marble stairs with their bright blue balustrades, the small tables and chairs still in the same places, the familiar paintings on the walls.

They reached the door to the drawing room. Would it be changed? she wondered.

Jeffers opened the door and announced. 'Lady Tinmore and Miss Summerfield.'

Two young gentlemen stood. One, of course, was Lord Rossdale, dressed in formal dinner attire, which made him look even more like a duke's heir. The other man was an inch or two shorter than Rossdale and fairer, with brown hair and blue eyes.

Jeffers continued the introductions. 'My lady, Miss Summerfield, allow me to present Lord Rossdale—'

The Marquess bowed.

'And Lord Penford.'

But Penford was so young!

He approached them. 'My cousins. How delightful to meet you at last.' His voice lacked any enthusiasm, however. He blinked at Lorene as if in surprise and stiffly offered his hand. 'Where is Lord Tinmore, ma'am?'

Lorene blushed, which was not like her. She might be reserved, but never sheepish. Unless Tinmore had cowed her into feeling insecure in company. Or perhaps she was as surprised as Genna that Penford was not their father's age.

'Lord Tinmore is ill.' Lorene put her hand in Penford's. 'A trifling illness, but he thought it best to remain at home.'

Penford quickly drew his hand away. 'I am delighted you accepted my invitation.' He glanced past Lorene and looked at Genna with a distinct lack of interest. 'And your sister.' He perfunctorily shook Genna's. 'Miss Summerfield.'

The stiff boor. Genna made certain to smile at him. 'Call me Genna. It seems silly to stand on ceremony when we are family.'

'Genna,' he repeated automatically. He glanced back to Lorene.

'You may address me as Lorene, if you wish,' she murmured.

'Lorene,' he murmured. 'My friends call me Dell.'

Which was not quite permission for Lorene and Genna to do so.

Rossdale stepped forward.

'Oh.' Penford seemed to have forgotten him. 'My friend Ross here is visiting with me over Christmas.'

'Ma'am.' Ross bowed to Lorene. When he turned to Genna, he winked. 'Miss Summerfield.'

She felt like giggling.

'Come sit.' Penford offered Lorene his arm and led her to a sitting area, with its pale pink brocade sofa and matching chairs that their mother had selected for this room. He placed her in one of the chairs and he sat in the other.

The Marquess gestured to Genna to sit, as well.

She hesitated. 'May I look at the room first?'

'By all means,' Penford responded.

'You lived here, I believe,' Rossdale said, remaining at her side.

'I did, sir,' she said too brightly.

So far he was not divulging the fact they'd met before. He stood politely while she gazed at another familiar plasterwork ceiling, its design mimicked in the octagon carpet below. Again, nothing was changed, not one stick of furniture out of place, not one vase moved to a different table, nor any porcelain figurines rearranged. She gazed at her grandmother's portrait above the fireplace, powdered hair and silk gown, seated in an idyllic garden.

Rossdale said, 'A magnificent painting.'

'Our grandmother.' Although neither she nor Lorene bore any resemblance to the lady. 'By Gainsborough.'

'Indeed?' He sounded impressed.

Genna had always loved the painting, but it was Gainsborough's depiction of the sky and greenery that fascinated her the most, so wild and windy.

'I am pouring claret. Would you like some, Genna?' Penford called over to her.

She felt summoned. 'Yes, thank you.'

She walked over and lowered herself on to the sofa. Rossdale sat next to her.

'Does the room pass your inspection?' Penford asked, a hint of sarcasm in his voice.

He handed her the glass of wine.

Was he censuring her for paying more attention to the room than the people in it? Well, how ill mannered of him! It was the most natural thing in the world to want to see the house where one grew up.

'It is as I remember it,' she responded as if it had been a genuine question. 'I confess to a great desire to see all the rooms again. We were in much turmoil when we left.' When he'd sent them packing, she meant.

Penford's face stiffened. He turned to Lorene, shutting Genna out. 'Do you also have a desire to see the house?'

Lorene stared into space. 'I have put it behind me.'

'I imagine Tinmore Hall is much grander than Summerfield,' he remarked.

Grander and colder, Genna thought.

'It is very grand, indeed,' Lorene responded.

Genna turned to Rossdale. 'I expect the house where you grew up would make both Summerfield House and Tinmore Hall look like tenants' cottages.'

His brows rose. Now *he* knew *she* knew his rank.

'Not so much different.' His eyes twinkled. 'Definitely grander, though.'

'Ross grew up at Kessington,' Penford explained to Lorene. 'You have heard of it?'

Her eyes grew wide. Now Lorenc knew Rossdale's rank, as well. Wait until Lorene told Tinmore whom he'd missed meeting.

'Yes, of course.' Lorene turned to Rossdale. 'It is in Suffolk, is it not?'

'It is,' he replied. 'And it is a grand house.' He grinned. 'My father should commission someone to paint it some day.'

He leaned forward to pour himself more wine and brushed against Genna's leg.

Secretly joking with her, obviously. What fun to flaunt a secret and not reveal it.

'I paint, you know,' she piped up, feigning all innocence. 'I even paint houses sometimes.'

'Do you?' Penford said politely. 'How nice to be so accomplished.'

Genna waited for him to ask Lorene her accomplishments, which were primarily in taking excellent care of her younger siblings for most of their lives. He did not ask, though, and Lorene would never say.

Genna could boast on her sister's behalf, though. 'Lorene plays the pianoforte beautifully. And she sings very well, too.'

Lorene gazed at her hands clasped in her lap. 'I am not as skilled as Genna would have you believe.'

'Perhaps you will play for us tonight,' Penford said, still all politeness.

'After dinner, perhaps?' Genna suggested.

'Perhaps after dinner you would show me the house, Miss Summerfield,' Rossdale asked. 'It would kill two birds with one stone, so to speak. Ease my curiosity about the building and give you your nostalgic tour.'

How perfect, Genna thought. Lorene would simply spoil her enjoyment if she came along and Lord Penford's presence only reminded Genna that all her beloved rooms now belonged to him. With Rossdale, she could enjoy herself.

She smiled. 'An excellent plan.'

Chapter Three

Ross enjoyed the dinner more than any he could recall in recent memory. Genna regaled them with stories about the house and their childhood years. She made those days sound idyllic, although if one listened carefully, one could hear the loneliness of neglected children in the tales.

Still, she made him laugh and her sister, too, which was a surprise. Heretofore Lady Tinmore had lacked any animation whatsoever. Dell was worse, though. He'd turned sullen and quiet throughout the meal.

It had never been Dell's habit to be silent. He'd once been game for anything and as voluble as they come. He'd turned sombre, though. Ross could not blame him. He simply wished Dell happy again.

In any event, Ross was eager to take a tour of the house with the very entertaining Genna.

After the dessert, he spoke up. 'I propose we forgo our brandy and allow Miss Summerfield her house tour. Then we can gather for tea afterwards and listen to Lady Tinmore play the pianoforte.'

Dell would not object.

'Very well,' Dell responded. He turned to Lady Tinmore as if an afterthought. 'If you approve, ma'am?'

'Certainly.' Lady Tinmore lowered her lashes.

She'd never let on if she did object, Ross was sure.

'What a fine idea! Let us go now.' Genna sprang to her feet and started for the door.

Ross reached her just as the footman opened it for her. She flashed the man a grateful smile and fondly touched his arm. These servants were the people she grew up with. Ross liked that she showed her affection for them.

They walked out the dining room and into the centre of the house, a room off the hall where the great staircase led to the upper floors.

'Where shall we start?' Ross asked.

Genna's expression turned uncertain. 'Would you mind terribly if we started in the kitchen? I would so much like to see all the servants. They will most likely be there or in the servants' hall. You may wait here, if you do not wish to come with me.'

'Why would I object?'

She smiled. 'Follow me.'

She led him down a set of stairs to a corridor on the ground floor of the left wing of the house. They soon heard voices and the clatter of dishes.

She hurried ahead and entered the kitchen. 'Hello, everyone!'

He remained in the doorway and watched.

The cook and kitchen maids dropped what they were doing and flocked around her. Other maids and footmen came from the servants' hall and other rooms. She hugged or clasped hands with many of them, asking them all questions about their welfare and listening intently to their answers. She shared information about her sisters and her half-brother, but, unlike her cynical conversation with Ross about her siblings, all was sunny and bright when she talked to the servants. So they would have no cause to worry, perhaps?

'Lorene—' she went on '*Lady Tinmore*, I mean— asked me to convey her greetings and well wishes to all of you. She is stuck with our host, I'm afraid, but I am certain she will ply me with questions about all of you as soon as we are alone.'

Ross remembered no such exchange between the sisters, but it was kind of Genna to make the servants believe Lady Tinmore thought about them.

Finally Genna seemed to remember him. She gestured towards him and laughed. 'Lord Rossdale! I do not need to present you, do I? I am certain everyone knows who you are.' She turned back to the servants. 'Lord Rossdale begged for a tour of the house, but really only so I could see all its beloved rooms again and make this quick visit to you. I am told little has changed.'

'Only the rooms that were your parents,' the housekeeper told her. 'Lord Penford asked for a few minor changes in your father's room, which he is using for his own. He asked for your mother's room to be made over for Lord Rossdale.'

Ross turned to the housekeeper. 'He needn't have put you to the trouble, but the room is quite comfortable. For that I thank you.'

Genna looked pleased at his words. 'We should be on our way, though. I am sure Lady Tinmore will wish to return to Tinmore Hall as soon as possible, so we do not overstay our welcome.' She grinned. 'I am less worried about that. I'm happy for our cousin to put up with us for as long as possible. I am so glad to be home for a little while.'

But, of course, it would never be her home again.

There were more hugs and promises that Genna would visit whenever she could.

Ross interrupted the farewells. 'Might we have a lamp? I suspect some of the rooms will be dark.'

A footman dashed off and soon returned with a lamp. Genna extricated herself and, with eyes sparkling with tears, let Ross lead her away.

When they were out of earshot, she murmured, 'I miss them all.' She shot him a defiant look. 'No doubt you disapprove.'

'Of missing them?'

'Of such an attachment to servants,' she replied.

He lifted his hands in protest. 'That is unfair, Miss Summerfield. What have I said or done to deserve such an accusation?'

She sighed. 'You've done nothing, have you? Forgive me. I tend to jump to conclusions. It is a dreadful fault. After this past year mixing in society, I learned to expect such sentiments. Certainly Tinmore would have apoplexy if he knew I'd entered the servants' wing. No doubt that is why Lorene stayed away.'

'Does your sister disapprove of fraternising with servants as well?' He would not be surprised. She seemed the opposite of Genna in every way.

'Lorene?' Her voice cracked. 'Goodness, no. But she tries not to displease Tinmore.' She shrugged. 'Not even when he could not possibly know.'

'What shall we see next?' he asked, eager to change the subject and restore her good cheer.

'I should like to see my old room,' she responded. 'And the schoolroom.'

They climbed the two flights of stairs to the second floor and walked down a corridor to the children's wing.

She opened one of the doors. 'This was my room.'

It was a pleasant room with a large window, although the curtains were closed. She walked through the space, subdued and silent.

'Is it as you remember?' he asked.

She nodded. 'Everything is in the right place.'

'You are not happy to see it, though.'

She shook her head. 'There is nothing of me left here. It could be anyone's room now.' She continued to walk around it. 'Perhaps Lorene knew it would feel like this. Perhaps that is why she did not wish to come.'

He frowned. 'I am sorry it disappoints you.'

She turned to him with a sad smile. 'It is odd. I do feel disappointed, but I also like that I am seeing it again. It helps me remember what it once was, even if the remembering makes me sad.'

Ross had rooms in his father's various residences, rooms he would never have to vacate, except by choice. For him the rooms were more of a cage than a haven.

'Let us continue,' she said resolutely.

They entered every bedroom and Genna commented on whose room it had been and related some memory attached to it.

They came to the schoolroom. She ran her fingers over the surface of the table. 'We left everything here.' She opened a wooden chest. 'Here are our slates and some of the toys.' She pointed to a cabinet. 'Our books will be in there.' She sighed. 'It is as if we walked out of here as children, probably to run out of doors to play.'

'To become Boadicea?' Ross remembered.

She smiled. 'Yes! Out of doors the fun began.' She clasped her hands together and perused the room one more time. 'Let us proceed.'

They peeked in other guest bedchambers, but she hesitated when they neared the rooms that had been her parents'. 'I certainly will not explore Penford's room.' She said the name with some disdain.

'You seem inclined to dislike my friend,' he remarked.

'Well, he might have let us stay here a while longer.' She frowned.

'Dell only inherited the title last summer. I believe your resentment belongs to his father.'

Her eyes widened. 'Oh. I did not know.'

Dell might not desire him to say more. Ross changed the subject. 'I have no objection to your seeing your mother's bedchamber,'

She recovered from her embarrassment and blinked up at him with feigned innocence. 'Me? Enter a gentleman's bedchamber accompanied by the gentleman himself? What would Lord Tinmore say?'

'This will be one of those instances where Lord Tinmore will never know.' He grinned. 'Besides, for propriety's sake we will leave the door open and I dare say my valet will be inside—'

Her eyes widened in mock horror. 'A witness? He might tell Lord Tinmore! We would be married posthaste, I assure you.'

She mocked the idea of being married, so unlike the other young women thrown at him.

Her expression turned conspiratorial. 'Although I am pining to show you something about the house, so we might step inside the room just for a moment.'

With no one else would Ross risk such a thing, for the very reason of which she'd joked.

He opened the door and, as he expected, his valet was in the room, tending to his clothes.

'Do not be alarmed, Coogan,' he said to his man. 'We will be only a moment.'

'Yes, Coogan.' Genna giggled. 'Only a moment.'

'Do you require something, m'lord?' Coogan asked. 'I was about to join the servants for dinner, but I can delay—'

'We are touring the house and Miss Summerfield wishes to show me something about the room,' Ross replied. 'Stay until we leave.'

Ross was glad to have a witness, just in case.

She stepped just inside the doorway and faced a wall papered in pale blue. She pressed on a spot and a door opened, a door that heretofore had been unnoticed by Ross.

'We'll be leaving now,' she said to his valet and gestured for Ross to follow her.

They could not have been more than a fraction of a minute.

As soon as he stepped over this secret threshold, she pushed the door closed. Their lamp illuminated a secret hallway that disappeared into the darkness.

'My grandfather built this house so that he would never have to encounter his servants in the house unless they were performing some service for him. He had secret doors put in all the rooms and connected them all with hidden passages. The servants had to scurry through these narrow spaces. We can get to any part of the house from here.' She headed towards the darkness. 'Come. I'll show you.'

Dell remained in the dining room with Lorene until they'd both finished the cakes that Cook had made for dessert. Their conversation was sparse and awkward.

He'd never met his Lincolnshire cousins, knew them only by the scandal and gossip that followed the family and had no reason to give them a further thought. He'd not been prepared for the likes of Lorene.

Lovely, demure, sad.

When he and Lorene retired to the drawing room, he was even more aware of the intimacy of their situation. What had he been thinking to allow Ross and the all-too-lively Genna to go off into the recesses of the house? Why the devil had Tinmore not simply refused the invitation? Why send his wife and her sister alone?

He realised they were standing in the drawing room.

She gestured to the pianoforte. 'Shall I play for you?'

'If you wish.' It would save him from attempting conversation with her, something that seemed to fail him of late.

She sat at the pianoforte and started to play. After the first few hesitant notes, she seemed to lose her self-consciousness and her playing became more assured and fluid. He recognised the piece she chose. It was one his sister used to play—Mozart's *Andante Grazioso*. The memory stabbed at his heart.

Lorene played the piece with skill and feeling. When she came to the end and looked up at him, he immediately said, 'Play another.'

This time she began confidently—*Pathétique* by Beethoven—and he fancied she showed in the music that sadness he sensed in her. It touched his own.

And drew him to her in a manner that was not to be advised.

She was married to a man who wielded much influence in the House of Lords. Dell would be new to the body. Ross was right. He needed to tread carefully if he wished to do any good.

When Lorene finished this piece, she automatically went on to another, then another, each one filled with melancholy. With yearning.

The music moved him.

She moved him.

When she finally placed her hands in her lap, they were trembling. 'That is all I know by heart.'

'Surely there is sheet music here.' He looked around the pianoforte.

She rose and opened a nearby cabinet. 'It is in here.' She removed the top sheet and looked at it. 'Oh. It is a song I used to play.'

'Play it if you like.' After all, what could he say to her if she stopped playing? His insides were already shredded.

She placed the sheet on the music rack, played the first notes and, to his surprise, began to sing.

I have a silent sorrow here,
A grief I'll ne'er impart;
It breathes no sigh, it sheds no tear,

But it consumes my heart.
This cherished woe, this loved despair,
My lot for ever be,
So my soul's lord, the pangs to bear
Be never known by thee.

Her voice was clear and pure and the feeling behind the lyrics suggested this was a song that had meaning for her. What was her *'cherished woe'*, her *'loved despair'*? He knew what his grief was.

She finished the song and lifted her eyes to his.

'Lorene,' he murmured.

There was a knock on the door, breaking his reverie.

The butler appeared. 'Beg pardon, sir, my lady.'

'What is it, Jeffers?' Dell asked, his voice unsteady.

'The weather, sir,' Jeffers said. 'A storm. It has begun to snow and sleet.'

Lorene paled and stood. Dell stepped towards the window. She brushed against him as he opened the curtains with his hand. They both looked out on to ground already tinged with white. The hiss of sleet, now so clear, must have been obscured by the music.

She spun around. 'We must leave! Where is Genna?'

'I sent Becker to find her,' Jeffers said.

'Well done, Jeffers. Alert the stables to ready the carriage.' Dell turned towards Lorene. 'You might still make it home if you can leave immediately.'

Lorene placed her hands on her cheeks. 'We did not expect bad weather.'

Dell touched her arm, concerned by her distress. 'Try not to worry.'

'Where is Genna?' she cried, rushing from the room. 'Why did she have to tour the house?'

Genna led Ross through dark narrow corridors, stopping at doors that opened into the other bed-chambers. On the other side, the doors to the secret passageways were nearly invisible to the eye. While they navigated this labyrinth, sometimes they heard music.

'Lorene must be playing the pianoforte,' Genna said.

The music wafting through the air merely made their excursion seem more fanciful.

It was like a game. Ross tried to guess what room they'd come upon next with the floor plan of the house fixed in his mind, but he was often wrong. Genna navigated the spaces with ease, though, and he could imagine her as a little girl running through these same spaces.

She opened a door on to the schoolroom. 'Is it not bizarre? The passageways even lead here. Why would my great-grandfather care if servants were seen in the nursery?'

'I wonder why he built the whole thing,' Ross said.

She grinned. 'It made for wonderful games of hide and seek.'

He could picture it in his mind's eye. The ne-glected children running through the secret parts of the house as if the passages had been created for their amusement.

'It even leads to the attic!' They came upon some stairs and she climbed to the top, opening a door into a huge room filled with boxes, chests and old furniture. Their little lamp illuminated only a small part of it.

Ross's shoe kicked something. He leaned down and picked up what looked like a large bound book.

'What is that?' she asked, turning to see.

He handed it to her and she opened it.

'Oh! It is my sketchbook.' Heedless of the dust, she sat cross-legged on the floor and placed the lamp nearby. She leafed through the pages. 'Oh, my goodness. I thought this was gone for ever!'

'What is it doing up here?' he asked.

'I hid it for safekeeping and then I could not remember where it was.' She closed it and hugged it to her. 'I cannot believe you found it!'

'Tripped over it, you mean.' He made light of it, but her voice had cracked with emotion.

When had he ever met a woman who wore her emotions so plainly on her sleeve? And yet…there was more she kept hidden. From everyone, he suspected. With luck the Christmas season would afford him the opportunity to see more of her.

She opened the book again and turned the pages. Illuminated by the lamp, her face glowed, looking even lovelier than she'd appeared before. Her hair glittered like threads of gold and her blue eyes were like sapphires, shadowed by long lashes. What might it be like to comb his fingers through those golden locks and to have her eyes darken with desire?

He stepped back.

For all the scandal in her family she was still a respectable young woman. A dalliance with her would only dishonour her and neither she nor he wished for something more honourable—like marriage.

The time was nearing when he would be forced to pick among the daughters of the *ton* for a wife worthy of becoming a duchess. Not yet, though. Not yet.

She looked up at him. 'What should I do with it?'

'Take it, if you wish. It is yours.'

Her brow creased. 'Would Lord Penford mind, do you think? He might not like knowing I was poking through the attic.'

He shrugged. 'I cannot think he would care.'

She stood and, clutching her sketchbook in one hand, brushed off her skirt with the other. 'We were not supposed to take anything but personal items.'

He pointed to the book. 'This is a personal item.'

She stroked it. 'I suppose.'

He crouched down to pick up the lamp. 'In any event, we should probably make our way back to the drawing room.'

She nodded.

He helped her through the door and down the stairs. She led him through the secret corridor down more stairs to the main floor where they heard their names called.

'Genna! Where are you?' her sister cried.

'Ross! We need you!' Dell's voice followed.

Genna giggled. 'They must think we have disappeared into thin air.'

'Does your sister not know of the secret passageway?'

'She knows of it, but we really stopped using it years ago.' She paused. 'At least Lorene and Tess did.' She seized his hand. 'Come. We'll walk out somewhere where we will not be seen emerging from the secret passageway.'

They entered another hallway, and Ross had no idea where they were.

'This is the laundry wing.' She led him to a door that opened on to the stairway hall, but before stepping into the hall, she placed her sketchbook just inside the secret passage.

'Genna!' her sister called again, her voice coming from the floor above.

'We are here!' Genna replied, closing the door which looked nearly invisible from this side. 'At the bottom of the stairs.'

Her sister hurried down the stairs, Dell at her heels. 'Where have you been? We have been searching for you this half-hour!'

Genna sounded all innocence. 'I was showing Lord Rossdale the house. We just finished touring the laundry wing.'

'The laundry wing!' Lady Tinmore cried. 'What nostalgia did you have for the laundry wing?'

'None at all,' Genna retorted. 'I merely thought it would interest Lord Rossdale.'

'I assure you, it did interest me,' Ross replied as smoothly as his companion. 'I am always interested in how other houses are run.'

Dell tossed him a puzzled look and Ross shook his head to warn his friend not to ask what the devil he was about.

'Never mind.' Genna's sister swiped the air impatiently. 'The weather has turned dreadful. Jeffers has called for the carriage. We must leave immediately.'

Genna sobered and nodded her head. 'Of course.'

Jeffers appeared with their cloaks and Ross hurriedly helped Genna into hers. As they rushed to the front door and opened it, a footman, his shoulders and hat covered with snow, was climbing the stairs.

'The coachman says he cannot risk the trip,' the footman said, his breath making clouds at his mouth. 'The weather prevents it.'

They looked out, but there was nothing to see but white.

'Oh, no!' Lady Tinmore cried.

Genna put her hands on her sister's shoulders and steered her back inside. 'Do not worry, Lorene. This could not have been helped.'

'We should have left earlier,' she cried.

'And you would have been caught on the road in this,' Dell said. 'And perhaps stranded all night. We will make you comfortable here. I will send a messenger to Lord Tinmore as soon as it is safe to do so.'

'We will have to spend the night?' Lorene asked.

'It cannot be helped,' Genna said to her. 'We will have to spend the night.'

Chapter Four

The lovely evening was over.

Although Lord Penford had tea brought into the drawing room, Lorene's nerves and Penford's coolness spoiled Genna's mood. Lorene was worried, obviously, about what Lord Tinmore would say when they finally returned and who knew why Penford acted so distantly to them? Why had he invited them if he did not want their company? Had he done so out of some sense of obligation? Even so, it was Lord Tinmore who'd compelled them to accept the invitation and she and Lorene certainly had not caused it to snow.

Not that it mattered. If Tinmore wished to ring a peal over their heads, reason would not stop him.

All the enjoyment had gone out of the evening, though.

Lord Penford poured brandy for himself and Rossdale and sat sullenly sipping from his glass while Rossdale and Genna made an effort to keep up conversation. With no warning Penford stood and announced he was retiring for the night. Rossdale was kind enough to keep Genna and Lorene company until the housekeeper announced that their bedchambers were ready. At that point they also felt they must say goodnight.

The housekeeper led them upstairs. 'We thought you might like to spend the night in your old rooms, so those are what we prepared for you.'

'Thank you,' Lorene said.

Genna gave the woman whom she'd known her whole life a hug. 'Yes, thank you. You are too good to us.'

The older woman hugged her back. 'We've found clean nightclothes for you, as well. Nellie and Anna will help you.' Nellie and Anna had served as their ladies' maids before they'd moved.

They bade the housekeeper goodnight and Genna entered her bedchamber for the second time that night. At least now there was a fire in the grill and a smiling old friend waiting for her.

'How nice it is that you can stay the night,' Anna said. 'In your old room. Like old times.'

'It is grand!' Genna responded.

Anna helped her out of her dress and into a nightgown.

'Come sit and I'll comb out your hair,' Anna said.

Genna sat at her old familiar dressing table and gazed in her old familiar mirror. 'Tell me,' she said after a time. 'What are the servants saying about Lord Penford?'

Anna untied the ribbon in her hair. 'We are grateful to him. He kept most of us on and we did not expect that. He does seem angry when he learns of some new repair to the house, but his anger is never directed at the servants.'

'He must be angry at my father, then,' Genna said. Did his anger extend to the daughters, too? That might explain why he was so unfriendly.

'I suppose you are right.' She pulled out Genna's hairpins and started combing out the tangles. 'He paid us our back wages, you know.'

Genna glanced at her in the mirror. 'Did he? How good of him.'

Paying their back wages was certainly something Lord Penford could have avoided if he'd chosen to. What could the servants do if he'd refused to pay them?

Anna gave her a sly grin. 'Why are you not asking about Lord Rossdale?'

Genna felt her cheeks grow hot. Why would that happen? 'Lord Rossdale? Whatever for?'

She stopped combing. 'Is he sweet on you? We were wondering.'

'He's not sweet on me!' Genna protested. 'Goodness. He's far beyond my touch. Besides, you know that I'm not full of romantic notions like Lorene and Tess. He knew I wanted to see the house so he asked for a tour.'

'So he said in the kitchen.' Anna resumed combing. 'I am still saying he's sweet on you.'

Genna stilled her hand and met Anna's gaze in the mirror. 'Please do not say so. At least not to anyone else. I admit Lord Rossdale and I do seem to enjoy each other's company, but it is nothing more than that and I do not want any rumours to start. It would not be fair when he has merely been kind to me.'

Anna shrugged. 'If you say so.'

As soon as Anna left, Genna started missing her. She missed all these dear people. Now she would have to get used to not seeing them all over again. It was so very depressing.

She stared at the bed, not sleepy one bit. All she'd do was toss and turn and remember when her room looked like *her* room. She spun around and strode to the door.

Like she'd done so many times when she was younger, she crossed the hallway to Lorene's room and knocked on her door.

'Come in,' Lorene said.

Genna opened the door. 'I came to see how you are faring. You were so upset about the weather and our having to spend the night.' How the tables had turned. Genna used to run to Lorene for comfort, now it was the other way around.

Lorene lowered herself into a chair. 'I confess I am distressed. What will he think?' She did not need to explain who *he* was. 'Knowing we are spending the night with two unmarried gentlemen without any sort of chaperon.'

Genna sat on the floor at her feet and took Lorene's

wringing hands in hers. 'We are home. Among our own servants. And Lord Penford and Lord Rossdale are gentlemen. There is nothing to worry over.'

Lorene gave her a pained look.

Genna felt a knot of anger inside. 'Will Tinmore… give you a tongue lashing over this?' Or worse, he might couch his cruelty in oh-so-reasonable words.

Lorene leaned forward and squeezed Genna's fingers. 'Do not worry over that! Good heavens, he is so good to us.'

Only when it suited him, though. He liked to be in charge of them.

Well, he might be in charge of Lorene, but Genna refused to give him power over her—even if she reaped the advantages of his money. She could not escape admitting that.

She smiled at Lorene. 'Let us enjoy our time back in our old rooms, then. Back *home*. Does it not feel lovely to be here?'

Lorene pulled her hands away and swept a lock of hair away from her face. 'I cannot enjoy it as you do, now that it is no longer our home.'

Genna secretly agreed. She did not enjoy seeing the rooms empty of any signs of her sisters or brother or herself, but she'd never admit it to Lorene. The best part of the house tour had been showing Rossdale the secret passages; the rest merely made her sad, just as Lorene had anticipated.

Genna stood. 'I love being back. I'm glad we can stay. I'll sleep in my old bed. I'll wake to sun shining in *my* windows. Cook will make us our breakfast again. It will be delightful.'

Lorene rose, too, and walked to the window. 'We had better hope the sun shines tomorrow.' She peeked out. 'It is still snowing.'

Genna gazed out on to the familiar grounds, all white now. 'We must not worry about tomorrow until it comes.' She turned to Lorene. 'How did you and Lord Penford fare while we toured the house?'

Lorene averted her face. 'I played the pianoforte.'

'We heard,' Genna said. 'You learned to play on that piano. How nice you were able to play on it again.'

'Yes,' Lorene replied unconvincingly. 'Nice.'

Cheering up Lorene was not working at all. It was merely making Genna feel wretched. 'Well, I believe I will go back to my room and snuggle up in my old bed. You've no idea how I've yearned to do so.'

Even if she feared she'd merely toss and turn.

She bussed her sister on the cheek and walked back to the room where she'd slept for years, ever since she'd left the nursery.

But once in the room, she found it intolerable. She paced for a few minutes, trying to decide what to do. Finally she made up her mind. She picked up a candle from the table next to her bed and carried it to the hidden door. She opened the door and entered the passageway.

She made her way downstairs and to the space where she'd left her sketchbook. As she picked it up and turned to go back to her room, the light from another candle approached. Her heart pounded.

'Miss Summerfield.' It was Lord Rossdale.

He came closer and smiled. 'I came to pick up your sketchbook. I see you had the same notion. I am glad you decided to keep it.'

She clutched it to her chest. 'I have not decided to keep it. I just wished to look at it in my room. I cannot take it back with me. It is too big to conceal and I do not wish to cause any problems.'

'I am certain Dell would wish you to have it,' he said.

She could not believe that. Even so, Lorene would probably worry about her taking it out of the house. 'I do not wish to ask him or to have my sister know. She would not like him bothered.' Genna was certain Lorene would not wish her to ask anything of Lord Penford.

Rossdale did not move, though, and the corridor was too narrow for Genna to get past him.

'Enjoy the book tonight, then,' he said finally. 'Come, I'll walk you back to your room.'

She laughed softly. 'More like you want me to show you the way so you do not become lost.'

He grinned. 'I am found out.'

He flattened himself against the wall so she could get by, but she still brushed against him and her senses heightened when they touched.

How strange it was to react so to such a touch. She did not understand it at all.

And she dared not think about it too much.

* * *

The next morning did indeed begin with the sun pouring in Genna's bedroom window. For a moment it seemed as if the last year had never happened. That was, until her gaze scanned the room.

Still, she refused to succumb to the blue devils. Instead she bounded from the bed and went to the window. Her beloved garden was still covered in snow, not only sparkling white, but also showing shades of blue and lavender in the shadows. The sky was an intense cerulean, as if it had been scrubbed clean of clouds during the night, leaving only an intense blue.

Genna opened the window and leaned out, gulping in the fresh, chilled air, relishing the breeze through her hair, billowing under her nightdress to tingle her skin.

'It is a lovely day!' she cried.

On a rise behind the house, a man riding a horse appeared. A grey horse and a grey-coated man.

Lord Rossdale.

He took off his hat and waved to her.

Imagine that he should see her doing such a silly thing. In her nightdress, no less! Perhaps he had heard her nonsense, as well.

She laughed and waved back before drawing back inside and shutting the window. She sat at her small table and turned the pages of her old sketchbook, remembering when life was more pleasant here.

Unfortunately, some of her drawings also reminded her of unhappy times. Hearing her father bellow about how much his daughters cost him, or rail against her mother who'd deserted them when Genna was small. Then there were the times when he'd consumed too many bottles from the wine cellar and she'd hidden from him. Her drawings during those times were sombre, rendered in charcoal and pencil, all shadowy and fearful.

Most of the pages, though, were filled with watercolours. Playful scenes that included her sisters and brother. Sunny skies, green grasses, flowers in all colours of the rainbow.

Her technique had been hopelessly childish, but, even so, her emotions had found their way on to the paper. The charcoal ones, obviously sad. The watercolours, happy and carefree.

A soft knock sounded at the door. Before Genna could respond, Anna opened the door and poked her head in.

She paused in surprise. 'Good morning, miss. I thought you would still be sleeping.'

Genna smiled. 'The sun woke me.' She closed the sketchbook and gestured to the window. 'Is it not a beautiful day?'

'It is, indeed, miss.' Anna entered the room and placed a fresh towel by the pitcher and basin Genna had used since a child. 'Mr Jeffers sent one of the stable boys with a message to Tinmore Hall.'

'That should relieve Lorene's mind.' Genna swung back to the window. 'How I would like it if I had my half-boots with me. I would love to be outside.' Even if she had her watercolours and brushes with her, she could paint the scene below and include all the colours she found in the white snow. That would bring equal pleasure.

She gazed out of the window again, wishing she were galloping across the snow-filled fields. On a grey horse, perhaps. Held by a grey-coated gentleman.

She turned away with a sigh. 'I suppose I might as well wash up. Then you can help me dress.'

Anna also arranged her hair in a simple knot atop her head.

When she was done, Genna stood. 'I might see if Lorene is awake yet.' She turned to Anna and filled with emotion again. 'I do not know when I will see you again.' She hugged Anna. 'I shall miss you!'

Anna had tears in her eyes when Genna released her. 'I shall miss you, too, miss. We all miss you.'

Genna swallowed tears of her own. 'I will contrive to visit if I can.'

She left the room, knowing she was unlikely to see it again, ever, and knocked on Lorene's door.

Lorene was alone in the room seated in one of the chairs. Doing nothing but thinking, Genna supposed.

'How did you sleep?' Genna asked.

'Quite well,' Lorene responded. Of course, Lorene would respond that way no matter what.

'Anna told me a messenger was sent to Tinmore Hall,' Genna assured her.

Lorene merely nodded.

Genna wanted to shake her, shake some reaction, some emotion from her, something besides worry over what Lord Tinmore would think, say, or do. She wanted her sister the way she used to be.

'Shall we go down to breakfast?' Genna asked.

Lorene rose from her chair. 'If you like.'

They made their way to the green drawing room where breakfast was to be served. Lord Penford sat at the table, reading a newspaper. He looked startled at their entrance and hastily stood.

'Good morning,' he said stiffly. 'I did not expect you awake so early.'

'We are anxious to return to Tinmore Hall,' Lorene said.

'Yes,' Penford said. 'I imagine you are.'

'*I* am not so eager to return,' Genna corrected. 'I have enjoyed my visit to our old home immensely.' She looked over the sideboard where the food was displayed. 'Oh, look, Lorene. Cook has made porridge! It has been ages and ages since I've tasted Cook's porridge!'

Becker, one of the footmen, attended the sideboard. Lorene made her selections, including porridge, and was seated next to Lord Penford at the small round breakfast table.

Becker waited upon Genna next, placing a ladle of oatmeal into a bowl for her. She added some cheeses, bread and jam.

'Thank you, Becker.' She smiled at him as he carried her plate to the table and seated her opposite her sister.

Penford sat as well although he did not look at either of them. 'I trust you slept well.'

Lorene hesitated for a moment before answering, 'Very well, sir.'

'Fabulously well!' added Genna. 'Like being at home.'

Lorene shot her a disapproving look, before turning to Penford. 'It was a kindness to put us in our old rooms.'

He glanced down at his newspaper. 'The housekeeper's decision, I am sure.'

Goodness! Could he be more sullen? 'I hope you did not disapprove.'

He shot her a surprised look. 'Why would I disapprove?'

She merely answered with a smile.

Why had he invited them if he seemed to take no pleasure in the visit? Unless his main purpose was to curry favour with Tinmore. If so, Genna was glad Tinmore had not accompanied them. Well, she was glad Tinmore had not accompanied them, no matter what Penford thought. Perhaps if Penford had been a more generous man, he might have left his cousins in the house to manage it in his absence. He might have come to their rescue instead of tossing them out of the only home they'd ever known and forcing Lorene to make that horrible marriage.

Lorene broke in. 'The porridge is lovely. Just as I remembered it.'

Penford's voice deepened. 'I am glad it pleases you.'

He put down his paper and darted Lorene a glance. 'I sent a man to Tinmore Hall early this morning. The roads are passable. You may order your coach at any time.'

He was in a hurry to be rid of them, no doubt.

'Might we have the carriage in an hour?' Lorene asked this so tentatively one would think she was asking for the moon instead of what Penford was eager to provide.

'Certainly.' Penford nodded towards Becker, who bowed in reply and left the room to accomplish the task.

Genna sighed and dipped her spoon into the porridge. She'd hoped to see Lord Rossdale one more time, but likely he was still galloping over the fields.

The rest of the breakfast transpired in near silence, except for the rattle of Lord Penford's newspaper and the bits of conversation exchanged between Genna and Lorene. Genna used the time to think about the house. Her time away had seemed to erase it as her home. Leave the place to the dour Lord Penford. Her life here was gone for ever. More of its memories had been captured in her sketchbook, but she had no confidence that it would ever return to her possession. Likely she would not even see Rossdale again.

When it came time for them to leave, the servants gathered in the hall to bid them goodbye, just as they had done when Genna and her sisters first removed to

Tinmore Hall. This time the tears did not fall freely, although many bid them farewell with a damp eye. Lorene shook their hands. Genna hugged each of them. Lord Penford stood to the side and Genna wondered if he felt impatient for them to depart.

When the coach pulled up to the front, Penford walked outside with them, without greatcoat, hat, or gloves. One of the coachmen helped Genna climb into the coach.

Lord Penford took Lorene's hand to assist her.

Lorene turned to him, but lowered her lashes. 'Thank you, sir, for inviting us and for putting us up for the night.' She lifted her eyes to him.

For a moment Penford seemed to hold her in place. He finally spoke. 'My pleasure.' He'd never seemed to experience pleasure from their visit. 'I shall remember your music.'

Lorene pulled away and climbed into the coach.

'Safe journey,' Penford said through the window.

As the coachman was mounting his seat, a horse's hooves sounded near. A beautiful silver-grey steed appeared beside the coach.

Rossdale leaned down from his saddle to look inside the coach. 'You are leaving already!'

Genna leaned out the window. 'We must get back.'

'Forgive me for not being here to say a proper goodbye.' His horse danced restlessly beside them.

Genna spoke in a false tone. 'I do not believe I shall forgive you.' She smiled. 'But thank you for allowing me to give you a tour of the house. It was most kind.'

He grinned. 'It certainly was more than I ever thought it would be.'

The coach started to move.

'Goodbye!' Genna sat back, but turned to look out the back window as the coach pulled away.

Rossdale dismounted from his horse and stood with Penford watching the coach leave.

They watched until the coach travelled out of their sight.

Chapter Five

Lorene fretted on the road back to Tinmore Hall. 'I wish we had not gone. He will have been frantic with worry when we did not return last night.'

Did she fear the effect of Tinmore's worry on his health or that he would blame her for their absence?

'He wanted us to go,' Genna reminded her. 'He ordered us to go.'

Lorene curled up in the corner of the carriage, making herself even smaller. 'Still, we should not have gone.'

Genna tried to change the subject. 'What did you think of our cousin, then? *Lord Penford*. Did you know he just inherited the title this summer?'

Lorene did not answer right away. 'I did not know that,' she finally said. 'Perhaps that was why he was so sad.'

'Sad?' Genna had not considered that. Perhaps he had not been disagreeable and rude. Perhaps he'd still been grieving. His father would have died only a few months before. She felt a pang of guilt.

'He's taking care of the house,' Genna said, trying to make amends, at least in her own mind. 'Anna said he paid the servants their back wages.'

'Did he?' Lorene glanced back at her. 'How very kind of him.'

Genna might have continued the conversation by asking what Lorene thought of Rossdale, but she didn't. She felt Lorene really wished to be quiet. Instead Genna recounted their tour of the house, intending to fix in her memory the details of each room they'd visited. More vivid, though, were Rossdale's reactions to those details. She'd enjoyed showing him the rooms more than she'd enjoyed visiting them.

Their carriage crossed over the bridge and the cupolas of Tinmore Hall came into view. The snow-covered lawn only set off the house more, its yellow stone gleaming gold in the morning sun. Genna's spirits sank.

She hated the huge mausoleum. The house hadn't seen a change in over fifty years. At least her mother had kept Summerfield House filled with the latest fashion in furnishings—at least until she ran off with her lover.

The carriage passed through the wrought-iron gate and drove up to the main entrance. Two footmen emerged from the house, ready to attend them. Moments later they were in the great hall, its mahogany wainscoting such a contrast to the light, airy plasterwork of Summerfield House.

Dixon, the butler, greeted Lorene. 'It is good you are back, m'lady.'

'How is Lord Tinmore?' she asked.

'His fever is worse, I fear, m'lady,' he responded. 'He spent a fitful night.'

Oh, dear. This would only increase Lorene's guilt.

'Did the doctor see him yesterday?' Lorene handed one of the footmen her cloak and gloves.

Dixon nodded. 'The doctor spent the night, caught in the storm as you were. He is here now.'

The doctor's presence should give Lorene some comfort.

'I must go to him.' Lorene started for the stairway. 'I ought to have been at his side last night.'

'He would not have known it if you were,' Dixon said.

Lorene halted and turned her head. 'He was that ill?'

'Insensible with fever, Wicky told us.'

'That is good, Lorene,' Genna broke in. 'He cannot be angry at you if he does not know you were gone.'

Lorene swung around. 'It is not good!' she snapped. 'He is ill.'

Genna felt her face grow hot. 'I am so sorry. It was a thoughtless thing to say.'

'And very unkind,' Lorene added.

'Yes,' Genna admitted, filled with shame. 'Very unkind. I am so sorry.'

Lorene turned her back on Genna and ran up the stairs.

Why could she not still her tongue at moments like these? She must admit she cared more about Lorene's welfare than Tinmore's health, but she did not precisely wish him to be seriously ill, did she?

She took a breath and glanced at Dixon. 'Is Lord Tinmore so very ill?'

His expression was disapproving. 'I gather so from Wicky's report.'

Genna deserved his disdain. By day's end the other servants would hear of her uncharitable comment and would call her an ungrateful wretch.

Which she was.

Over the next three days Genna hardly saw Lorene, who devoted all of her time to her husband's care. Genna would have happily assisted in some way—for Lorene's sake, not Tinmore's—but no one required anything of her and anything she offered was refused. She kept to her room, mostly, and amused herself by drawing galloping horses with tall, long-coated riders. She could never quite capture that sense of fluid movement she'd seen that day when she'd gone to make a painting of Summerfield House.

She had just finished another attempt and was contemplating ripping it up when there was a knock at her door. Her maid, probably. 'Come in,' she called, placing the drawing face down on her table.

'Genna—' It was Lorene.

Genna turned and rose from her chair. 'How is—?' she began.

Lorene did not let her finish. 'He is better. The

fever broke during the night and now he is resting more comfortably.'

'I am glad for you,' Genna said.

Lorene waved her words away.

Genna walked over to her. 'You look as if you need rest, too. Might you not lie down now?'

Lorene nodded. 'I believe I will. I just wanted you to know.'

'Thank you.' Genna felt careful, as if talking to a stranger. 'I am glad to know it.'

Lorene turned to leave, but a footman appeared in the corridor.

'My lady, two gentlemen have called to enquire after his lordship's health,' he said. 'Lord Rossdale and Lord Penford.'

Genna's heart fluttered. She would be excited for any company, would she not? Of course, they had not come to call upon her.

Lorene put a hand to her hair. 'Oh, dear. I am not presentable.' She turned to Genna. 'Would you entertain them until I can make myself fit for company?'

'Certainly. Anything to help.' Genna turned to the footman. 'Where are they?' There were so very many rooms in this house where visitors might be received.

'I put them in the Mount Olympus room,' he replied.

The room with the ceiling and walls covered with scenes from mythology, cavorting, nearly naked gods, all painted over a century before.

'Very good,' Lorene told him. 'Have Cook prepare some tea and biscuits.'

'Tea?' Genna said. 'Offer them wine. Claret or sherry or something.'

Lorene pursed her lips. 'Very well. Some wine, then, as well as tea and biscuits.'

The footman bowed and rushed off.

Lorene glanced at Genna.

'I can go down directly.' Genna took off the apron she wore to cover her dress and hurried to wash the charcoal off her fingers. She dried her hands. 'I'm off!'

Ross craned his neck and stared in wonder at the ceiling. It looked as if the mighty Zeus and all the lesser gods surrounding him might tumble down on to his head.

'This is quite a room,' he remarked. 'I am reminded of our Grand Tour—the palaces of Rome and Venice. Remember the murals? On every ceiling it seemed.'

'A man cannot think. The room fills the mind too much,' Dell responded.

Ross grinned. 'We did not do much thinking in those days, did we?'

Dell nodded, his face still grim. 'None at all, I recall.'

Ross perused the ceiling and walls again. 'In those days we would have been riveted by the naked ladies.' He stopped in front of one such figure, a goddess who appeared as if she would step out from the wall and join them.

Dell paced. 'Remind me again why we were compelled to come here?'

Ross had already explained. 'You wanted to become acquainted with Lord Tinmore, so calling to enquire after his health is only polite, especially after his illness kept him away from your dinner.'

The door opened and both men turned. Ross smiled. It was Genna, the one person he'd hoped to see when he concocted this scheme to call at Tinmore Hall.

Genna strode over to them. 'Rossdale. Penford. How good of you to call. My sister will be here in a few minutes. She has ordered refreshment for you, as well.'

Dell frowned. 'Lord Tinmore is still ill, then?'

'Lorene can better answer your questions.' She gave Dell a cordial smile. 'But, yes, Tinmore remains unwell.'

She gestured to the gilt stools cushioned in green damask that lined the walls of the room. 'Do sit.'

The room was in sore need of a rearrangement of furniture more conducive to conversation, Ross thought. A style more in tune with the present.

'Tell me, how is the weather?' Genna asked politely. 'I see our snow still covers the fields. Was it not terribly cold to ride this distance?'

'Not so terribly cold.' Ross kept his expression bland. 'I suspect some people would consider walking this far even when it is cold outside.' He darted a glance her way and saw she understood his joke.

'We felt it our duty to enquire into Lord Tinmore's health,' Dell said solemnly.

'How very good of you,' she responded, her voice kind.

Ross gave her an approving look.

'How were the roads?' she asked.

Dell shrugged. 'Slippery in places, but the horses kept their footing.'

'I think they relished the exercise,' Rossdale added. He'd relished it, as well.

She looked at a loss for what else to say. He fished around to find a topic and rescue her from having to make conversation.

She beat him to it. 'Tell me, do you plan to stay at Summerfield House for Christmastide?'

'At present that is our plan,' Dell responded.

Genna looked surprised. 'Do you not travel to visit your families?'

Dell averted his gaze and Rossdale answered. 'We decided to avoid all that.'

He hoped his tone warned her not to ask more about that. Dell's grief at the loss of his entire family was still raw. It was why Ross had elected to pass up a Christmas visit to his father at Kessington Hall. So he could be with his friend at such a time.

That and because he preferred his friend's company to the politically advantageous guests his father always invited.

'What are your plans?' Ross asked her.

She sighed. 'Lord Tinmore plans a house party.

Several of his friends will come to stay.' She did not seem to look forward to this. 'Guests should arrive next week.'

'No, they will not.' Her sister entered the room. Genna and the gentlemen stood. 'How do you do, sirs? It is kind of you to call.'

Dell's voice turned raspy. 'How—how fares Lord Tinmore?'

Lady Tinmore glanced up at him, then gazed away. 'He is better. The fever broke, but he remains too weak to receive callers.'

'We do understand,' Dell said stiffly. 'Please send our best wishes for his recovery.'

Lady Tinmore darted another glance at him. 'I will. Thank you, sir.'

Dell seemed uncomfortable around these sisters. Not ready for even this relatively benign social call?

Genna turned to her sister. 'What did you mean the guests will not arrive next week?'

Her sister replied, 'Tinmore has asked that the house party be cancelled. His secretary is to write to the guests today.'

The refreshments arrived. Ross and Dell accepted glasses of wine and offers of biscuits.

Ross stepped away while Lady Tinmore poured for Dell. To his delight, Genna joined him.

He wanted a chance to speak to her. 'Are you disappointed about the house party?' he asked.

She laughed. 'Not at all. I do not rub well with Lord Tinmore's friends.'

Her sister heard her and snapped, 'It is cancelled because Lord Tinmore needs the time to recover. He has been very sick, Genna.'

'I know that, Lorene,' Genna said softly.

Ross felt for her. No one liked being reprimanded in front of others.

He took a sip of his wine. 'Tell me about this room, Lady Tinmore. It is quite unusual.'

'It is called the Mount Olympus room,' Lady Tinmore responded, sounding glad to change the subject. 'Depicting the Greek gods. My husband said it was painted over one hundred years ago by the Italian muralist, Verrio. He painted a similar scene even more elaborate at Burghley House. And one at Chatsworth, as well. My husband prefers this one, though.'

Ross noticed Genna gazing at the walls and ceiling as if seeing them for the first time.

'It is hard to imagine one even more elaborate,' he said diplomatically. 'Although it does remind me of rooms we saw in Rome and Florence and Venice.'

'You've visited Rome and Florence and Venice?' Genna's eyes grew wide.

'We did indeed,' Ross replied. 'On our Grand Tour. You would have appreciated the fine art there.'

'Lord Tinmore's grandfather and great-grandfather collected many fine pieces of Italian art. They are hung in almost every room of this house,' Lady Tinmore said almost dutifully.

'They are?' Genna looked surprised.

Dell drained the contents of his wineglass and

placed it on the table. 'We must take our leave.' He spoke to Lady Tinmore, but did not quite meet her eye. 'I do hope Lord Tinmore continues to improve.'

'Thank you,' she murmured.

Ross bowed to her. 'It was a pleasure seeing you again, ma'am.' He turned to Genna. 'And you, Miss Summerfield. I hope we meet again.'

'Yes.' Genna smiled. 'I would enjoy that.'

Perhaps he could convince Dell to call upon Lord Tinmore again. Or he could call upon the gentleman himself, although he had less reason to do so and no interest in meeting the man. He merely wanted to see Genna again.

And he still must devise a way to deliver her sketchbook to her as he had promised.

Before Ross could say another word, Dell strode out of the room as if in a hurry. Ross was compelled to follow, although he did so at a more appropriate pace.

He also turned back to the ladies when he reached the door. 'Good day, ma'am. Miss Summerfield.'

When he caught up to Dell in the hall, Dell had already sent the footman for their greatcoats, hats and gloves.

'What the devil was the rush?' Ross asked him.

'We were intruding.' Dell did not meet his eye. 'Tinmore is still ill. Sick enough for him to cancel his house party. The last thing Lady Tinmore needs are callers.'

'She did not seem to mind,' Ross insisted.

The footman brought their coats and assisted in

putting them on. 'Your horses are being brought from the stable.'

They waited in uncomfortable silence until the horses were outside the door.

They were on the main road from the estate before Ross spoke. 'What is amiss, Dell?'

'Amiss?' he shot back. 'I told you. We were intruding. I should not have allowed you to talk me into this visit.'

Ross spoke in a milder tone. 'I did not see any indication that we were not welcome. Lady Tinmore seemed very gracious. I think she appreciated our concern for her husband.'

'She was gracious,' Dell admitted, sounding calmer. 'She was—' He cleared his throat. 'Perhaps we might call again. In a week or so, when we are certain of Tinmore's recovery.'

Genna and Lorene waited at the window until they saw Rossdale and Penford ride away.

Lorene then turned to tidy up the wineglasses and plate of biscuits, putting them back on the tray, something for which her husband would chastise her if he knew of it.

Acting like a servant, he would say.

Genna liked those old habits of Lorene's—her tendency to take care of things and save others the trouble.

Genna put her hands on her hips and stared at the

Mount Olympus mural. 'I had not noticed before, but this really is a remarkable painting.' Verrio had painted the perspective so skilfully the figures in the painting appeared to be stepping into the room. Remarkable.

A footman had stepped into the room, ready to take the tea tray away.

Genna walked out of the room with Lorene. 'How serious is Lord Tinmore's illness?' she asked. 'I confess, I was surprised he cancelled the house party.'

'He is very weak, but his breathing is less laboured.'

The footman opened the door for them and Genna wondered what he thought about her ladyship tidying the room.

Lorene continued talking. 'If he had not cancelled it today, there would not have been enough time for letters to reach everyone. He did not want guests arriving with him lying abed. He said I should have known to cancel the house party two days ago.'

'Did he?'

And if Lorene had cancelled it, he would have been angry at her for interfering with his plans. But Genna would not say so to Lorene, who was still too sensitive on the subject of her husband. Genna missed being able to speak her mind to Lorene, but even more she wished she could ease Lorene's hurt feelings. Lorene would never complain to her, though.

They entered the hall and started up the stairway.

'How did you find Lord Penford?' Genna asked instead. That seemed like a safe subject.

Lorene avoided looking at her. 'What do you mean?' Her voice was sharp.

That took Genna by surprise. 'No special reason. You thought him sad before. I wondered if that was why he seemed so uncomfortable.'

'I think he realised it was not a good day to call,' Lorene said, as if defending him.

Genna had not intended any criticism of the man. 'Perhaps.' Better to agree than risk an argument. 'I suspect you are right.'

They reached the first floor where Lorene's set of rooms were located. And Lord Tinmore's.

'Is there anything I can do for you, Lorene?' Genna asked.

'Nothing,' her sister said.

'You will rest this afternoon, then?' Lorene still looked very fatigued.

'I will.' Lorene smiled wanly. 'I believe I will have dinner sent up to my room. May I tell Cook you will not expect to be served at the table?'

'Of course you may!' Genna assured her. 'A simple plate will do very nicely for me. Whatever is on hand.'

She was not the servants' favourite at any time, even though she tried never to put them to too much trouble for her. Like expecting a full meal prepared and served to her alone.

She reached over to buss Lorene's cheek. 'Promise you will rest.'

Lorene nodded.

Genna walked up another flight of stairs to her bedchamber. As she entered the room, a wave of loneliness washed over her. She had never felt lonely at Summerfield House—well, almost never. But here she felt so very alone.

She hadn't felt lonely with Rossdale. In fact, she'd felt happy, as if she'd found a real friend.

Right now, he felt like her only friend.

Chapter Six

Having dinner in the dining room was no pleasure. Lord Tinmore recovered well over the next few days, well enough to dress for dinner and to expect his wife and her sister to do the same. Genna complied, of course, and placed herself on her best behaviour. She was well capable of being agreeable at mealtime, especially when Lord Tinmore expected an audience rather than conversation.

They dined in the formal dining room, but at one end of the table. Lord Tinmore sat at the table's head. Lorene sat to her husband's right and Genna to his left. He was a little deaf in his left ear so there was little need for Genna to speak. Mr Filkins, his secretary, who was nearly as old as he, also dined with them. Filkins was seated next to Lorene, the side of the table upon which Tinmore focused most of his attention.

By the time the main course was served Tinmore had exhausted a recitation of the frequency of his cough, the colour of his phlegm and the irregularities of his bowels, to which Mr Filkins made appropriately sympathetic comments.

He went on to lament his decision to cancel the house party.

'I now see I will be quite well enough,' he said. 'I should have known I would recover swiftly. I have a strong constitution.'

'That you do, sir,' agreed Mr Filkins. 'But you had to decide quickly and I believe you made the most prudent of choices.'

'Yes,' Tinmore readily agreed with him. 'Besides, what is done cannot be undone.' He pointed his fork at Genna. 'Although I had high hopes for you, young lady. There was many a good catch invited to that party.'

Yes. Eligible men of Tinmore's age looking for a young wife to take care of them and their sons and grandsons looking for a dowry big enough to tempt them.

'A lost opportunity,' Genna said.

'What?' Tinmore cupped his ear.

'A lost opportunity,' she said louder.

Tinmore stabbed a piece of meat with his fork and lifted it to his mouth. After he chewed and swallowed it, he glanced at Lorene. 'You never told me about the dinner with Lord Penford.'

How like Tinmore to accuse rather than merely ask.

'You were so ill, I put it entirely out of my mind,' Lorene said.

'Put it out of your mind? Something as important

as all that? Where is your head, my dear?' He took another bite of meat and waved his fork at her. 'Well, how was it? Were you treated well?'

Lorene responded as if she'd been asked with some kindness. 'We were treated very well, I assure you. Were we not, Genna?'

Genna nodded. 'Very well.'

Lorene went on, 'Although Lord Penford was disappointed you were unable to attend.'

Tinmore looked pleased at that. 'What did he serve?'

Goodness. Genna hardly remembered. Lorene, though, provided a rather thorough list of the courses. Genna wondered if she made up some of them.

'Was he a reasonable fellow, this Penford?' he went on to ask. 'I knew his father.' He would have seen the late Lord Penford in the House of Lords last Season. 'I have great hopes of turning the son to my views. Get them while they are new, you know.'

Mr Filkins laughed appreciatively.

'He was very amiable,' Lorene said. 'Although he and his friend did not talk politics with us at all, did they, Genna?'

'Not at all,' Genna agreed.

Tinmore straightened. 'His friend? Who was this friend?'

'Lord Rossdale,' Lorene responded.

Tinmore half-rose from his seat. 'Rossdale? Rossdale? The Duke of Kessington's son?'

'Yes, that is who he was,' Lorene responded. 'He was very nice, as well.'

'The Duke's son?' He pounded his knife down on the table. 'You should have told me you dined with the Duke's son.'

'Well, you were ill,' Genna said.

Tinmore turned to her. 'What, girl? Speak up. Do not mumble.'

She raised her voice. 'You were ill!'

He ignored her response. 'Kessington is the last man I would wish to offend. We must do something about this immediately!'

'I do not believe Lord Rossdale was offended,' Lorene assured him. 'He offered kind condolences over your illness when they called here the other day.'

'The Duke's son called here the other day?' Tinmore's face was turning red.

Lorene reached over and patted his arm. 'Do not make yourself ill over this. I am sure they understood completely that you were too ill to receive them. Perhaps we can invite them for dinner one night when you are a little stronger.'

'Dinner. Excellent idea,' Tinmore said.

'Excellent idea,' Mr Filkins agreed.

Tinmore pointed the knife towards him. 'But we must not wait. Must do something immediately.'

'Might I suggest a letter?' Mr Filkins offered. 'I will pen something this very night and if it meets with your approval it can be delivered to Lord Rossdale in the morning.'

'A letter. Yes. A letter is the thing.' Tinmore popped a piece of potato into his mouth. 'But address it to Penford. He was the host. Make certain you mention Rossdale in it.'

'I quite comprehend, sir,' the secretary said. 'An excellent point.'

Genna smiled to herself. At least she would see Rossdale again.

'In fact,' Tinmore went on, 'invite them for Christmas Day.' He turned to his wife. 'Do you know if they are staying through Christmastide?'

Lorene nodded. 'That is what they told us. Through to Twelfth Night, at least.'

'Ha!' Tinmore laughed. 'We shall have a house party after all. At least Christmas dinner with elevated company.' He tossed a scathing look at Genna. 'Rossdale is not married. But you come with too much baggage to tempt him.'

Baggage?

The sins of her mother and father, she supposed. As well as her sisters and brother. She'd not done anything to deserve society's censure.

At least not yet.

On Christmas Day Ross and Dell made an appearance at the parish church for morning services and later in the day rode over to Tinmore Hall in Dell's carriage. The invitation to Christmas dinner had been somewhat of a surprise, albeit a welcome one for Ross. He was eager to call upon Genna again and curious to meet the formidable Lord Tinmore. Dell seemed less enthusiastic. Less enthusiastic than he'd been when first he'd invited Tinmore to dinner. Then he'd thought it prudent to ingratiate himself to the old lord, but now he seemed to relish meeting the man as much as one might look forward to having a tooth pulled.

The nearer the carriage brought them to Tinmore Hall, the bigger Dell's frown seemed to grow.

'Are you certain it will not be thought presumptuous to bring presents?' Dell asked.

Gifts had been Ross's idea. 'Presumptuous? Guests always brought my father gifts for his Christmas parties.'

Dell shot him a glance. 'Then if Tinmore seems offended, you must tell him that it was your father's custom.'

'I will.' Ross grinned. 'I dare say that will make the practice quite appreciated.'

The roof line of Tinmore Hall came into view in all its Elizabethan glory. As they passed through the gate, a herd of deer bounded across the park, their hooves kicking up clods of snow from the patches that still dotted the grass.

'At least it is merely a dinner and not a house party,' Dell said. 'I would detest having to spend the night.'

That would not have brought pleasure, would it? Ross agreed silently. No secret passages to explore. No surprise meetings when others were abed. Still, a conversation with Genna would prove stimulating. The closer Christmas Day came, the more withdrawn

Dell had become. Ross supposed his friend remembered what his Christmases used to be like.

The carriage drew up to the entrance and four footmen emerged, forming a line to the carriage door. They were ushered into the hall, their cloaks taken and packages carried behind them as the butler led them to the Mount Olympus room and announced them.

The room was fragrant with greenery and spice. Garlands of evergreen were draped around the windows, holly, red with berries, lined the mantelpiece. Bowls of apples sat on the tables. Ross glanced up. Mistletoe hung in the doorway.

Seated in the huge room were Lord Tinmore and his wife, an incongruous pair. Tinmore, who must have been in his seventies at least, had the pallor and loose skin typical of an aged man who'd lost whatever looks he might have once possessed. He was thin, with rounded posture, but still his presence seemed to dominate the room. His wife, on the other hand, was a beauty in her prime. Flawless skin, rich dark hair, clear eyes and pink lips. A figure any man would admire, but she seemed a mere shadow in the wake of her husband's commanding presence.

Ross preferred her sister, who sparkled with life.

Tinmore, using a cane, rose from his chair. 'Good to see you. Good to see you. Happy Christmas to you.'

Ross and Dell crossed the room to him.

Lady Tinmore stood at her husband's side and made a more personal introduction. 'May I present my cousin, Lord Penford, and his friend, Lord Rossdale?'

Dell bowed. 'A pleasure, sir, to meet you.'

'And you, sir,' Tinmore said to Dell. He turned to Ross. 'Knew your grandfather. A decent man.'

'I have always heard so.' Ross hardly remembered his grandfather. The only image he could conjure up was of a remote figure, always busy, too busy to bother with an inquisitive, energetic boy. Rather like his father became after Grandfather died.

'Please, do sit,' Lady Tinmore said. 'We have refreshments.' She turned towards the fireplace where a bowl sat on the grate. 'Wassail, for you.'

A footman in attendance ladled wassail into a glass, which Ross took gratefully. The carriage ride had given him a thirst.

Tinmore asked about the carriage ride. The conditions of the road were discussed and the weather, of course, and the fine quality of the drink. The church services and sermons were compared, a devious way for Tinmore to discover whether they had attended the services at their parish. Tinmore had not attended church, but his wife and her sister had.

And where was her sister?

He took the first opportunity to ask. 'Will we have the pleasure of Miss Summerfield's company today?'

Lady Tinmore frowned slightly. 'She should be here. I dare say something has detained her.'

'I am here!' Genna burst into the room, her arms

laden with packages wrapped in brown paper and string. 'I was wrapping gifts.'

'Gifts?' Tinmore said disparagingly.

Ross rose from his chair. 'We also brought gifts. My father always insisted on gifts on Christmas Day.' He looked around. 'Although I am not quite sure what has become of them.'

Tinmore gestured to a footman, who bowed and left the room.

Genna placed her packages on a table and walked up to Dell and Ross. 'How delightful you could be with us today.' She smiled. 'Happy Christmas!'

Ross shook her hand. 'Happy Christmas, Miss Summerfield.'

Tinmore had not stood at her entrance. 'You are late, girl.'

Her smile stiffened. 'I do apologise, sir. I fear the wrapping took longer than I had anticipated.'

She sat on the sofa next to her sister, which placed her next to Ross's chair. She glanced at him as she sat and her smile softened again.

'I hope you have not been extravagant, girl,' Tinmore said. 'I do not provide you an allowance for frivolities.'

How ungentlemanly of Tinmore to make it a point that her allowance came from him.

She lowered her voice. 'I assure you. I was not extravagant.'

The footman handed her a glass of wassail and she took a sip.

Dell asked a question about the next session of Parliament and Ross was grateful to him for deflecting Tinmore's attention from Genna.

Not wanting to spend the holiday discussing politics, Ross turned to the ladies. 'The room smells and looks like Christmas.'

'It was Lorene's doing,' Genna said. 'I think it turned out lovely.'

'Lovely, indeed.'

Lady Tinmore's cheeks turned pink at the compliment. 'Genna helped.'

Genna grimaced. 'She means I supervised the gathering of the greens. The decoration was completely up to Lorene.'

'You did well, ma'am,' he said.

Genna gazed around the room and looked as if she was trying to stifle a laugh. 'It is a bit incongruous, though, do you not think? All these Roman gods amidst greenery meant to celebrate the Christian holiday.'

'The gods appear to be joining in the revelry,' he responded.

It was amusing that this room in particular was used to entertain guests on this special day, especially because this house must have several other drawing rooms that would be suitable. Was this chosen as the most impressive?

Lady Tinmore's brows knitted and Ross suspected she did not see the humour so evident to her sister.

Lady Tinmore changed the subject. 'We will eat

dinner early. In a few minutes, perhaps. I hope that will be to your liking?'

Ross took a sip of his wassail. 'I am usually ready to eat at any moment of the day, so whatever you have planned will suit me very well.' He glanced at Genna. 'Perhaps after dinner there will be time for you to give me a tour of this house.'

She smiled. 'I would be pleased to do so.'

They'd had time enough to finish the wassail when Dixon announced dinner.

Mr Filkins, Tinmore's secretary, had not been included in the meal. Genna supposed the poor man was eating in his room alone on this day, which did not seem at all right to her.

The conversation was not as lively or amusing as it had been when she and Lorene had shared a meal with Rossdale and Penford at Summerfield House. It was dominated by Lord Tinmore and, as such, did not include Genna. She was seated across from Rossdale, but unable to speak with him. If only he'd been seated at her side they might have been able to have a little private conversation.

'Your father is Whig, is he not, Rossdale?' Tinmore asked.

'Very,' Rossdale responded.

'And yourself?' Tinmore went on.

'Me?' Rossdale responded. 'I am not in politics.'

'But you must have a party, a set of beliefs?' Tinmore took a bite of roast goose.

'Must I?' he answered. 'I can see no reason at the moment. When my father dies, I will choose, but I am in no hurry to do so.'

'Odd thing, not declaring your party.' Tinmore turned to Penford. 'And you, sir? Do not say you are Whig.'

The Whigs advocated reform, to give more power to the people and Parliament and less to the monarchy.

Penford nodded. 'I must say so, at least in desiring to ease the suffering of our people. There is more suffering to come, I fear, now that the war is over.'

'Now that the war is over, we must protect our property and the prices of our crops. That is what the Corn Laws are all about.' Tinmore landed a fist on the table for emphasis.

The Corn Laws fixed the prices of grain and imposed tariffs to prevent imported grain from undercutting those prices.

'I do understand, sir,' Penford replied. 'But I fear the high prices will cause many to go hungry.'

Tinmore turned to Rossdale. 'I suppose you were against the Corn Laws. Your father certainly held out until the last, but we won him to our side.'

'I did not have to make the choice,' Rossdale said. 'But it would be hard to vote for a hardship for so many.'

Tinmore jabbed a finger in Rossdale's direction. 'If our farms fail, we all go hungry.'

Had Rossdale's father voted against his beliefs? 'It

must be very difficult to choose,' Genna said. 'Especially when one does not know what the future will bring.'

'Humph!' Tinmore said. 'What do you know of such things?'

She had forgotten for a moment. Tinmore did not expect her to have opinions.

Rossdale spoke up. 'I quite agree with Miss Summerfield. Those in Parliament must live with many difficult decisions. It can be a great burden.'

Rossdale stood up for her? When was the last time anyone had done that for her?

Tinmore straightened in his chair. 'It is a great privilege! And one's duty!'

'I agree it is both of those things, as well,' Rossdale responded.

Tinmore seemed unexpectedly at a loss for words.

Ross rescued him, as well. 'Sir, I must tell you I am intrigued by this house. I have heard there is much to admire here.'

Tinmore swelled with pride. 'The first Earl of Tinmore was in the service of Queen Elizabeth. In her honour, the house was designed like the letter E, which might not be apparent to you. One can see it is shaped like an E if one climbs to the roof, though.'

'I should like to see that,' Rossdale said.

'I'll have Dixon take you around after dinner.'

'We do not need to trouble your butler. Miss Summerfield gave me a tour of Summerfield House. I am certain she will do a fine job of showing me Tinmore Hall.'

Genna felt herself go all warm. First he stood up for her; now he complimented her.

Tinmore waved his fork. 'Dixon will do it. The girl knows nothing of this house.'

Genna tensed, but tried to keep her voice composed. 'Then I should like to go along, if I may. To learn what Dixon can teach me.'

'Suit yourself,' Tinmore said, swallowing another bite of goose and smiling ingratiatingly towards Rossdale. 'I'll have Dixon take you around after tea.' He signalled to the butler who then had the footmen remove the main course. 'Time for the pudding,' Tinmore said.

Chapter Seven

After the pudding, Genna and Lorene left the gentlemen to their brandy and retired to the drawing room again.

'Do be careful, Genna,' Lorene warned as they walked to the Mount Olympus room. 'You know how he is. And I do not believe he is as recovered as he makes us believe. His temper is easily piqued, I fear.'

How did Lorene know? Had he lost his temper with her? 'I am being careful. I forgot myself for one moment, that is all.'

'Being late did not help matters either,' Lorene added.

'Yes, I realise it.' Genna doubted Tinmore cared whether she'd been present or not. 'I do wonder, though, why he is not throwing me at these two *eligible* gentlemen. He is so eager for me to make a match and here they both are.'

She meant it as a joke, but Lorene answered her in all seriousness. 'He thinks they are too high for you, Genna. Marrying you would not give either of them any advantage.'

Lorene's words stung. 'I was not being serious. Do you not think I know they are too high for me?'

They entered the room and sat on the sofa where they had been before dinner. Genna's back was stiff and with effort she kept her hands still in her lap. She could not think of a word she wished to say to her sister, at the moment.

Or rather, she could not think of a civil word she wished to say.

Once upon a time she would have shared with her sister that she had no plans to marry, that she intended to make her own way in the world unshackled by any man. But Lorene's decision to marry Tinmore had altered matters. Lorene and she did not look upon the world with the same eyes.

'What are these gifts you are giving?' Lorene asked, breaking the silence.

'They are gifts,' Genna said. 'You discover the gift when you open it, not before.'

Lorene's brow furrowed. 'You have gifts for Lord Rossdale and Lord Penford?'

'For our guests, you mean? Yes, that was rather the point of it all.' Although she would have given Lorene her gift before the day was over, even if there had been no guests.

Lorene bit her lip. 'I do hope Lord Tinmore finds them appropriate.'

What were the chances of that? 'Do not worry, Lorene. They are mere trifles.'

The footman brought in tea and they lapsed into silence again. Genna occupied herself by staring at the paintings that covered the walls of the room, studying Verrio's use of colour, of movement and illusion. Whatever room she had found herself in these last few days she'd examined the paintings. How had she not allowed herself to see them before?

Ross felt as if he was sitting at his father's table with all Tinmore's talk of the politics of the day. Ross was not oblivious to the issues facing the country now that the war was over and he was not indifferent, but while his father was still alive he had no role to play in deciding such matters as what should be taxed, what prices should be fixed and what tariffs imposed. He also did not have to consider the consequences of whether he voted aye or nay. His day would come for all this, but now it was in the hands of others.

Tinmore slapped the table with the palm of his hand. 'The power must remain with the King and the aristocracy! We shall never go the way of France!'

His words became lost in a paroxysm of coughing. His butler quickly poured more brandy for him.

He downed the drink in one gulp. 'Shall we join the ladies?' His voice still choked.

'Excellent idea.' Ross tried not to sound too eager—or sarcastic.

Tinmore leaned heavily on his cane as he led them

back to the drawing room. His butler followed rather solicitously.

The ladies looked up at their entrance.

'Would you like tea, gentlemen?' Lady Tinmore asked as they approached.

Lawd, no, thought Ross. More tea, more conversation.

'They don't want tea,' Lord Tinmore snapped. He signalled to the butler. 'Bring more brandy.'

The butler bowed and left the room.

In Ross's mind, the Earl had imbibed quite enough brandy already. He glanced at Lady Tinmore, who looked both chastened and concerned. Genna merely looked furious. Even Dell looked displeased.

Such a disagreeable man, especially to his wife and her sister.

The brandy was brought quickly and poured by the butler.

Ross detested the pall brought on by Tinmore's ill humour. He'd be damned if he let the evening go on like this. 'Shall we open the presents?' Tinmore would not dare contradict him.

Few men contradicted the son of a duke.

'If you desire it,' Tinmore agreed, sipping his brandy.

Genna turned to Ross. 'Do you mind if we open my gifts first? They really are mere trinkets.'

Ross smiled at her. 'If it pleases you, Miss Summerfield.'

She jumped out of her seat. 'It does, indeed!' She rushed over to the table where she'd placed her pack-

ages and brought them over. Handing them out, one to
her sister, one to Dell, one to Ross. Even one to Tinmore, who, after all, provided her with lovely clothes,
a roof over her head and an allowance.

'Please, do open them.' Her eyes sparkled in anticipation.

Dell was the first to open his. 'It is Summerfield
House!'

The gift was a small framed watercolour of Summerfield House, obviously painted by Genna. It was
not the one with the wild colours that she'd made the
day he'd met her, though. This one showed snow on
the ground and candlelight shining from the windows.

'It shows the night of your dinner party,' Genna
said.

'So it does.' Dell looked up at her.

'I painted it for you,' she said.

He gazed at it appreciatively. 'It is a fine remem-
brance of that evening.'

Genna beamed with pleasure.

Ross opened his next. Another watercolour of a
similar size, this one of a man on a galloping horse,
his greatcoat billowing behind him. It was meant to
be him, he realised, riding Spirit. He caught her eye
to show he knew.

'I surmised that any gentleman would like a picture of a horse,' Genna explained.

So it was to be just between them that she'd drawn
him?

He grinned. 'I like it very much.'

She smiled back, her face radiant.

Lord Tinmore tore open his gift next. His was smaller. He looked at it without comment.

'It is a miniature of Lorene,' Genna said.

She'd made a very small ink-and-watercolour painting of her sister and placed it in a frame small enough to be carried in the pocket of a coat.

Tinmore turned to his wife. 'It does you no justice, my dear. Amateur work.' He tossed it aside and it fell on the carpet by Dell's feet. 'When we go to London I will commission a proper portrait of you from the finest miniature artist in town. Perhaps Cosway or Engleheart are still painting. If not, someone quite as renowned.'

Genna's cheeks turned red, as if she'd been slapped in the face. She might as well have been.

Ross was too outraged to speak. How unspeakably rude and cruel to both women.

Dell picked up the small painting and looked at it. 'I disagree, Tinmore.' He turned to Genna. 'Well done, Miss Summerfield. This is a charming likeness of your sister.' He placed it carefully on the table, catching Lady Tinmore's eye as he did so.

She immediately glanced away. 'Let—let me open mine,' she said, her voice shaking and her fingers tremulous. 'Oh, Genna!' Lady Tinmore turned her small painting around for the others to see.

It showed four children, a boy and three little girls, playing at a folly, the folly where Ross and Genna had taken refuge from the weather.

'It is us,' whispered Genna.

Her sister looked up at her with glistening eyes. 'Look how happy we were.'

Tinmore tapped his cane on the carpet. 'We should allow our guests to present their gifts, since they have gone to the trouble.' He glanced at the butler who gestured to a footman to bring the gifts to them.

'I fear our gifts will pale in comparison to such thoughtfulness on Miss Summerfield's part,' Ross said. 'As you shall see.'

Ross took the gifts from the footman and handed one to each of them. Even in the wrapping, it was pretty obvious what he and Dell had brought for Lord Tinmore.

The man opened it eagerly. 'Cognac. Remy Martin 1780!'

'From my father's cellar,' Ross said.

Tinmore gushed. 'This is a fine gift indeed. A very fine gift. Even finer that it came from the Duke's cellar.'

'Open yours, Lady Tinmore,' Dell said.

It was a large and heavy box that she balanced on her knees. When she opened the box, she gasped, 'The music!'

Dell spoke, 'I am merely returning what is yours.'

She lifted each sheet of music as if it were as precious as jewels. 'I did not think to bring the music with me when we left Summerfield House. You have restored it to me.'

'Look,' Genna said, 'some are the pieces from which we first learned to play.'

'Lovely memories,' Lorene murmured.

Genna looked up. 'It is my turn, I suppose.' She untied the string and opened her box. 'My sketchbook!'

'Again, we merely return what is yours,' Dell said.

Ross had talked Dell into bringing Genna's sketchbook and presenting it as a gift. He had, after all, promised to return it to her. It was Dell who thought of the piano music, though.

Genna opened the book and glanced at some of the pages before closing it again and clasping it to her breast. 'I am so happy to have it. I thought it lost for ever.' She faced Ross and her smile widened. *Thank you*, she mouthed.

Ross turned to Lord Tinmore. 'See, sir, nothing precious.'

Tinmore looked affronted. 'I assure you, the cognac is quite precious!'

Ross had brought it for Dell and rather wished the two of them had made short work of it instead of leaving it with this disagreeable man who did not even have the courtesy to offer to share it with them.

Ross suddenly could not stand to be in this man's presence another second.

He stood. 'I desire to prevail upon your butler for the house tour now. I have a great need to stretch my legs.'

Tinmore was still examining his bottle of cognac, turning it around in his hands. He looked up and smirked at Ross. 'I am certain Dixon would be delighted to start the tour.' He snapped his hand to his butler. 'Dixon, show Lord Rossdale the important rooms of the house, the state rooms.'

Dixon bowed. 'Very good, sir.'

Ross glanced at Dell. 'Do you come, too, Dell?' Perhaps Dell needed a break from this disagreeable man, as well.

Dell darted a glance at Lady Tinmore and shook his head. 'I am content to stay.'

Genna rose from her chair. 'I will go.' She faltered and turned to Tinmore. 'You gave your permission, sir.'

Tinmore waved her away. 'Go, then.'

'This way, m'lord,' Dixon said, leading the way.

When they crossed the threshold, Ross glanced up at the mistletoe, but this would certainly not be an opportune time to take advantage.

Besides, it would send the wrong message to her.

Instead he whispered to her, 'Tinmore is unpleasant and cruel. I am sorry for you and your sister.'

'I am able to bear it,' she whispered back, 'but I worry about Lorene.'

'We will begin at the hall,' the butler said, cutting off more conversation.

Genna inclined her head towards the butler. 'Dixon will repeat anything we say to each other.'

Ross took the warning and stepped away from her.

The hall, the first room seen when one entered the house from the main entrance, was wainscoted in dark mahogany and its walls were adorned in armament of early times, when it was important that a lord show his military strength. Though the swords, battleaxes, lances, rapiers and pikes were arranged in decorative patterns, the sheer numbers were a warning.

'You can see,' the butler intoned, 'the power that has always been a part of the Earls of Tinmore.'

Rossdale Hall had an armament room with twice as many weapons on display and countless more stored away in an attic somewhere, but Ross did not mention that fact.

'Depressing, is it not?' murmured Genna just loud enough for Ross to hear.

Dixon gestured to a huge portrait of a gentleman on the left wall. 'This is the first Earl of Tinmore, a favourite of Queen Elizabeth and one of her trusted advisors. He was given this land and title as a reward for his faithful service to the Queen.'

The first Earl had the pointed beard, ruff and rich velvets of his era.

'And on the right is his Countess.'

The portrait matched the size of the first Earl of Tinmore's. His Countess wore a black gown with an even wider white ruff and huge puffed sleeves.

'The house has over one hundred rooms…' Dixon said.

He led them from salon to dining room to gallery and Ross made no more attempt to talk with Genna. This house tour had none of the delight of her tour of Summerfield House. His only consolation was that they were free of Tinmore's company.

And he could watch Genna.

In each room, Genna paid close attention to the paintings. The house contained an impressive array of them. Most were Italian, as Tinmore had suggested. Ross recognised the style from the Grand Tour he and Dell had taken in their youth, but there was also an impressive number of Dutch paintings, classical sculpture, and later portraits by Lawrence and Reynolds.

What was she thinking as she examined the artwork? Ross wondered. Her mind was alive, he could tell, but he did not have an inkling what was passing through it.

He rather liked that.

Tinmore waved a hand towards the pianoforte. 'Play for our guest,' he demanded of his wife.

Dell steeled himself. He'd managed to act as if he was not affected by Lorene, but he did not know how long he could tolerate Tinmore's company. He would have fled the room with Ross and Genna, but he could not bear to leave Lorene alone with him.

Foolish. She was his wife. She would be alone with him the moment they left for Summerfield House.

She rose from her sofa and gracefully moved to the pianoforte in one corner of the room. The pianoforte was a work of art unto itself, like the walls of the room with their Roman gods spilling over each other. Trimmed in ebony and gold, the pianoforte sparkled in the candlelight, as dreamlike as the Mount Olympus scene.

Dell held his breath as her hands touched the keys. Since the night she had played for him at Summerfield House, he could not get her music out of his head—or the vision of her playing it. It came back to him during moments of solitude when he could not keep himself busy enough to stop thinking.

She began with the Beethoven piece she had played for him before, the one that revealed to him all her sadness and loneliness and so reminded him of his sister. It took a few bars of the music to transport her and then her lovely face glowed as if the music had lit her from within. He had to close his eyes from the sheer beauty of her.

'No. No,' her husband interrupted. 'Do not play your gloomy nonsense!'

She stopped with a discordant note and her back stiffened.

Tinmore had downed another glass of brandy. How many had he consumed? Dell and Ross prided themselves on being able to empty a few bottles at night, but where they'd restrained themselves, Tinmore had indulged.

'Our guest does not want to hear this.' He pounded on the carpet with his cane.

'I assure you I do wish to hear whatever your wife chooses,' Dell said through clenched teeth.

Tinmore smirked at him. 'You need not be polite, Penford. She can play something cheerful. Something fitting for Christmas Day.'

She paused for a moment, as if collecting herself,

before she played the first notes of *Here We Come A-wassailing.*

Lord Tinmore started to sing, *"'Here we come a-wassailing among the leaves so green—'"*

Another fit of coughing overtook him.

Lorene rose and hurried over to him. 'My lord, you are ill again.'

Dell poured him a cup of tea, tepid now. Better tea than more brandy. He handed it to Tinmore without milk or sugar. Tinmore gulped it down and the coughing eased, but his breathing was laboured.

'You are wheezing.' Lorene placed a hand on Tinmore's forehead. 'Let me help you to your room.'

Tinmore pushed her hand away. 'Stop fussing. Think of your duty, woman. We have a guest. You stay and entertain our guest. Wicky will take care of me.' He motioned for the footman attending the room to approach. 'Help me to my room and get Wicky for me.'

'His valet,' Lady Tinmore explained.

Dell did not care who tended to Tinmore.

The old Earl hobbled out of the room with the footman bearing his weight. His coughing came back, echoing behind him.

This damned man. How could he be so churlish towards his wife, even while she showed him great solicitude? How did she bear moments like this, being callously dismissed and rebuffed?

She still faced the door from which her husband

exited. Dell indulged in his desire to gaze at her, so graceful, so perfect.

Lawd! Why should this woman be married to such a man?

He raised his arm, wanting to comfort her, but he had no right. He had no right to even speak to her about her husband.

But he could not help it. 'Does he always speak to you so?'

She turned and lifted her eyes to his. 'Quite often.'

'He should not,' he answered in a low voice. 'You do not deserve it.'

She lowered her lashes. 'It is kind of you to say so.'

There was so much more he wished to say. He wanted Tinmore to go to the devil and never do her feelings an injury again.

Instead the two of them stood there, less than an arm's length apart. Too close. Much too close.

He could not help but reach out and touch her arm. 'Would you play the Beethoven piece for me?' he murmured. 'I would very much like to hear it again.'

She nodded. 'Of course.'

She returned to the pianoforte and began *Pathétique* and the notes of the music transformed into sheer emotion. He could not quiet the storm inside him. As she played he walked back to the chair where he had been sitting, spying on the table the miniature Genna had painted of her. Lorene's back was to him and, for the moment, there was no one else in the room. He picked up the miniature and placed it in his coat pocket.

When she finished *Pathétique*, she turned to him. 'Do you mind if I play some of the music you brought to me?'

'Not at all,' he responded. He picked up the box and brought the sheet music to her. She set it on the piano bench and started to look through it.

'Some of this is so frivolous,' she said. 'Some too simple.'

'Like what?' he asked.

'King William's March,' she responded. 'This is one of the first pieces I learned to play.'

She put the sheet of music on the stand and played the crisp lively notes. He stood behind her and watched the confident movement of her fingers on the keys and was glad that the music had led her to something more cheerful. When the piece was done her mood seemed to have lifted.

She looked through her box again. 'Let us look for a nice song!'

'The wassail song?' he asked.

She laughed. 'No, not that one.' She continued to riffle through the pages. 'This one.' She handed him a sheet.

'Barbara Allen?' He placed it on the stand. 'Even I know that one.'

She placed the box on the floor and moved over on her bench. 'Then sit and sing it with me.'

They sang the old song together, her voice high and crystalline; his deeper.

In Scarlet town where I was born
There was a fair maid dwelling...

The song was a tragedy, two lovers dying.

She played other pieces of music from her box, all songs of thwarted love, it seemed. He remained at her side, watching her, joining in on the songs when he knew them. Time seemed suspended as her music went on.

'You select one,' she said, handing him the box.

He picked out *The Turtle Dove*. She played and he sang.

Fare you well, my dear, I must be gone,
And leave you for a while,
If I roam away I'll come back again,
Though I roam ten thousand miles...

He sang to the end of the song:

O yonder doth sit that little turtle dove,
He doth sit on yonder high tree,
A-making a moan for the loss of his love,
As I will do for thee, my dear.

When he finished, she placed her hands on the bench at her sides, but continued to stare at the piano keys. The room turned very quiet.

He touched her hand, a bare touch with only two fingers entwined with hers. He was merely feeling sympathy for her, was he not? She was a relation of sorts so it stood to reason he would care about her.

Very slowly she faced him and met his gaze.

Dell stopped thinking.

She leaned towards him, still holding his eyes.

The door opened and Genna's laughter reached their ears.

Genna and Ross entered the room.

'We are finished with the tour!' Genna said.

Dell stood up and moved away from the pianoforte. 'And we must take our leave,' he said.

'Now?' Ross looked surprised.

'Yes—now—' Dell sputtered. 'Lord Tinmore took ill again. We should leave. Now.'

Chapter Eight

London—February 1816

Six weeks later Genna sat behind her sister in the recesses of Lord Tinmore's box at the Royal Opera House. Onstage was *Don Giovanni* and all the *ton* were keen to see it—and to be seen seeing it. Thus, the boxes were packed with ladies in silks and gentlemen in impeccably tailored formal dress. Those in the orchestra were not so fashionably dressed, but those people mattered very little to the fashionable world.

Genna loved to see the fashionable clothes the London ladies wore. Genna, though, considered it important to set herself off from the latest fashion, with a twist on whatever was the rage. She and Lorene used a modiste who used to be their sister Tess's maid. Nancy was a particularly creative collaborator in Genna's quest to express herself in her dress.

Her wardrobe, of course, was possible only through

the benevolence of Lord Tinmore, a fact which nig-
gled at Genna's conscience a little, even though he
considered her dress mere pretty packaging to attract
suitors. Tinmore's intention was to marry her off this
Season. Genna was just as determined to resist.

If she could only hold out this Season. In the autumn she would turn twenty-one and then she intended to do as she pleased.

In the meantime she would enjoy the Season's entertainments, like this lovely opera, so filled with humour and drama. The Season was hardly at its height,
but more of the fashionable elite arrived every day
and more and more were hosting balls, breakfasts,
or musical soirées.

Not that Genna expected to be invited to many of
them. Tinmore was a generation or two too old to be
on everyone's guest list and Genna was certain many
hostesses seized on any excuse to keep from inviting
the scandalous Summerfield sisters.

'Look! Look there!' Tinmore cried above Leporel-
lo's solo. 'I do believe that is the Duke of Kessington.' He lifted his mother-of-pearl opera glasses to
his eyes. 'Yes. Yes. It is. Rossdale and Penford are
in his company.'

Rossdale. Her heart skittered.

She knew there was a chance she would see Rossdale during the Season. It was unlikely they would
attend the same entertainments, but it was possible
that their paths would cross somewhere like this. She
hardly knew what greeting to expect from him, if he

deigned to greet her at all. He and Penford had left so abruptly on Christmas Day. They quit Lincolnshire entirely within that same week, she'd heard, even though they'd said they would stay past Twelfth Night.

Something must have offended them. What other explanation could there be? Something must have happened while she and Rossdale were touring the house. Lorene professed to know nothing, but Genna did not know whether to believe her or not.

She'd missed Rossdale. She fancied him her friend and Genna had enjoyed his company more than anyone she could remember.

Although perhaps he'd merely been kind to a silly chit with scandalous parents and siblings.

'Who is Tinmore talking about?' her sister Tess leaned over to ask.

Another of the delights of London was the opportunity to see Tess, who now stayed in town most of the time with her husband and his parents, Viscount and Viscountess Northdon.

Genna answered her. 'He is talking about our cousin, Lord Penford, and his friend. They sit in the Duke of Kessington's box.'

'Our cousin attends the opera with a duke?' Tess's brows rose. 'Impressive.'

'His friend is the Duke's son,' Genna explained.

The Duke's box was positioned almost as advantageously as the King's box, which seemed a great distance from Genna at the moment.

Once she would have told Tess about every moment with a man like Rossdale, but since Lorene married and turned their world on its ears, Genna had become too used to keeping secrets.

Tess glanced at the Duke's box again. 'Lorene told me you had dined with our cousin, but I did not know about his friend.'

Genna joked, 'I suppose Lorene and I are so accustomed to lofty acquaintances that it quite slipped our minds to tell you.'

Tess laughed. 'Who would ever have thought any Summerfield sister would be acquainted with a person of such high rank?'

'Indeed.' Though he might pretend not to know her now.

Ross saw Tinmore gazing at his father's box through opera glasses. Whether Dell saw Tinmore, too, Ross could not tell. He didn't dare ask either. Ever since Christmas night Dell had acted very strange. First he'd insisted they leave Tinmore Hall abruptly, then he'd decided to quit Lincolnshire entirely. Ross thought he would have left on Boxing Day if he could have, but it took a little longer than that to complete his business there.

Ross asked once what had happened to make Dell so adamant about leaving. Dell told him he did not want to risk having to be in Tinmore's company again. Neither he nor Ross could abide the man, but Ross had been disappointed that their visit was cut so short. He'd have risked a few moments in Tinmore's company if it meant spending more time with Genna. He'd at least hoped they would have had a chance to discuss the house tour or the artwork she'd examined that night.

Now every time he saw a painting, even the familiar ones in his father's town house, he thought of her. Would she see the painting as he did? Would she learn something from the artist's technique?

He must confess, he'd never given artistic technique a thought until meeting her, until seeing her wild use of colour in that watercolour of Summerfield House.

Was she in Tinmore's box? he wondered. He could not see her and he certainly did not wish to call upon Tinmore during the intermission if she were not present.

Could he renew his friendship with Genna here in London? He did not see how. Eligible men and marriageable women could not simply enjoy one another's company without wagging tongues putting them both in parson's mousetrap.

On stage Don Giovanni attempted to seduce Zerlina. *'This life is nought but pleasure,'* he sang in Italian.

But life was not all pleasure, Ross thought. For many there was nothing but suffering. He and Dell had visited some of the Waterloo wounded who'd been in Dell's regiment, men merely hanging on to life by a thread. He'd brought them bottles of brandy, but what they'd really wanted was food for their families. He'd seen to that later. Those families would never go hungry again.

If his father the Duke knew of his charity, he'd scoff and insist that the real solutions lay in Parliament. To his father, Parliament and its politics were everything. Even the guests the Duke had selected to share his box were chosen to bring some political advantage. Ross was not even sure his father and his wife paid any attention to the marvel of this opera.

What about merely inviting friends because you enjoyed their company? And why not help suffering individuals now? What was wrong with doing things his own way, not like his father?

Ross and Genna were alike in that way. They both wanted to choose their own way.

Ross stared at Giovanni, so determined to do as he wished, as reprehensible as his wishes were. Ross's desires were not reprehensible. He wished to do good for people. But the important thing to him was to assist by his own choice, not someone else's, not what the politics of the situation would require of him.

He shifted his gaze to Tinmore's box. Somehow he'd cross paths with Miss Genna Summerfield again. Why not?

When the opera was over the crowds spilled on to the street where the carriages were lined up to gather them. A fine mist of rain dampened the air and kept most of the crowd waiting in the shelter behind the Opera House's columns.

Genna stood with Tess and her husband, Marc Glenville, a few feet from Tinmore and Lorene, who remained under the portico. The rain was too thin to be of much concern and, after the close air and crowds inside the theatre, Genna relished the night air. The lamplight shone on the wet pavement and cobbles, making a play of light and dark that captivated her. How did artists paint such reflections?

Something else to try. There was always something about art that she discovered she did not know. Thanks to Rossdale, she'd begun to look at the paintings around her more carefully to try to answer some of these questions.

She took a breath.

Rossdale. Where was he? Somewhere in the crowd? Odd to know he was so close. It made her skin tingle with excitement.

'What is the delay?' she heard Tinmore complain. 'I distinctly told the coachman to be at the head of the line. I detest waiting.'

Next to her, Tess gave an exasperated sigh. 'At least it is not pouring rain.' She clasped her husband's arm. 'It feels rather refreshing out here.'

Marc smiled and held her even closer. 'It does look as if we are in for a bit of a wait.'

'We could walk back faster,' Genna said.

'I would not mind,' Tess said.

Most of those from the orchestra seats seemed to be doing just that, filling the streets and blocking the carriages.

Tess hummed. 'Do you not have the music still in your head? I do.'

'It was good music,' her husband agreed.

Genna held on to the costumes, the stage designs and the colours and patterns of the theatre itself.

'Miss Summerfield?' A low masculine voice sounded behind her.

She turned. 'Lord Rossdale!' Her insides skittered with something like joy.

He tipped his hat and bowed. 'I thought that was you.'

'Rossdale! Rossdale!' Tinmore called out. 'Saw you in the theatre. You and your father. Give him my regards.'

Rossdale turned slowly and merely nodded to Tinmore before turning back to Genna. 'I hope you are well, Miss Summerfield.'

She smiled. 'I am always well, sir!' Her voice dropped. 'It is good to see you.'

She caught his gaze for a moment, when Tess, standing right beside her, said, 'Genna?'

'Oh.' She gestured from Tess to Rossdale. 'Tess, may I present Lord Rossdale, with whom we became acquainted when he visited Lincolnshire. My sister, Mrs Glenville.'

Tess smiled at him. 'Lord Rossdale.'

Tess's husband spoke up. 'Rossdale. Good to see you again.'

'And you, Glenville.' He shook Marc's hand. 'Under better circumstances, yes?'

Marc glanced at his wife. 'Much better circumstances.'

'There it is!' Tinmore shouted. 'There is our carriage. Do not tarry!' He walked quickly, his cane tapping loudly on the pavement.

Genna exchanged a glance with Rossdale.

He stepped back. 'Goodnight, Miss Summerfield.' He nodded to Tess and Marc. 'Goodnight.'

'Make haste!' Tinmore called from the carriage door. 'I do not wish to remain here all night.'

They had no choice but to rush to the carriage.

Genna took a glance back as she was assisted into the carriage, but Rossdale seemed to have melted into the crowd.

Shortly after Lord Tinmore's carriage pulled away, Ross climbed into his father's carriage.

'Is Dell with you?' his father asked. They had all been invited to a supper after the opera.

'He is making his own way,' Ross replied.

Dell had left him right after the performance. Rather abruptly, Ross thought.

'I wanted to talk to him about this income-tax business,' the Duke said. 'We must settle this question. It is vital.'

Income taxes had been high during the war with Napoleon and now, with the peace, the citizens were eager for some relief.

'I heard much discussion among the others who called upon our box during the intermission,' the

Duchess said. Ross's father's second wife was perhaps even more serious about politics than was his father.

The carriage started to move.

Ross, though, had heard his father's discussion of the income tax—and the Duchess's—many times since joining them in London. He'd contributed all his thoughts on the subject already. Not that his father credited his opinion.

He turned his thoughts instead to Genna. To devising some way to see her again soon.

It was possible that eventually they would be invited to the same social affair, but that was leaving too much to chance. He needed to figure out a way to see her soon and he knew just how to arrange that.

'I heard something as well,' he began. 'Well, not so much heard, but noticed.'

'Something of importance?' his father asked sceptically.

His father believed Ross was merely pleasure-seeking, but, then, his father never knew Ross to do anything of importance. He never knew of Ross's voyages across the channel during the war, transporting spies like Glenville, Genna's brother-in-law, and of bringing exiles to safety. He certainly did not know of his assistance to Waterloo veterans and their families.

'Do you recall that Dell and I had some acquaintance with Lord Tinmore when we were in Lincolnshire?' Ross asked.

'That unpalatable fossil?' his father spat.

Ross suppressed a smile. His father did have a way with words. 'The very one. I ran into him tonight right before the carriage came. He asked me to give you his regards.'

His father peered at him. 'Ross, Tinmore's regards are of no importance to me.'

'I think they are,' Ross countered. 'The thing is, Tinmore is dazzled by you. He acted the complete toad-eater when Dell and I saw him in Lincolnshire. I believe he fancies being one of your set. I think he'd be easily swayed to vote with you if he had the impression you favoured him.' This was half-true at least. Tinmore was enamoured of being in the company of a duke—or even his son. Whether he'd change his vote was total speculation.

Ross's father nodded thoughtfully. 'You might be correct. And if I secure his vote, those old cronies of his might follow suit.' He shook his head. 'No. If I befriend him now he'll think I am merely seeking votes.'

Which was precisely what his father wished to do.

'Be subtle,' Ross urged. 'Do not approach him directly. Invite him to some of your entertainments.'

The Duchess, who had been listening with keen interest, spoke up. 'Invite him...I believe it could work, although I hesitate to include that fortune-hunter wife of his.'

'I can ease your concern on that score,' Ross said quickly. 'Lady Tinmore is actually a mild-mannered, well-meaning woman. I think you might actually take a liking to her.'

'Is she?' The Duchess's brows rose. 'Difficult to believe. Everyone knows her mother was as wanton as they come even before she ran away with a foreign count.' She leaned forward. 'You know people say each of the Summerfield daughters were fathered by different lovers. And there is that bastard son. And Summerfield lost his fortune, of course.'

Leave it to the Duchess to know all the gossip there was to know.

'I also heard the bastard son married Lord Northdon's daughter,' she went on. 'A patched-up affair that was, I am certain. Northdon packed them off to some farm in the Lake District.'

How did she retain all this information?

'I do not dispute the sins of the parents,' Ross said. 'And I have never met the son. But the daughters are not cut from the same cloth.' Genna was an original, that was certain, but he saw nothing wanton in her. 'They would not embarrass you.'

She leaned back on the seat. 'I confess I am curious about them.'

'Invite them to your musicale next week,' he suggested.

Her mouth turned up in a calculating grin. She turned to the Duke. 'Shall we?'

He returned her expression. 'By all means.'

Chapter Nine

The invitation to the Duchess of Kessington's musicale was quite unexpected, but it put Lord Tinmore in raptures. He became nearly intolerable. From the moment he'd opened the gold-edged invitation bearing the Kessington crest his warnings and instructions had been incessant. He was convinced that Lorene or Genna would behave improperly and would prove to be an embarrassment to him.

Genna had no fears that she and Lorene would offend anyone. Tinmore's capacity to be objectionable, though, was another story altogether.

Along with a litany of dos and don'ts in the society of dukes and duchesses, Tinmore desired to select what gowns they were to wear and how they ought to style their hair. Goodness! He would probably have put them in stomachers and powdered wigs.

Somehow Lorene had been able to prevent that ghastly idea. It was a good thing, because Genna would have refused to wear whatever Tinmore selected, even if it had been her finest dress.

On the night of the musicale, with the assistance of Nancy, their modiste, they managed to look presentable, but that hardly eased Tinmore's nerves. When their carriage pulled through the wrought-iron gates of Kessington House on Piccadilly, he was nearly beside himself.

'Now remember to curtsy to the Duchess and, whatever you do, do not open your mouths. The less you say the less chance you will utter some drivel.'

They entered the hall, a semicircular room all white and gold with marble floors and cream walls with gilded plasterwork. The curve of the room was repeated in the double-marble staircase, as was the gold. Its wrought-iron banister was gilded, the curves appearing again in its design.

A footman in fine livery took their cloaks and another led them toward the sounds of people talking and soft violin music playing.

The butler announced them, 'Lord and Lady Tinmore. Miss Summerfield.

Genna noticed heads turn towards them. Because of Tinmore or because two of the scandalous Summerfield sisters had arrived? She lifted her chin and allowed her gaze to sweep the room. Its walls were covered with huge paintings and mirrors, its ceiling a marvel of plasterwork design. Hanging from the ceiling was the largest crystal chandelier she had ever seen. The room was all pattern and opulence.

Tinmore impatiently tugged at her arm to follow him to where His and Her Graces greeted other guests who had arrived just before them. Rossdale stood next to them and caught Genna's eye as they approached.

He smiled and she knew the smile was just for her.

Tinmore effusively greeted the Duke and thanked the Duchess for including them. He made a big show of presenting Lorene to them before mumbling, 'My wife's sister, Miss Summerfield.'

'Very good of you to come,' the Duke said. 'I trust we will have some time to talk before the night is through.'

'It would be my honour.' Tinmore bowed.

The Duchess smiled graciously at Lorene and Genna. 'I must learn who your modiste is. Your appearance is charming. Charming.'

Rossdale stepped forward, extending his hand to Tinmore. 'Good of you to come, sir.'

'Rossdale.' Tinmore shook his hand eagerly. 'Good to see you again. Looking forward to this evening.'

Rossdale also took Lorene's hand. 'Welcome, ma'am. I dare say there should be some people you know here. Your cousin is here somewhere.'

'Lord Penford?' she said. 'Yes, I already glimpsed him.'

Finally he clasped Genna's hand and even through her glove she could feel his warmth and strength. 'Miss Summerfield. I hope you will allow me to show you the art work in this house. We have a considerable collection.'

She was so happy to see him, but feared it would

show. She glanced at the paintings gracing the walls instead. 'I can see that already! There are so many wonderful paintings here.'

He released her. 'I took time to learn of them so you will be impressed with me.'

She laughed.

Tinmore took her arm and pulled her away. 'Do not waste the gentleman's time.'

'She is not—' Rossdale started, but other guests arrived and he had to turn away.

Tinmore led Genna and Lorene through the throngs of people and deposited them in a corner before insinuating himself into a group of other lords probably discussing their political matters.

'Do you suppose anyone will speak to us?' Lorene asked. 'I cannot help but feel this company is too high for us. Why were we invited, I wonder?'

'I wonder, too.' Did Rossdale have anything to do with it?

Two of the ladies seated nearby gave them curious looks. Did they disapprove of their being invited?

Lorene nodded to them and smiled sweetly. How could anyone not adore her sister?

Genna turned her attention to the painting on the wall behind them, a portrait of an old man in a turban. This was not an Italian artist, she would guess by the clothing and the style of painting. The colours were dark and the figure seemed to blend into the background, although his face seemed bathed in light.

'Lady Tinmore.' A male voice came from behind. Genna turned. It was Lord Penford.

'How do you do, sir,' Lorene said, her voice barely audible.

'Penford!' Genna said lightly. 'Are you going to speak to us? No one else has dared!'

'I thought I might take you around and introduce you,' he said.

It was what Tinmore ought to have done.

'How very nice of you, Cousin.' Out of the corner of her eye Genna saw Rossdale working his way through the crowd. 'Take Lorene around. I wish to study these paintings a little longer.'

Neither he nor Lorene acted as if she'd said something odd. They left her. A footman brought her a glass of champagne which delighted Genna, who had only tasted the bubbly light wine two or three times during the last Season.

The two ladies seated nearby glanced at her again. They were of an age with her parents, Genna guessed. Perhaps they knew Genna's mother and father. If so, no wonder they stared.

Genna used Lorene's response and smiled at them. They smiled back. Did they wish her to speak with them? Genna could not tell.

No matter. Rossdale was coming closer.

'You are here alone,' he said when he reached her.

She turned to the wall. 'I was studying this painting. It is not Italian, is it?'

He grinned. 'Good girl. It is Dutch. Rembrandt.'

She looked at it again, more closely. 'I have never seen a Rembrandt. Look how he paints the black cloak of the man. It blends into the background, but it is still clear it is a coat if you look closely.'

He nodded. 'Do you wish a tour of the other paintings in the room?' he asked.

She glanced at the ladies nearby who looked her way again. 'I am afraid it would look odd with all your guests here.' She leaned closer to him. 'Tinmore might have apoplexy if I do anything to draw attention to myself. He has a great fear that Lorene and I will do something to mortify him.' She huffed. 'Of course, as soon as he could, he left us in this corner. I suppose he thought we would stand here like statues.'

He inclined his head. 'I saw Dell introducing your sister to other guests. Would you like me to introduce you?'

She giggled. 'Let Tinmore worry that I'll do something objectionable in your company.'

He started with the two ladies who had made her and Lorene an object of interest. 'May I present Miss Summerfield, sister-in-law to Lord Tinmore? Miss Summerfield, the Duchess of Archester and the Duchess of Mannerton.'

Genna executed a perfect curtsy. 'Your Graces. I am honoured to meet you.'

The Duchess of Archester peered at her. 'I knew your mother, Miss Summerfield.'

And she probably knew about all her mother's lovers and how her mother had left her children with a father who cared nothing for them and ran off with a foreign count.

'Did you, ma'am?' Genna smiled and held her gaze steady.

'I knew her quite well,' the Duchess said. 'How is she faring? I hope she is in good health.'

Genna managed to keep her composure. 'I have not seen her for many years.' Since she was three years old. 'But my sister, Mrs Glenville, met her in Brussels last summer. By her report my mother is in good health and prospering.'

'Is she still with Count von Osten?' asked the Duchess of Mannerton.

Was this any of their concern?

'Yes, she is.' Genna still smiled. 'My sister reports they are quite happy together.'

She was not about to give them the satisfaction of imagining her mother going to rack and ruin by leaving a loveless, desolate marriage for a man who loved her and could give her everything she desired.

Except her children.

To her surprise, though, the Duchesses looked pleased. 'I am delighted to hear it,' the Duchess of Mannerton said. 'A bad business it was, but she found her way in the end.'

Rossdale asked if the Duchesses needed anything and if they were enjoying themselves while Genna still reeled from this reaction to her mother.

'I cannot believe it,' she said as Rossdale escorted her away. 'I think they actually liked my mother. I thought they were looking at Lorene and me because they disapproved of us.'

'Perhaps they knew your mother well enough to realise she did the right thing,' he said.

She stiffened. 'Right for her, perhaps.'

He walked her around the room and introduced her to guests who were not deep in conversation. It seemed as if most of the guests were high in rank or important in government and all were quite uninterested in her.

'Ah, Vespery is here,' Rossdale said. 'Now, he is someone you must meet.'

He brought her over to a rather eccentrically attired gentleman, his neckcloth loosely tied, his waistcoat a bright blue. His black hair was longer than fashionable, very thick and unruly. As were his eyebrows.

The gentleman's eyes lit up upon seeing Rossdale.

'Rossdale, my lad,' he said. 'Are you in good health?'

'Very good, Vespery.' Rossdale turned to Genna. 'Miss Summerfield, allow me to present Mr Vespery to you.'

'How do you do?' Genna extended her hand, over which Vespery blew a kiss.

'Charmed,' the man said.

'Vespery is a friend of the Duchess's,' Rossdale explained. 'He is painting portraits of her and my father.'

'You are an artist!' The first true artist she'd ever met.

His eyes assessed her. 'Are you in need of an artist? Please tell me you wish to have your portrait painted. I would be more than delighted to immortalise you on canvas.'

She laughed. 'I am not important enough to be immortalised.'

'Miss Summerfield is an artist herself,' Rossdale told him.

'Are you?' Vespery's rather remarkable brows rose.

Genna rolled her eyes. 'An *aspiring* artist is more precise. But I am very serious about it.'

Vespery leaned forward. 'Do tell me. What is your medium?'

'Watercolours,' she replied. 'But only because I've never been taught how to use anything else.'

At that moment the Duchess of Kessington came up to Rossdale. 'I need you Rossdale. I must take you away.'

The Duchess took him out of earshot. 'What are you about, Ross? Spending all your time with the Summerfield girl? We have other guests.'

'Is that why you took me away?' Ross frowned.

'You know how it will look if you favour one young lady.' She kept her smile on her face. 'Especially a Summerfield.'

'Both Lord Tinmore and her sister left her standing alone,' he said. 'There is no one of her acquaintance here. Would it not be rude to leave any guest in that circumstance?'

'Well, be careful,' the Duchess said. 'You would

do well to join some of the conversations among the peers tonight. These are very important times, you know. You will learn much from the experience of these gentlemen.'

'Constance.' He looked her directly in the eye. 'Do not tell me what I must do.'

She released his arm. 'I speak for your father.'

Ross doubted that. Although her father and she were perfect partners, both working hard to further his political power and influence, Ross was reasonably certain his father was motivated by duty to the country and its people. Ross feared the Duchess merely liked power and influence for its own sake.

Ross's father married Constance when Ross was in school. Her connection was to his father and his role in society, not to Ross. It was fortunate that she had no interest in mothering Ross, because no one could replace the mother he had adored. The duty in which Constance revelled was what had killed his mother.

Ross scanned the room and found his father deep in conversation with his cronies. Tinmore, who looked very gratified, was included.

'I dare say the Duke has not given me a thought since the party began,' Ross told her. 'So do not tell me he has spoken of me to you.'

'You are impossible.' She swept away.

Ross glanced towards Genna, who seemed to be delighted to be in conversation with Vespery. As much as he hated to admit it, the Duchess was correct that people would notice if he spent the whole of the evening in Genna's company. He must make the rounds of the room and speak with other guests before returning to her. That should keep his father's wife satisfied.

He approached Dell, who still remained at Lady Tinmore's side, obviously not feeling the same obligation to limit his time with any one person.

'Is Dell taking good care of you?' he asked Lady Tinmore.

She blushed, although why she should blush at such a statement he could not guess.

'He has been very kind,' she said.

Ross glanced over at her husband, who was listening intently to something Ross's father was saying. 'Lord Tinmore seems quite preoccupied.'

'Indeed,' she said. 'I fear Lord Penford took pity on me. I am grateful to him.'

Dell looked like a storm ready to spew lightning and thunder.

'I know some ladies who might be very interested to speak with you.' Ross meant the Duchesses Archester and Mannerton.

'Would you like that?' Dell asked her.

'Of course.' She lowered her lashes. 'And it would free you from having to act my escort.'

Dell nodded, but Ross could not tell if he wanted to be rid of Lady Tinmore or not. Nor could he tell what Lady Tinmore really wished.

Lady Tinmore took Ross's arm and Dell followed.

Ross presented Lady Tinmore to the Duchess of Archester and the Duchess of Mannerton. 'The Duchesses told your sister that they knew your mother,' he told Lady Tinmore.

'Come sit with us, dear.' The Duchess of Archester patted the space next to her on a sofa.

Ross bowed and he and Dell walked away.

'Tinmore appears to have forgotten his wife,' Ross remarked.

'Yes.' Dell's voice was low. 'I thought it my duty to step in.' He took two glasses of champagne off a tray offered by a passing footman and handed one to Ross. 'Cousin and all. Why ever did your stepmother invite them?'

'Do not call her my stepmother.' Ross had told him this many times. She was his father's wife, but not any sort of mother to him. 'She invited them at my suggestion.'

'Your suggestion?' Dell gaped at him.

Ross shrugged. 'I had a desire to see Miss Summerfield again.'

'Miss Summerfield?' Dell took a sip of champagne. 'I am surprised.'

'Are you?' Ross responded. 'She is refreshing.'

Dell's brows knit. 'Your father will not approve, you know.'

'There really is nothing for him to approve or disapprove,' Ross said. 'I merely enjoy her company.'

'Will you court her?' Dell asked.

'I do not intend to court anyone,' Ross replied.

'You know that. I am in no hurry to be leg-shackled or to be shackled to a title. Time for that later.' His father was in good health. The need to produce an heir and be about the business of a duke was some years away yet.

Dell put a stilling hand on Ross's arm. 'Take care not to trifle with that young woman. She's got enough of a trial merely living with Tinmore. Besides, she's barely out of the schoolroom.'

'She's not as young as all that. She'll reach her majority within a year.' A friendship with Genna was sounding more and more impossible.

But it should not be. They should be free to be friends if they wished to.

'Take care, Ross,' Dell said. 'Tinmore means for her to be married. And he is just the sort to force the deed, if you give him any reason.'

Genna could not help but keep one eye on Rossdale. She fancied she could tell precisely where he stood in the room at any time. It made her heart glad merely to be in the same room with him, knowing he would eventually speak to her again. In the meantime what could be more delightful than to be in the company of a true artist, a man who made his living by painting! There was so much she wanted to ask Vespery, so much of his knowledge and skill she wished to absorb.

She asked him about the paintings.

'What of this one?' She pointed to a nearby landscape, a pastoral scene with a cottage, a stream, horses and a wagon, cattle, men working.

He pulled out spectacles and perched them on his nose. 'This painting? This painting is Flemish, of course.'

She wondered how one could tell a Flemish painting from a Dutch one. Although even she had been able to tell the Dutch painting was not Italian.

'It is a Brueghel, I believe,' he went on. 'Jan the Younger, if I am not mistaken. There were several generations of Brueghels. Some of them painted fruit.'

'How old is it?' she asked.

'Oh, possibly two hundred years old. Seventeenth century.'

She looked at it again.

Vespery moved closer to the painting. 'Notice the composition. All the triangles.'

She stared at it. 'Yes! The roof of the cottage. The shape of the stream. Even the tree trunks.' Patterns. Like the pattern of curves in the hall of this house. 'It makes it pleasing to look at.'

She wished she could find Rossdale and tell him what Vespery had taught her.

She glanced around the room and saw Rossdale speaking to an older woman and a younger one, possibly the older woman's daughter. The excitement in her breast turned into a sharp pain.

Why should she ache? Rossdale was merely speaking to a young woman who was his social equal.

Genna could not aspire to be anything but a friend
to him, not that they could manage a friendship in
London during the Season when everyone and everything centred on marriageable young ladies finding
eligible gentlemen to marry.

Chapter Ten

The musicale was announced and the guests filed out of the drawing room.

Genna excused herself from Vespery. 'I should find my sister.' No doubt Tinmore would leave her to walk into the music room alone.

She found Lorene near where Tinmore had first deposited them.

'I have had the most remarkable conversation with two duchesses,' Lorene said when Genna reached her. 'You spoke with them, too, Rossdale said. They knew our mother.'

The Duchesses of Archester and Mannerton. 'Yes. I did.'

'They knew her when she eloped with Count von Osten. I must tell you all about it later.' Lorene glanced around the room.

Tinmore had attached himself to another grey-haired gentleman and was leaving the room, but Lorene did not remark on it. Genna walked with Lorene as if it was the most natural thing in the world to be left without an escort.

Except Lord Penford appeared. 'I will escort you ladies to the music room.'

They followed the other guests to another huge room, this one painted green with cream accents and more gold gilt at the border of the ceiling and along the chair railing on the walls. Chairs upholstered in a brocade the same shade as the walls were lined up facing an alcove whose entrance was flanked by two Corinthian columns, their elaborate ornamentation painted gold.

'This is a lovely room,' Lorene exclaimed.

'Let me find you seats,' Penford said.

Tinmore hobbled up to them. 'There you are!' he said peevishly. 'Come. Come. Let us sit.'

Penford stepped back and when Genna next glanced his way, he'd disappeared.

'Here. Sit here.' Tinmore gestured with his cane.

They were near the centre of the room, several gentlemen having chosen seats in the back and Tinmore knew better than to take the front seats that more properly went to those of higher rank. On each chair was a printed card edged in gold like the invitation had been. It listed the program.

When everyone was seated, the butler stood at the front of the alcove and announced the program. 'Mozart's Quintets in D Major and G Minor.'

He backed away and five musicians entered the alcove through a door hidden in the wall, two violins, two violas and a cello. They sat and spent a few minutes tuning their instruments before beginning the first piece.

Lorene gasped and leaned forward, her colour high and the hint of a smile on her face. Genna silently celebrated. Her dear sister was awash in pleasure from the beautiful music. It was a joy to see her so happy. Genna glanced around the room, looking for Rossdale.

He stood in the back of the room, his arms folded across his chest, looking perfectly comfortable—and slightly bored. And very handsome. How lovely to have a handsome friend.

But she must not be caught staring at him.

She turned her attention instead to the lovely array of colours of the ladies' gowns, like so many flowers scattered about. She looked for patterns and shapes, but, unlike the symmetry of the room's decor, the guests were a mishmash. How would one put a pleasing order on a painting of this event?

Feeling like a hopeless amateur, she gave up and closed her eyes.

To her surprise she heard a pattern of sounds in the music, a repeated melody, but as soon as she identified it, the music changed and the pattern was lost. Sometimes it came back; sometimes a new pattern of notes emerged. Frustrating.

After talking with Vespery she'd entertained the idea that all art used pattern. Hearing it in the music expanded the idea. But then Mozart broke the pattern and her idea seemed suddenly foolish.

She opened her eyes again and looked around her.

Lord Tinmore leaned on his cane, his eyes closed and his breathing even. The music had put him to sleep. Goodness! She hoped he would not snore.

Rustling in the back suggested that other guests were restless. Lorene, though, was rapt and that was enough for Genna.

She wanted to glance behind her to see Rossdale's reaction to the music, but she feared it would be noticed.

When the first piece finished there was a short intermission during which the musicians left the room and the footmen served more champagne.

Some guests rose from their seats, but Lorene and Genna remained seated. Tinmore woke, but his eyes remained heavy.

'What did you think of the music?' Genna asked her sister.

'I thought it marvellous.' Lorene said. 'I wonder if there is sheet music for piano. I should love to learn it.'

'Perhaps we can visit the music shops and find out.' The shopping was another of the delights of London. There was a shop selling anything one could imagine.

After a few minutes the glasses were collected and the musicians returned to the alcove.

They began to play.

This piece was not as light-hearted as the first. It was melancholic. Sorrowful.

It reminded Genna of all she had lost. The home in which she'd grown up. Her mother.

And now her sisters and brother whose lives really did not involve her any more.

She blinked rapidly. She would not give in to the blue devils. She would not. No matter how dismal her life became. She was in London, a city of many enjoyments. She would enjoy as many as she could and would take it as a challenge to thwart any of Tinmore's plans for her to marry.

She would do just as she pleased.

The last movement began, a slow cavatina. It was a veritable dirge, pulling Genna's spirits low again. Then the music paused and Genna braced herself against a further onslaught of depression.

Instead, the music turned ebullient. Genna almost laughed aloud in relief as the notes danced cheerfully along, brushing away all that darkness.

That was what she would do. She'd brush away the darkness, make her own happy life and leave the rest behind.

She smiled and dared to glance back at Rossdale.

Ross scanned the supper room, although he knew precisely where Genna sat. Lord Tinmore had brought his wife and her sister into the supper room, but Ross's father had called him over to his table and Tinmore never looked back. The ladies were again left alone. Ross had been ready to cross the room to them, but both Dell and Vespery approached their table and sat with them. So he made the rounds again, but kept his eye on her, determined to spend a little more time with her before the night was over.

He moved through the room and finally stopped at their table.

Genna smiled up at him. 'Might you sit with us a little while?'

'I would be pleased to,' Ross answered truthfully. 'I do not believe I have sat down since the evening began.'

'Not even during the Quintet,' she stated.

'I stood in the back.' He turned to Lady Tinmore. 'Did you enjoy the performance?'

Lady Tinmore certainly had appeared as if she had. Of all the guests, she was the one whose attention to the music did not waver.

Her face lit up. 'Oh, yes! I do not know when I have so enjoyed music.'

He was baffled. The music had been competently played by the musicians and the pieces were pleasant enough. 'Why do you say so?'

'The first piece. In D major. It lightened my heart. There were so many musical ideas in it that I could not see how Mozart would be able to make it into a coherent whole.' She smiled. 'But, of course, he did.' She looked at the others. 'Did you not think so?'

'I listened for patterns of melody,' Genna said. 'But as soon as I heard one, the music changed to something else.'

'That is what I mean! So many ideas,' her sister cried. 'Please someone say they heard what I heard.'

Vespery threw up his hands. 'I do not analyse. I merely listen.'

Dell's chair had been pulled back as if he were not quite a part of this table. He stared into his glass of wine. 'I thought it complex. And beautiful.'

Lady Tinmore nodded. 'Yes,' she whispered. She looked shyly at Ross. 'What did you think?'

'I agree it was pleasant to listen to.' Music had never captured his interest. Neither had art of any sort, really. He liked what he saw or not, liked what he heard. Or not.

'What of the second piece?' Genna asked. 'That was not pleasant.'

'Beautiful.' Vespery raised a finger. 'But not pleasant.'

'But there were so many surprises in it!' Lady Tinmore cried. 'Like those harsh chords in the minuet.'

One thing Ross could say. Lady Tinmore had suddenly come to life. She had a personality after all. And emotion. Hidden, he supposed, because of her overbearing yet neglectful husband.

Genna spoke up. 'I thought I should be driven to a fit of weeping by those movements. Right when I was beginning to completely despair, that happy ending came.'

'Yes!' her sister cried. 'Was that not marvellous?'

Ross liked both the Summerfield sisters, he decided.

Lord Tinmore appeared at the table, but he spoke only to Ross. 'Rossdale, I was just telling your father, the Duke, that this was a most competently played musical evening. I am honoured to have been in the audience.'

Ross saw Genna cover her mouth, but her eyes danced. Tinmore did not notice. His attention was only on Ross. He also did not see Dell pull his chair further back and slip away.

'Kindly said, Tinmore,' Ross responded.

'I fear, sir, that I must bid you goodnight,' Tinmore went on. 'I already bade goodnight to your father and the Duchess. I hope that my years will excuse me to you and your family. Fatigue plagues me.'

They were leaving? He'd hardly had time to speak to Genna.

'Come!' Tinmore snapped to his wife and Genna. 'We must leave now.'

Lady Tinmore rose. 'I must thank the Duke and Duchess first.'

'They do not want to be bothered, I assure you,' Tinmore said. 'I said all that was required.'

All the life glimpsed a moment ago seemed drained from Lady Tinmore now. Genna looked red-faced with anger.

This boor.

Ross put on a smile he did not feel. 'I must agree with your wife, sir. My father and the Duchess take great offence when guests do not bother to thank them. I will accompany your wife and her sister to bid their farewells. You rest here.'

As Ross offered his arms to each of the ladies,

Tinmore looked at Vespery and demanded, 'Who are you?'

Ross did not wait to hear Vespery's reply.

When they stepped away from the table, Genna murmured, 'It was nonsense.'

'What was?' Ross asked.

'He fell asleep during the whole concert,' she said. 'He did not hear it competently played at all.'

Ross inclined his head to her. 'I noticed. I could see from the back.'

She giggled.

'Want to hear more nonsense, ladies?' Ross asked.

'Indeed!' Genna said.

Her sister remained subdued.

He stopped and looked from one to the other. 'My father and the Duchess do not care a fig if you bid them goodnight.'

Genna's eyes sparkled. 'Oh, you are trying to make me laugh out loud!'

Yes. He definitely wanted to see more of Genna Summerfield.

Because she made him want to laugh out loud, too.

The next morning Ross strode down Bond Street and entered a shop he had never set foot in before. Mori and Leverne's Music Shop. He'd passed it countless times on his way to Gentleman Jackson's Boxing Salon, but he'd never had a reason to enter it before.

He had a whim to purchase sheet music to the

Mozart pieces performed at the Duchess's musicale to give to Lady Tinmore. It seemed the one thing that made her happy. He'd present it to Lord Tinmore for his wife and no one would think anything of that, not that any member of the *ton* would know of it. Tinmore would take it as a compliment to him, Lady Tinmore would receive some pleasure from it and perhaps Genna would also be pleased with him.

He stood inside the door without a clue how to find the piece he desired. The music seemed to be arranged in aisles, filed in some order that escaped him.

The clerk stood behind a counter at the far end of the shop, speaking to two ladies.

As Ross approached one of the ladies turned and broke into a smile. 'Rossdale!'

Genna. And her sister.

'What a surprise to see you!' Genna said. 'We came looking for the music from last night's musicale, but the last copy was sold just this morning.'

'I am terribly sorry,' the clerk said. 'The gentleman came early when the shop opened. You might try Birchall's down the street.'

'We did try there,' Lady Tinmore said.

So much for his idea of giving the music to her.

'What are you here for, Rossdale?' Genna asked. 'Do not tell me you were searching for the same music.'

Very well. He would not tell her. 'I was considering a gift,' he said.

Her smile faltered. 'Oh.' She seemed to recover,

though. 'Perhaps we can help you. What sort of music did you have in mind?'

He shrugged. 'Perhaps something by Mozart. For the piano.'

'Ah!' said the clerk. 'I have some over here.'

'Help him, Lorene,' Genna said. 'You will be able to tell him what music is best.'

Lady Tinmore acted as reserved as usual. 'If you like.' She lowered her lashes.

'I would be grateful,' Ross said.

She riffled through the sheets of music the clerk indicated. 'Here is one.' She pulled out the sheet and studied it. 'A piano sonata. Number eleven.'

She handed it to him and he glanced at the page. He could follow almost none of it. 'Do you have this music?' he asked her.

'No,' she replied. 'I merely think it would be a pretty one to play.'

He handed the sheets to the clerk. 'I will purchase this one.' He gave his information to the clerk.

Upon learning where the bill was to be directed, the clerk became even more solicitous. 'Allow me to place this in an envelope for you, my lord.'

'Did you want to look for something else?' Genna asked her sister.

Lady Tinmore shook her head.

Ross, music in hand, walked with the ladies to the door. At the door, though, he stopped and handed the envelope to Lady Tinmore. 'This is for you, ma'am,' he said.

'For me?' Some expression entered her face.

'Lorene!' Genna broke into a smile.

'But, why?' Lady Tinmore asked.

'For being the guest last night who most enjoyed the concert,' he replied.

And to give her some happiness since she certainly did not have that in her marriage.

Ross opened the door and held it. Lady Tinmore walked out first.

Genna paused and looked up at Ross. 'Take care, Lord Rossdale. You might make me like you very much.'

He grinned. 'There must be worse fates than that.'

Although what good would it do them to like each other? Unless they could spend time together.

He was determined to figure out a way, but unless he made a formal gesture, he could not even call upon her. All he could do was wait until they saw each other by accident, like this, or were invited to the same parties. And who knew when that would be?

Chapter Eleven

What was he thinking? They were together now. Ross could contrive to spend more time with Genna, even if her sister was also present.

'Where are you ladies bound after this?' he asked when they were out on the pavement.

'I believe we will go home,' Lady Tinmore said.

Genna looked disappointed. Perhaps she wanted more time together, as well. He was not surprised they were of one mind.

'May I escort you?' he asked.

Genna's eyes pleaded with her sister. The walk back to Curzon Street and Tinmore's town house would be a short one, but to accompany them would be more enjoyable than if he simply left them here.

Lady Tinmore lowered her lashes. 'If you like.'

Genna smiled.

As did Ross.

He offered his arm to Lorene, who, as a countess, had precedence. Genna walked next to her.

They strolled past the shops on Bond Street and turned on Bruton Street.

'Are you enjoying your Season in London?' Ross asked in a polite tone.

'Yes, quite,' Lorene answered agreeably.

He leaned over and directed his gaze at Genna. 'And you, Miss Summerfield?'

Genna appeared for a moment to be doing battle with herself. Trying not to say something she really wanted to say.

Her words burst forth. 'To own the truth, I am feeling a bit restrained.' Apparently what she wanted to say won out. 'There is so much to do and see here in town and, as I cannot go out alone, I am confined to the house.'

'Genna!' her sister chided.

'Well, it is true,' Genna protested hotly.

They had reached Berkeley Square.

Ross deflected the impending sisterly spat. 'Shall we do and see something right now?' he asked. 'Here is Gunter's. Shall we stop and have an ice?'

Lady Tinmore's brows knit. 'I do not know if we should.'

'It would be respectable,' Ross said. 'I would not have asked otherwise.'

'Oh, let's do, Lorene.' Genna pleaded. 'It will be fun.'

Lady Tinmore looked as if she were being dragged to a dungeon instead of the most fashionable tea shop and confectioner in Mayfair.

'Very well,' she finally said.

Genna skipped in apparent delight.

'The day is overcast, though, as well as being chilly,' Ross said. 'Let us not eat in the square under the trees. We should go inside.'

They entered the shop and sat at a table.

A waiter stepped up to serve them. 'Sir? Ladies?'

'What would you like?' Ross asked Genna and her sister.

'Not an ice,' Lorene said. 'Not on such a cold day. I shall have tea.'

Genna huffed. 'I do not care how cold it may be, I am having an ice!'

The waiter handed them cards that had the flavours printed on them. 'Your choice, miss.'

Genna read part of the list aloud. 'Barberry, elderflower, jasmine, muscadine, pistachio and rye bread…' She handed the card back to the waiter. 'I shall be adventuresome. I will try the rye-bread ice.'

'Rye-bread ice,' repeated the waiter in a voice that showed her exotic choice was commonplace for him. 'And you, sir?'

'Pineapple,' Ross said.

The waiter bowed and left.

'Pineapple?' Genna looked at him in mock disapproval. 'That is not very daring.'

'It is what I like,' he explained.

'But how do you know that you will not like another flavour better unless you try it?' she asked.

'Genna fancies whatever is new and different,' her sister said.

'You make me sound frivolous,' Genna complained, but she turned to Ross and laughed. 'What am I saying? Lorene is correct! That is me! Liking whatever is new and different.'

Therein was her charm. 'And you are eager to see new and different sights while you are here?' he asked.

'I am eager. Not very hopeful, though.' She frowned and her face tightened in frustration. 'I think I might be content to do anything but stay in the house.'

'Genna!' her sister again chided. 'You must not say such things. They can be misinterpreted. You'll sound fast.'

'Oh, I think Lord Rossdale knows what I mean,' she said with confidence. 'I just want to *do* things. The places I see do not even have to be new. Something I've liked before and wish to do or see again would be fine.'

'Like what?' he asked.

'Well.' Her mouth widened into an impish smile. 'Like having an ice at Gunter's.'

He liked her humour. 'What else?'

Lady Tinmore answered for her. 'Genna wishes to see Napoleon's carriage at the Egyptian Hall.'

Ross laughed inwardly. He wanted to see Napoleon's carriage, as well.

'I do wish to see it!' she protested. 'Who would not?'

'It has created quite a stir,' he admitted.

Genna gave Lorene a smug look. 'See, Lorene, I am not the only one.' Lorene folded her arms across her chest and glanced away.

He had no idea what to do with sisterly disputes. He had no brothers or sisters. It was one of the reasons his father was so eager for him to marry and produce an heir.

Perhaps if his mother had lived it would have been different. Perhaps there would have been little sisters or brothers for him to spat with.

Genna went on. 'I would love to see everything in the Egyptian Museum. I also want to see Astley's Amphitheatre, the menagerie at the Tower, and—' She paused and looked away. 'I want to see the Elgin Marbles.'

She was game for everything.

Like his mother had been.

Until his father inherited the title and the burden of that responsibility fell upon him. And her.

'You cannot see the Elgin Marbles,' Lady Tinmore said. 'No one can. They are stored away until Parliament decides whether or not to purchase them for the British Museum.'

They were stored at Montagu House.

Their ices and Lady Tinmore's cup of tea were brought to them.

Genna dipped into hers eagerly. And made a face, but she took another spoonful and another.

Ross's spoon was poised to taste his. 'How is it?'

She put on a brave smile. 'It is—it is—it is…'

She faltered. She finally laughed. 'It is quite dreadful, actually.'

Her sister murmured, 'Of course it is.'

Ross pushed his untouched pineapple ice towards her. 'Here. Have mine. I only ordered it so you would not have to eat alone.'

She looked at it longingly, then pulled it the rest of the way towards her. 'Oh, thank you! I love pineapple ices.'

Her sister stood and Ross quickly stood, as well.

'I believe I will choose some confections to bring to Lord Tinmore,' she said.

'Shall I assist you?' he asked.

'Not at all. The clerk will help me.'

There was a clerk behind a counter who had just assisted someone else.

Ross sat again as Lady Tinmore walked away.

'She is purchasing confections for Lord Tinmore,' he repeated, finding it difficult to believe.

Genna's countenance turned serious. 'She tries very hard to please him. An impossible goal, I believe.'

He thought he ought to be careful what he said. 'Tinmore is very…critical…of her.'

She swallowed a spoonful. 'He is an awful man, but do not say so in front of her. She will defend him.'

He was puzzled. 'She has a regard for him?'

She shook her head. 'Not in the way you mean. She is grateful to him for marrying her. She married him so that my sister Tess, my brother and I would have a chance to make good matches and not be required to be governesses or ladies' companions, or, in my brother's case, to stay in the army and be sent some place terrible like the West Indies.'

'She married him for you and your sister and brother?' Marrying for money took on a different meaning in that case.

She nodded and glanced over at her sister. 'Although I never wanted any of it. I won't use his dowry, no matter what Tinmore thinks.'

'Surely you wish to marry, though,' he said.

She scoffed. 'With no dowry, I cannot expect to marry, but that does not trouble me. I do not wish to marry.'

'How would you live, then?' he asked.

Young ladies of good birth had few choices in life except to marry. The few they had were dismal. Ladies' companions or governesses, as she'd said.

'Well, if you must know, I wish to make my living as an artist. Like your Mr Vespery.' She took another spoonful.

'You wish to paint portraits?' That was how Vespery made his living.

'I would prefer to paint landscapes, but I doubt that will bring me enough money.' She shrugged.

He smiled. 'Ones with purple skies and blue grass?'

She laughed. 'I doubt that sort of landscape would bring me any income at all!' She glanced down at her almost finished ice. 'I have so much more to learn, though. I do not even know how to paint in oils.'

Maybe Vespery could be persuaded to give her lessons, Ross thought. But would Tinmore allow such a thing?

She smiled and took the last bite. 'I can always become a lady's companion. I would make a good one, do you not think?'

He grinned. 'You would keep some lady on her toes, that is true.'

Lady Tinmore walked back to the table, a small package in hand. Ross stood.

'I believe we should go, Genna,' she said.

Genna rose. 'Thank you, Lord Rossdale. That was a lovely interlude.'

'My pleasure.'

It was his pleasure, a pleasure to have a candid conversation with an intelligent young woman who enjoyed new experiences as much as he did. He was not going to leave their next meeting to chance. After he delivered Genna and her sister to the town house on Curzon Street, he would make another call nearby. The Duchess of Archester was planning a ball in two weeks' time. He would wager she could be persuaded to invite the daughters of her old friend, Lady Summerfield.

After Rossdale left Genna and Lorene at their door and the footman carried away their cloaks, Lorene turned to Genna. 'Do you not think you are acting a bit too free with Lord Rossdale?'

She should have known Lorene would have something to say about her behaviour. Too often her husband's words seemed to be coming out of Lorene's mouth.

'Too free? I do not take your meaning.'

They started up the stairs.

'You say too much. About wanting to go to the Egyptian Museum, and Astley's and all. Might he not take it you want an invitation from him?'

She made herself laugh. 'Perhaps I did! How else am I going to do things unless someone invites me?'

'Not the son of a duke!' Lorene cried. 'You must not mistake his father's interest in Lord Tinmore for the son's intention to court you.'

Sometimes Lorene could sound every bit as dispiriting as her husband.

She continued up the stairs, a few steps ahead of her sister. 'I like Lord Rossdale. And I think he likes me. But he is not going to court me. It is not like that.'

No one would court her if she had anything to do with it. Tinmore could not force her to marry. She just needed a little more time to be ready to forge her own way.

Lorene went on. 'You must not speak so familiarly to gentlemen. It is not the thing to do. You must be careful. The last thing we want is to be the objects of gossip.'

Of scandal.

Genna did not have the horror of gossip and scandal that her two sisters did. She did not care what others thought of her.

Had her mother been like her?

If she should ever again be in the company of the Duchesses of Archester and of Mannerton, she would ask them.

They were met on the first floor by the butler. 'A package arrived for you, my lady.'

'For me?' Lorene sounded surprised.

'It is in your sitting room.' He bowed.

Lorene had a parlour near to her bedchamber where she could receive callers—if anyone called on her, that was.

'Let us go see what it is!' Genna cried, the sharp words between them forgotten.

They rushed to the sitting room. On the tea table was an envelope very similar to the one Lorene held in her hand, the music Rossdale had purchased for her. She placed that envelope on the table and picked up the other. It was tied with a ribbon like a gift. A card was stuck underneath the ribbon.

Lorene pulled the card out and read it. She handed it to Genna.

'"*For your enjoyment*",' Genna read. She looked up at Lorene. 'It is not signed.'

Lorene opened the envelope and pulled out sheets of music. She gasped. 'The Mozart pieces from the musicale last night!'

'Oh, my goodness,' Genna exclaimed. 'It must have been purchased by that gentleman the clerk mentioned. Who could it be?'

Lorene traced her fingers along the lines of music, a strange, soft expression on her face. 'I do not know.'

Not Tinmore, that was for certain.

Two weeks later Lord Tinmore, Lorene and Genna were invited to the Duchess of Archester's ball, the first important ball of the Season. It was a coup Tinmore credited to his new alliance with the Duke of Kessington, Rossdale's father. He was more certain than ever that Lorene or Genna would embarrass him completely, so every dinner for over a week had been consumed with his incessant instructions.

He insisted both Genna and Lorene have new ball gowns, as if they would not want a new gown themselves. Their modiste made certain their dresses were beautifully fashionable. Genna's was a pale blue silk with an overdress and long sleeves of white net. The hem of the skirt was trimmed in white lace as were the neckline and cuffs.

Tinmore insisted that a hairdresser be hired as well, but Genna disliked what the man did. She had her own maid take down her hair and rearrange it to a style less fussy and more comfortable for her. She wound up with curls around her face and the rest pulled high on her head. A long string of tiny pearls was wrapped around her head and up through the crown of curls.

Lorene's gown was white muslin embellished with gold embroidery that shimmered in the candlelight. She wore a gold-and-diamond band in her hair and diamonds around her neck. Her usually straight hair had been transformed into a mass of curls. How anyone could look at another lady there, Genna did not know. Her sister took her breath away.

When they were announced at the ball, Genna felt secure in their appearance—and totally mismatched with the grey-haired, wrinkled man who escorted them. They first waited in a line to greet the Duke and Duchess of Archester. When it was finally Genna's turn, the Duchess greeted her warmly.

The Duke held on to Genna's hand for a moment. 'You are the image of your mother, young lady,' he said with feeling.

Genna felt a stab of pain. She could not remember what her mother looked like.

She curtsied. 'Thank you, your Grace.' What else could she say?

Tinmore quickly whisked them away from the Duke and Duchess.

As they crossed the ballroom floor, Tinmore whispered, 'There will be some eligible men here, girl. I expect you to be on good behaviour. Make a good impression. I have already spoken to some gentlemen on your behalf, so you will have some dance partners.'

Genna forced a smile. 'I never want for dance partners, sir.'

She had no intention of encouraging his matchmaking. She was perfectly capable of having a good time all on her own.

'Now, do not come bothering me if I am in conversation,' he whispered to Lorene. 'It will likely be about a matter of importance. There will be other ladies for you to speak to. Make certain you are agreeable.'

Lorene was always agreeable, Genna wanted to say, but Tinmore left them before she could open her mouth.

'There are so many people here!' Lorene looked around nervously.

Genna scoured the room. 'Good! Perhaps Tinmore's gentlemen will not be able to find me. If I spy them coming, I'll hide behind a jardinière of flowers.'

'He merely wants to see you settled,' Lorene said defensively.

'He wants me out of his house so he can have you all to himself,' Genna retorted in good humour, although she really meant it.

She caught sight of two men walking towards them. 'Here are two gentlemen we know.'

Rossdale and Penford.

Rossdale smiled. 'Good evening, ladies.'

Lord Penford merely nodded and asked, 'May I get you some refreshment?'

Genna saw liveried servants carrying glasses with what she hoped was champagne. 'Yes, Penford. Thank you.'

Was he Lorene's secret admirer?

Impossible. Genna could not tell whether or not Penford even liked Lorene. He was all obligation, Genna feared.

'Are you available for the first set?' Rossdale asked Genna.

Her heart danced in her chest. 'I am.' There was no one she would rather dance with.

He turned to Lorene. 'Will you be dancing, ma'am? Perhaps you will favour me with a set?'

Now Genna's heart melted. He'd included her sister who desperately deserved to enjoy herself.

Lorene's eyes darted towards where her husband was conversing with other men. 'I am not certain if I should.'

'Of course you should,' cried Genna. 'It is a ball and you look so lovely many gentlemen will want to dance with you.'

Penford came up and handed her and Genna a glass of champagne.

'Dance the second set with me,' Rossdale said. 'Then you may retire if you wish.'

'Oh, say yes, Lorene!' Genna said impatiently.

She lowered her eyes. 'Very well.'

By the time they finished the champagne, couples were lining up for the first dance. Rossdale took Genna's hand to lead her on to the dance floor. Genna turned back to smile at her sister. She felt a little guilty for leaving Lorene, but Penford, taciturn as he was wont to be, stood by her side and was some company, at least.

Genna filled with excitement. To see Rossdale again. To be dancing with him. To have a friend.

Ross smiled as they faced each other in the line, waiting for others to join.

The music started and the couples at the head of the line began dancing their steps and figures. Each couple would repeat the figures, couple by couple, down the line.

'Do you enjoy dancing?' Ross asked Genna, although it was clear she did.

Her colour was high and her eyes sparkled.

'I do indeed.' she responded. 'It is so lively. And I love how pretty it is when all the couples perform the figures together.'

Ross mostly considered dancing a social obligation, but it was impossible not to catch Genna's excitement and enjoy himself along with her. There was a rhythm to it, a pattern, he found pleasant, especially if he forgot anything but the dance.

And Genna.

He noticed that Dell and Lady Tinmore had joined the line. When he and Genna came together in the figures, he said to her, 'Your sister dances.'

'I noticed,' she replied as the dance separated them.

It brought them together again.

'Do you suppose Penford felt an obligation?' she asked.

His answer had to wait until they came together again. 'That is what he says.'

'I am delighted she is allowing herself some fun,' Genna said. 'I wonder if Tinmore even notices.' They parted and came together once more, turning in a circle. 'I hope she thinks of nothing but the dancing.'

He decided to offer Genna what she wanted for her sister—a chance to think of nothing but the dancing. He did not attempt more than a comment or two after that.

The sets often lasted a half-hour or more and this one was no exception. Ross usually succumbed to boredom after the first ten minutes, but this time he was not even aware of how much time had passed.

When the music stopped, he stood facing Genna again. They both stared at each other as if shocked the dance had ended. Finally she curtsied, he bowed, and he took her hand to return her to where she had stood with her sister.

Her step quickened when they neared her. 'Was that not lovely?' she asked.

Lady Tinmore darted a glance at Dell, who quickly looked away. 'Lovely. Yes.'

A footman bore a tray with champagne and they each took a glass.

It made perfect sense for Ross to remain with Genna and her sister. He would be dancing with her sister the next set, but after that he must leave them and dance with others. He could swing back for a second dance. Two dances were the limit unless he wished for there to be speculation about a betrothal between them.

He glanced around the room and saw his father's wife standing with the Duchess of Mannerton. His father was deep in conversation with the Duke of Mannerton and Lord Tinmore was hovering around the edges of these higher-ranking men. His father's wife, on the other hand, kept tossing disapproving looks Ross's way.

Another reason why he must leave Genna and seek out other partners. The Duchess could be a formidable enemy if she so chose and he certainly did not wish her to choose Genna as an enemy.

A young gentleman with whom Ross had a passing acquaintance, approached them.

He bowed to Genna. 'Miss Summerfield, how good to see you.'

She smiled at him. 'Why, good evening, Mr Holdsworth.'

Holdsworth was the younger son of Baron Holdsworth. He could not be more than twenty-one, more of an age with Genna than Ross, who was nearing thirty.

Holdsworth nodded nervously to Ross and Dell, who easily outranked him.

His attention returned to Genna. 'Are you engaged for the next set? If not, would you do me the honour of dancing with me?'

'Yes, of course, Mr Holdsworth,' she responded

right away. 'I remember dancing with you last Season. I enjoyed it very much.'

The young man beamed with pleasure. He bowed and withdrew.

Ross's mood turned sour.

'Do you know Mr Holdsworth?' she asked Ross. 'I should have introduced you, shouldn't I?'

'I am acquainted with him,' Ross answered.

'He is quite fun to dance with, as you will see.' She laughed. 'Very energetic.' She leaned closer to his ear. 'And he is not one of Lord Tinmore's choices.'

Ross frowned. 'Tinmore has chosen who will dance with you?'

'Widowers with a dozen children to manage or younger sons needing the dowry Tinmore offers.' She glanced around the room. 'I shall avoid them if I am able.'

Lorene glared at her. 'Genna, may I speak with you for a moment?'

Her sister drew Genna aside. 'What are you saying to Rossdale about Lord Tinmore—?'

Ross could not hear the rest.

He turned to Dell, who looked preoccupied. 'How are you faring, Dell?'

'Well enough, I suppose.' Dell composed his features, but only briefly. His eyes shone with pain. 'Actually, not well at all. I need some respite.'

'Is there anything I can do?' Ross asked. He'd been surprised that Dell had danced at all. In fact, he was surprised Dell had agreed to come. These social events were not easy for him.

'No. Nothing.' Dell glanced towards Genna and her sister. 'Please make my excuses to the ladies.' He turned and walked away without waiting for Ross's agreement.

Both sisters, looking somewhat heated, returned to where Ross stood. Neither looked very happy.

'Dell had to excuse himself,' he told them. 'He bids you goodnight.'

'Oh?' Genna glanced at her sister. 'I do hope he comes back.'

'Was there anything amiss?' Lady Tinmore asked. 'He appeared upset.'

'He is not yet completely recovered from the loss of his family,' Ross replied. 'It strikes him unawares at times.'

'What happened to them?' Genna's face looked pinched.

'They were killed in a fire. All of them,' he said in a low voice.

Lady Tinmore gasped.

'You and your sisters and brother, Lady Tinmore, are all the relations he has left,' he added.

The musicians signalled the next set and couples began to line up on the dance floor. Mr Holdsworth strode over eagerly and extended his hand to Genna, who seemed to have lost her sparkle.

He ought not to have spoken. Both ladies immediately grasped the enormity of Dell's loss and were affected by the news.

Ross turned to Lady Tinmore. 'This is our set, I believe.'

She glanced up at him and for a moment he thought she would start weeping. 'You do not have to dance with me, Lord Rossdale. I—I feel it is almost unseemly to dance after hearing…' Her voice trailed off.

'Forgive me,' he said. 'This was not the proper time to tell you of Dell's loss. He would be vexed with me if he found out I ruined this ball for you. Please dance with me.'

She nodded.

They took their place in the line not far from Genna and Mr Holdsworth.

Lady Tinmore noticed him looking Genna's way.

He changed the subject. 'I hope you and your sister settled your quarrel.'

'Quarrel?' She could not quite meet his eye. 'She has such lively spirits. Sometimes she is too forward and her tongue runs away with her.'

Ross responded, 'I admire your sister's forthrightness. It is a refreshing change from those who only say what is expected.'

'Then do understand. She is not trying to get you to court her.'

The music had begun and the first figures were starting down the line of dancers.

He knew that. Even from his first meeting with Genna, he knew she was not trying to trap him into marriage. But it depressed him to hear her sister say it aloud.

It was Genna's and Mr Holdsworth's turn to dance. They were quite well matched in lively steps and grace, which somehow did not please him. Genna seemed to regain some of her former enthusiasm, though.

At the end of the set, Lady Tinmore thanked him and added, 'I do hope Lord Penford returns to the ballroom.'

He bowed to her. 'I hope so, as well.'

He escorted her back to the place they'd been standing and she lowered herself into a nearby chair. 'I believe I will sit for a while.'

'Shall I bring you some refreshment?' he asked, although he also watched Genna and Mr Holdsworth still on the dance floor talking together.

'I would love something to drink.' Lady Tinmore fanned herself.

He brought her a glass of champagne and noticed Genna leaving the dance floor.

'I see your sister is returning to you,' he said to Lady Tinmore. 'I must take my leave.'

She thanked him again for the dance and said goodbye.

He made himself walk through the ballroom and converse with various people he knew. His father was doing the same, as was his father's wife, but they had an agenda—to turn as many members of Parliament as possible to their way of thinking. Important work, but when did his father ever simply enjoy himself? His father used to smile and laugh and be willing to do things just for the doing of them.

Ross spied Genna conversing with yet another young man. A man who looked to be in his forties—one of Lord Tinmore's choices, perhaps?—hung around her for a bit, but gave up trying to get her attention away from the young buck. A quadrille was called and the young man escorted her to the dance floor.

Ross asked the daughter of one of his father's closest allies to dance the quadrille with him, which certainly would meet with the Duchess's approval. The young lady was in want of a partner and Ross did not wish to leave her a wallflower.

But he intended to get a second dance with Genna before the night was through.

Unless another gentleman claimed her first, that was.

Chapter Twelve

After the quadrille, Ross noticed Genna leave the ballroom. She disappeared into the ladies' retiring room and he waited in the corridor to catch her when she came out.

The door opened and Genna peeked carefully around before stepping into the corridor. She seemed in no hurry to return to the dancing.

He approached her from behind. 'Genna?'

She jumped and put her hand on her chest when she saw it was him. 'Oh, Rossdale! You startled me. I thought you were someone else.'

'Who?' One of the young men who occupied her time?

She waved a hand. 'Oh, one of Tinmore's widowers. I am eager to avoid him.'

He took her arm. 'Then let's not return to the ballroom.'

He led her outside on to a veranda. The Duke of Archester's town house was one of the few in Mayfair to have a garden of any size behind it. They were not the only ones to seek a quieter, more secluded place. Other couples stood close together on the veranda or on benches in the garden. After the close, warm air of the ballroom, the chilly March air felt welcome, although Ross doubted that all the couples outside were merely seeking fresh air.

Genna inhaled deeply. 'Oh, how nice. I can breathe out here.'

It occurred to him that she smiled at him the way she smiled at her other dance partners. He didn't like that thought, though. 'You appeared to be having a good time dancing.'

She sobered. 'I am having a good time, although I cannot help thinking about Lord Penford. Has he returned to the ballroom?'

'Not that I've seen.' It pleased him that she felt concern for his friend.

Her lovely forehead knitted.

'Do not let it spoil your enjoyment, though. He would not wish that and I should feel quite regretful that I spoke of his family.'

She nodded. 'I have enjoyed the dancing.' She slid him a sly smile. 'So far I have not had to dance with any of the men Tinmore picked to court me.'

'Is he so determined to get you married?' he asked.

She nodded. 'But I only have to get through this Season. I will be twenty-one soon and I can go my own way.'

He thought about her desire to become an artist.

It was a daring choice. Women artists were rare, but some had made a good living with their art.

She shivered and he led them to a corner more protected from the cool air.

She gazed at him with curiosity. 'But what of you? There seem to be several young ladies with whom to dance. Are you not looking to make a match?'

He stiffened. 'I am in no hurry to take on that responsibility.'

She peered at him. 'You do not seem the sort to wish to shirk responsibility.'

'Perhaps responsibility is not the proper word.' How could he explain? 'My station dictates that a match should be a carefully considered one. Advantageous to both parties.'

Her expression turned sympathetic. 'How dreadful.'

He was not ready to explain it all, though. 'I know I must marry and produce an heir. It is my duty. I know I will have to bear the mantle of the title eventually, but my father is in excellent health. There is no reason for me to rush. There is so much more I wish to do.'

Her face relaxed. 'Like what?'

What did he wish to do? Since the war's end, he hadn't been sure, although there certainly was plenty to do for the returning soldiers. With the war's end, several regiments would disband and the soldiers would return home without a pension and many without a trade to support them.

He'd already cast Genna and her sister into the

dismals by talking of Dell's loss; he certainly did not wish to depress her further with the plight of the soldiers.

'I'd like to travel, perhaps,' he said instead. Who would not wish to travel? 'Visit Paris, for one thing. The rest of the Continent. Maybe return to Rome and Venice.'

Her eyes lit up. 'And see the works of art there! Would that not be wonderful?'

Lately, because of Genna, he'd been noticing the artwork wherever he went. He'd like to learn more, appreciate it more.

She laughed. 'Here I am, pining merely to see the sights of London. You are thinking of the world!'

He smiled. 'Not the world, perhaps.' Although he was intensely curious about the Colonies. 'But certainly the Continent. Do a Grand Tour all over again, but widen my horizons.'

She sighed. 'You did a Grand Tour?'

'With Dell,' he said. 'We have been friends since we were boys.'

'How lovely!'

A footman came to the veranda door. 'Supper is being served.'

'We missed the supper dance,' she said, sounding relieved.

'You wanted to miss it?' he asked.

She grinned. 'One of Tinmore's widowers was searching for me. That is why I left the ballroom. Imagine being trapped with him through supper.'

'You know this gentleman?'

She nodded. 'Tinmore introduced us last Season, but he was not out of mourning yet, so he's been encouraged to court me now.' She glanced away and back again. 'He is a perfectly nice man. I do not mean to make a jest of him. I merely do not want him to court me. There are so many ladies who would love to marry him, but I would feel imprisoned.'

Other couples crossed the veranda and re-entered the house.

'Would you consider it undesirable to be trapped with me through supper?' he asked.

Her gaze rose to meet his. 'I can think of no one else I would rather be trapped with.'

Sitting with Rossdale for supper was a delight. With anyone else she would have restrained herself and taken care what she said, but with Rossdale she felt free to say anything. Even better, she was not beneath the watchful eye of her sister, who she finally spied in a group of other ladies and gentlemen. And Lord Penford.

She was relieved to see Lord Penford back.

After supper some of the young gentlemen with whom she became acquainted the previous Season engaged her to dance. Lord Rossdale asked her for the last dance.

A waltz.

It was exciting that the Duchess of Archester allowed the waltz, still considered scandalous by some.

Genna usually did not relish the less lively dances, but she did love to dance the waltz. She liked being free of the lines of the country dances or the squares of the quadrilles. You stayed with your partner throughout the whole dance. With the right partner, the waltz was heaven.

And Rossdale was the right partner.

When the music began, they walked on to the dance floor with hands entwined and, finding a place, faced each other. She curtsied. He bowed. She put her hands on his shoulders. He placed his hands at her waist. Her heart fluttered.

Why did her body react so when he touched her? She could only think that it was because they liked each other so well and were as alike as two peas in a pod.

He led her in the dance, moving in a circle together.

Usually in the waltz, Genna relished the sight of the couples all turning on the dance floor, the ladies' dresses like spinning flowers. This time, though, she could not take her eyes off Rossdale. She was taller than fashionable, but it hardly mattered when dancing with him. She had to tilt her head to see his face and she much preferred that to staring at the top of some gentleman's head.

Especially because Rossdale's lovely eyes and smiling mouth made her feel happy inside.

Staring only at him made the rest of the room a blur. Genna felt as if they were alone in the room, moving to the music, like one unit. She was tired from the dancing and giddy from a bit too much champagne and it all felt like a lovely dream, one she did not want to end.

But end it did. The music stopped and it took a moment longer for Genna to tear her eyes from his.

'What a lovely way to end a ball,' she murmured.

He nodded.

He took her hand and they walked through the guests, looking for her sister. Or Tinmore. How lucky Genna had not seen Tinmore during the whole ball. That in itself had contributed to the night's enjoyment.

Lorene had returned to where Tinmore had originally left them and she stood with poor Lord Penford, although they were not speaking to each other. Lorene had danced many of the dances, Genna had been glad to see.

'There you are,' Genna cried. 'Did you dance the waltz?'

Lorene glanced at Penford. 'Yes. We did.'

Goodness. Penford even asked her to dance the waltz.

'I would have been without a partner otherwise,' Lorene added.

'We have had such a nice time,' Genna said, squeezing Rossdale's hand before he released hers. 'I must find the Duchess and thank her for including us.'

'I had an opportunity to speak with her,' Lorene said. 'I did convey our thanks.'

Genna laughed. 'I was too busy dancing.'

Penford inclined his head towards the door of the ballroom. 'Lord Tinmore is bidding you to come.'

Tinmore was leaning on his cane with one hand and waving the other. He looked very impatient.

'I wonder where he was all this night,' Genna said.

Lorene pulled her arm. 'Come, Genna.'

She turned and smiled at Rossdale and Penford. 'Goodnight!'

Ross and Dell watched the Summerfield sisters rush to where Lord Tinmore was beckoning.

'You spent a great deal of time with Miss Summerfield,' Dell said.

'As much as possible.' Ross slid him a sideways glance. 'And you with Lady Tinmore, I might add.'

Dell frowned. 'By happenstance.'

Ross clapped his friend on the shoulder. 'I am glad you came back.'

Dell nodded.

Dell was living with him in Ross's father's house while the shell of his burned London town house was restored.

'The thing is, I like them. I like both of them,' Ross said.

'They are not what I expected,' Dell said. 'I will agree to that.'

The two men followed the crowd out of the ballroom, taking their time, having no reason to hurry. They caught up with his father and the Duchess. His father's wife had remained in the ballroom the whole time, making her rounds and keeping an eye on Ross's activities. His father spent most of the time in the card room, where Ross imagined Tinmore stayed, as well.

His father and the Duchess joined them and they all stood waiting for the carriage.

Ross's father pointed to him. 'Brackton's daughter.' His father spoke as if their conversation had begun earlier than this moment. 'She'd be a good match for you. Marquess's daughter. A step up for her. Good family, too.'

Obviously the Duchess had reported to his father that he'd danced with Lady Alice.

'I danced with her, sir,' Ross said. 'I did not make an offer.'

'You should,' his father responded. 'You are not getting any younger and neither am I.'

Ross glanced towards Dell, who averted his gaze. Both had heard this conversation before. 'I am not ready to consider marriage,' Ross said. 'Not yet.'

'What are you waiting for?' his father snapped.

'There are things yet I wish to do.' He never discussed his activities with his father and certainly not with the Duchess. They both assumed he merely caroused.

His father sliced the air with his hand. 'Marry. Beget an heir. Then do as you wish until the title is yours.'

Ross gave him a scathing look. 'Do you hear yourself? What sort of marriage would that be for the woman?'

'If the woman is a proper partner, she will understand,' the Duchess said. 'She will have her duty, as well.'

'Do not spout any romantic nonsense,' his father said.

'I was not planning to.' Ross's anger rose.

Once his father had engaged in romantic nonsense. When Ross's mother had been alive. When it had been just the three of them. His father had loosened his reserve and expressed the love and affection he had for both his wife and son. When Ross's grandfather died and his father inherited the title, everything had changed. His father grew distant, always busy, too busy. Too busy to notice when Ross's mother became ill.

'No romantic nonsense,' his father repeated more softly. To Ross's surprise what looked like pain etched the corners of his father's eyes. His father gave him a fleeting bleak look that told him his father, indeed, remembered those halcyon days when he and Ross's mother engaged in romantic nonsense.

The Duchess did not see. She was too busy looking smugly at Ross. 'You need a wife who will understand that being a duchess is not play. It is serious business.'

Ross understood, though. A duchess needed to be more like her, more in love with the title than the man, because she had to run her own enterprise, something for which his gentle mother with her freedom of spirit had not been suited.

His father's countenance hardened again. 'You have waited long enough, Ross. This is the Season. No more tarrying.'

The carriage arrived and they all climbed in.

The next day Lorene and Genna called upon the Duchess of Archester to thank her for the ball. They stayed only fifteen minutes. Tinmore had made such a fuss about how they should behave with decorum that Genna said very little during the visit. Several other ladies and gentlemen had also called, including Mr Holdsworth, who left at the same time as Genna and Lorene.

'May I walk with you?' the young man asked.

Lorene nodded and walked a little ahead of them.

'It is a lovely day, is it not?' Mr Holdsworth said.

He continued to utter the sort of polite conversation that contained very little of interest to Genna. He was also visibly nervous, which puzzled her. They were acquainted. What was there to be nervous about?

She found herself comparing him to Rossdale, which was rather unfair. Rossdale had years on him and the experience with it. Rossdale made her laugh. Rossdale listened. He talked to her about art. Did Mr Holdsworth even know she painted watercolours?

They reached the corner of Curzon Street.

'May—may I call upon you, Miss Summerfield?' His voice shook.

Ah! She understood now. He wanted to court her.

Why on earth would he want to court her? There was so much more he could see and do before settling down to marry. So many more young ladies to meet who would suit him better.

She slowed her pace. 'Oh, Mr Holdsworth!' She spoke in exaggerated tones. 'If it were up to me, I would say yes, because we have such fun dancing together. But Lord Tinmore would never allow it. He is looking for someone much grander for me.'

Holdsworth looked wounded, as well he should. She'd just told him he was not good enough because of something he could do nothing about—the status of his birth. Better that, though, than telling him he simply did not interest her.

'Do tell me you understand, Mr Holdsworth,' she said pleadingly. 'I should not like Tinmore to ruin our friendship.'

He brightened a little. 'I do understand.'

They reached the door of the town house.

His brow furrowed. 'You do not think Lord Tinmore will change his mind? I will have money.'

She shook her head. 'It is status with him, you see.'

'I value your candour.' He bowed. 'And I must bid you good day.'

'Good day, Mr Holdsworth.'

He walked away with shoulders stooped.

Lorene glared at her. 'What are you about, Genna? Lord Tinmore would find Mr Holdsworth perfectly acceptable, I am certain.'

'But I do not find him acceptable, Lorene,' she said.

'Why not? He's the son of a baron. And he's a very nice young man.'

Maybe that was it. Genna felt years older than Mr Holdsworth. 'You know I would run rings around him. Why make him miserable being stuck with the likes of me? And what happened to all your romantic notions? Were you not the one who wanted Tess and Edmund and me to marry for love?'

'Of course I did,' Lorene shot back. 'I still do, but—'

Tess and Edmund did not marry for love. They married to escape scandal. It was just by sheer luck they found happiness and who knew how long it would last?

'Then do me the honour of allowing me my own choice of a husband.' Or no husband at all.

'Well.' Lorene huffed. 'Do not say it is Lord Tinmore who must approve your choice.'

'I had to say something,' she said. 'Would you have me wound the poor fellow? Say I simply do not fancy him?'

'It would be more honest,' Lorene countered. 'But let us not debate this at the door to the town house. We can continue inside.'

Where the servants would hear and report whatever they said to Lord Tinmore.

A footman attended the door and took their things. 'A gentleman to see you, Miss Summerfield. He is waiting in the drawing room.'

'To see me?' Her spirits plummeted. One of Tinmore's widowers, no doubt. 'Who is it?'

'Lord Rossdale,' the footman said.

She smiled. 'How delightful!' She started to climb the stairs to the drawing room.

Lorene hurried to catch up with her. 'I should come with you.'

To chaperon? She'd been alone with Rossdale more than once.

But she would not argue. 'Of course.'

When they entered the room, he was standing and gazing at one of the paintings on the wall. He turned at their entrance.

'Why, hello, Rossdale,' Genna said. 'How nice of you to call.'

He bowed. 'Lady Tinmore. Miss Summerfield.'

'Would you care to sit, sir?' Lorene said. 'Shall I send for tea?'

He held up a hand. 'No, please do not go to that trouble. I will only stay a minute.' He turned to Genna. 'I merely stopped by to ask if you would care to take a turn in the park with me this afternoon.'

She grinned at him, but looked askance. 'I do not know, sir. It depends upon your vehicle...'

He smiled in return. 'A curricle. Nothing too fancy, though. It will have a matched pair, however.'

She pretended to think. 'A matched pair, you say?'

'Matched chestnuts.'

She sighed. 'Oh, very well.' Then her grin broke out again. 'I would be honoured to. Really.'

He nodded. 'Three o'clock?'

Four was the fashionable hour.

'Yes.' Her voice turned a bit breathless. 'I will be ready.'

'Then I must take my leave.' He bowed again.

When he left, Lorene shook her head. 'I do not understand you. The way you talk.'

'Oh, Lorene.' Genna groaned. 'It is all in fun. Rossdale knows that.'

Her sister gave her an exasperated look. 'If you wish to gain his interest, it is no way to talk to him, though.'

'I am not trying to gain his interest,' Genna retorted. 'As you have said many times, he is too far above me.'

Besides, she knew Rossdale's desire was to avoid marriage.

Lorene's brows rose. 'Then why would he ask you to take a ride in the park?'

'I think he is taking pity on me.' Why else? 'I did moan to him about wanting to go places and see things.'

'Well…' Lorene turned to leave the room '…do heed your behaviour on this outing. Lord Tinmore's new connection to the Duke of Kessington is important to him.'

After Lorene left the room, Genna said, 'Oh, yes. Lord Tinmore's well-being is of the utmost importance to us all.'

Chapter Thirteen

Ross pulled up to the Tinmores' town house in his curricle with its matched chestnuts. Gone were his days of driving high flyers and racing down country roads. Those had been exhilarating times, but, once experienced, he'd no need to repeat them. His curricle was the latest in comfort and speed, though he'd not tested how fast he could push it.

He suspected Genna would not care if he pulled up in a mere gig.

His tiger jumped off and held the horses while he knocked on the door.

As the footman let him inside, Genna was coming down the stairs, putting on her gloves. 'I saw you drive up.'

She wore a pelisse of dark blue and a bonnet that matched, nothing too fussy.

'Shall we go, then?' he asked.

'Absolutely!' she cried. 'I am ready.'

He helped her into the carriage. She pretended to examine it. 'I suppose this will have to do.' She sighed.

He took the ribbons from his tiger and climbed in next to her. 'It must do, because it is the only one I possess.'

She blinked at him. 'Truly? A duke's son with only one carriage?'

He smiled. 'All the others belong to my father.'

She laughed. 'All the others! At Summerfield House we had one pony cart and one coach.' Her smile fled. 'My father had a curricle.'

He'd prefer her laughing. 'Shall we take a turn in Hyde Park?'

She smiled again. 'By all means.'

The park was mere steps away from Curzon Street. They entered through the Stanhope Gate. Right inside the gate, he stopped the curricle and the tiger jumped off. He'd pick him up again on their way out. He drove the curricle towards the Serpentine. The weather was overcast and a bit chilly, not the best, but at least it was not raining.

'There is a rug beneath the seat,' he told her. 'Let me know if you feel cold.'

'I like it,' she said. 'It feels so good to be out of doors.'

He turned to her. 'And you are one to set up your paints while the snow is falling.'

She protested, 'Not fair! I packed up when it began to snow.'

'That you did.'

He'd guessed correctly that the Park would be thin of other vehicles at this hour. He'd wanted to be as private with her as possible. He waited until they'd passed the Serpentine, where some children were playing under the watchful eyes of their nannies and others were feeding the ducks.

'You probably wondered why I asked you for this ride—' he began.

'No.' She looked surprised. 'I didn't wonder.'

'I have a proposition for you.'

'A proposition?' She pretended to look shocked.

'It will indeed be shocking,' he said. 'But hear me out.'

The carriage path was edged with shrubbery and there were no other vehicles in sight. He slowed their pace.

Her expression conveyed curiosity, nothing more. This was why he could ask what he planned to ask. She would not take advantage, nor would she assume more than he intended.

He continued. 'I have a plan that will get us both through the Season without feeling like commodities in the marriage mart.'

Her interest kindled. 'Indeed?'

'It will also give you the freedom you desire, freedom to explore London, and it will satisfy my father who has begun to pressure me into marriage.' He glanced to the horses who were plodding along.

'What is this plan?' she asked.

'We become betrothed.'

She stared at him, but did not speak.

He quickly added. 'Betrothed. Think of it. If we

are betrothed, I could escort you all around London. We could see the sights you wish to see. Do the things you wish to do. The cost of doing so would be no object.'

Her brows knitted. 'But a betrothal means becoming married. You just implied you do not wish to marry.'

'Not any more than you,' he responded. 'I said *betrothed*, not married. We would not have to marry. You could cry off, but not until you turn twenty-one and are free to do as you wish.'

And he had the funds to be certain she could do as she wished, but now was not the time to offer her money, not when she might misconstrue his intent. He meant merely to help her become the artist she wished to be. At least one of them would be free to do as they wished.

'No one would know it was not a real betrothal,' he added. 'It would be our secret.'

She stared at him again.

He actually began to feel nervous inside. 'Tinmore would see it as a feather in his cap if you were betrothed to a duke's son. He would stop sending you suitors.' Had he misread how daring she might be? 'There might be a little scandal. I fear you might receive some criticism for ultimately refusing me, but it is also likely that it will be assumed I was at fault.'

'What would your father say?' Her voice lacked enthusiasm.

He shrugged. 'What could my father say? He has

been pressuring me to marry and it would seem as though I was doing what he asked of me.'

'But surely he has someone else in mind besides me. My father was a mere baronet.'

'That is the beauty of it,' he explained. 'He cannot complain that I've become betrothed, but he is likely not to complain when you cry off.'

'Because I am not suitable for you.' She turned away and he feared he might have offended her.

'Betrothed,' she murmured.

He gazed at the horses and gripped the ribbons. 'I will understand if you do not wish this.'

She swivelled back to him, seizing his arm as she did so. 'Betrothed?'

He dared look at her again.

Her eyes were sparkling. 'A pretend betrothal.'

'Yes. To free us both.'

A smile lit up her face. 'It is a capital idea! We can go anywhere, do anything and no one will wonder over it.'

'That is the idea. We can enjoy this Season in a way that would have been impossible before.'

At their social engagements they would be free to be together the whole time. They could dance more than two dances. No greedy suitors would bother her; no matchmaking mamas would throw their frightened or eager daughters at him.

She frowned. 'I do not like the idea of keeping secrets from my sisters.' She paused and broke into a smile again. 'Why do I worry? They both kept secrets from me.'

He tilted his head. 'Then you say yes?'

She took a breath and he thought she would say yes. Instead she said, 'Let me think about it a little.'

'Take all the time you need,' he responded, disappointed. A delay usually meant no.

He flicked the ribbons and the horses moved faster. They continued to circle the park, turning at the Cumberland Gate and proceeding along the pcrimeter of the park.

She finally spoke again. 'Would—would you take me to see places like the Egyptian Museum and Astley's Amphitheatre?'

He glanced at her. 'It would be my pleasure to do so.'

She fell silent again for so long Ross felt like fidgeting.

'You do realise, I could make you honour your promise to marry me,' she said in a serious tone. 'You would be taking a great risk.'

He turned to her again. 'But you won't. You are not the sort to break your word.'

Her eyes glowed as if satisfied by his response.

'You realise *I* might make you honour your promise,' he countered.

Her eyes danced in amusement. 'But you won't. You are not the sort to break your word. Besides, I have the right to cry off.'

They rode on, nearing the Serpentine again.

She bit her lip. 'Do you think that we can stretch it out until I am twenty-one?'

'When is your birthday?'

'October.'

He nodded. 'We can stretch it out that long.'

She shifted in her seat, as if setting her resolve. 'Then let us do it, Rossdale! Let us have this false betrothal. We'll fool everyone and have a lovely time of it!'

He turned to her and grinned and, to his surprise, had an impulse to embrace her. He resisted it.

'Then you had better call me Ross, if we are to be betrothed,' he said instead.

She laughed. 'Ross. And you'll call me Genna.'

He wouldn't tell her he'd been thinking of her as Genna since that first meeting.

Genna threaded her arm through Ross's and squeezed her cheek against his shoulder. 'I already feel as if I am set free. No longer can Tinmore dictate to me. I can simply direct him to you.'

'I should speak to him first,' Ross said. 'Ask his permission.'

She bristled. 'He is not my guardian. He has no say in who I marry, no matter what he thinks.'

'No,' he agreed. 'But let us use his arrogance. Appeal to his vanity. Let him think he has some say. If he believes he has given his permission, he is less apt to question the validity of the betrothal. He'll be less apt to exert control over your activities.'

She nodded. 'I see your point, though it rankles

with me.' It was really no different than the way she'd always handled Tinmore, though. Make him think she would do as he desired, but really do what she pleased. 'Promise me one thing, though.'

He turned his head to glance at her. 'What?'

'Promise me you will refuse the dowry he has offered me.' She did not want Tinmore to think his money had any influence, even on this pretend-betrothal.

'Genna.' He looked her straight in the eye. 'We are not really to be married. The dowry makes no difference, because I will never receive it.'

'It makes a difference to me.' Her voice rose. 'I want Tinmore to know that I do not need his dowry money, that it had nothing to do with you proposing to me. It is bad enough I must accept his money for my dresses and such.'

She had to admit that Tinmore's money had given her a rather comfortable life these last two years. She had as many dresses as she could want, food aplenty and enough spending money to keep her in paints and paper. It was the cost to Lorene that ate at Genna's insides.

Ross nodded. 'I promise you that if the subject of the dowry comes up, I will refuse it.'

'The subject will come up. Tinmore will want you to know what a huge sacrifice he has made for me.'

He glanced at her and back at the road. 'Then I will make a very convincing refusal.'

While he was attending to the road and the horses, Genna had a chance to study him in detail. His was a strong profile, high forehead, gracefully sloping masculine nose, strong jaw and lovely thick brows and lashes. She loved that his face was expressive when he wished it to be and devoid of all expression when he did not.

She was so lucky, so fortunate that he would do her this great favour. Certainly she would receive more benefit from it than he. Tinmore's dictates that she marry would be silenced now, because Tinmore would think she was marrying Rossdale.

Ross.

The mere thought of his name brought flutters inside her. These sensations, all so new to her, were a puzzle and one she did not wish to examine too closely. She just wanted to enjoy his friendship.

This plan of his made it so they could be friends.

'So you will call upon Lord Tinmore tomorrow.' She had to keep talking or the flutters would take over.

'Correct.'

She did not mind keeping this secret from Tinmore and the rest of the world, but this was another huge secret to keep from Lorene and Tess. She'd told them nothing of her intent to be an artist or her determination to refuse marriage to anyone. This would distance them from her even further.

'Will you tell Lord Penford the truth?' she asked.

He thinned his lips and took his time to answer her. 'I would like to tell Dell,' he said finally.

She frowned. Since learning he'd lost his family in a fire, Genna's heart went out to him, but she still was not certain how he felt about her and Lorene. Sometimes Penford looked at them as if he wished they were in Calcutta, but at other times he behaved in a most thoughtful and attentive manner.

'Surely he will not approve of our scheme,' she said. 'Who would?'

'Even if he does not approve, we can trust him to keep the secret.' Ross met her eye. 'I would trust him with my life. In any event,' he added, 'we may need an ally.'

But if Penford disapproved, would he be an ally? She examined Ross's face.

If she embarked on this plan of theirs, she must trust Ross. 'Very well. You may tell Lord Penford.'

'Do you wish to confide in your sisters?' he asked.

She shook her head. 'I shall wait to announce this betrothal to Lorene, though,' she said. 'And to Tess and Marc.'

They fell into silence again until they neared the Stanhope Gate. Ross signalled to his tiger to get on the back and in what seemed like the blink of the eye, they pulled up to the town house.

The tiger jumped down again and held the horses while Ross helped Genna out of the curricle and walked her up to the door. When the footman opened the door, Ross bid her good day and she skipped inside, wanting to dance through the hall and up the stairs. How could she be expected to contain her exuberance?

Once in her room, she gave in to her impulse and spun around in joy.

Until there was a knock at her door. 'Come in,' she said tentatively.

Lorene entered. 'I saw Lord Rossdale pull up. How was your outing?' Her voice was filled with expectation.

Genna felt a great pang of guilt. She was about to lie about the lie they were going to tell everyone. 'It was lovely. We do get along famously, so there was a great deal to talk about.'

'Did you get any notion of why he asked you?' Lorene persisted.

'None except companionship.' This was not precisely a lie. Companionship was what they'd agreed upon, was it not?

The next day Ross called upon Lord Tinmore. When the butler announced him to Lord Tinmore in his study, Tinmore's head was bowed. It snapped up at the footman's voice. The old man had fallen asleep.

When Ross approached the desk, Tinmore fussed with the papers there as if he had been busy with them. He tried to stand.

Ross gestured with his hand. 'Do not stand, sir. No need of ceremony with me.'

'Kind of you, Rossdale. Kind of you,' Tinmore muttered. 'And how is your father? And the Duchess? In good health, I hope?'

'In excellent health,' Ross replied. 'And you, sir?'

'Excellent!' he repeated. 'Could not be better.' Tinmore sat back in his chair.

Ross wasted no time. 'I know you are a busy man, sir, so I will not waste your time with prattle. I have come to talk with you about Miss Summerfield.'

'What?' Tinmore straightened. 'What has the girl done now?'

Tinmore's automatic disapproval chafed. 'You assume she has done something of which you would disapprove?'

Tinmore's expression turned smug. 'Why else would you come here?'

'To ask your permission to marry her.'

Tinmore recoiled as if Ross had struck him in the chest. 'Marry her!'

Genna would like that reaction. Sheer surprise.

'Yes,' Ross stated. 'Marry her. Assuming she will accept me, that is.'

'Accept you?' Tinmore continued to look dumbfounded. 'She's naught but the daughter of a baronet. She's not fit—'

Ross's anger flared. 'I assure you, she is my choice.' He glared at the man. 'I might remind you that you married the daughter of a mere baronet.'

'An entirely different matter, sir!' Tinmore said indignantly. 'An entirely different situation.'

Ross inclined his head. 'In any event, I wish to become betrothed to Miss Summerfield and I would like your permission to ask her to marry me.'

'I would not refuse you.' Tinmore shook his head.

'But I feel an obligation to your father to advise you against this idea.'

This man was intolerable. He ought to be looking after Genna's best interests, not the best interests of a duke's son.

'Then I will be obliged to explain your reticence to my father, sir. I thought you would be pleased to unite our families.' Let him ponder that. 'What will he conclude but that you do not desire to be so closely connected?'

Tinmore's eyes bulged. 'No. No. No. I do not mean that. I would not offend— Mustn't think so. Mustn't think so.'

'Then I have your permission?'

The Earl still looked reluctant, but he finally nodded his head. 'Yes. Yes, my boy. If that is what you want.'

'I want her,' Ross said. Hearing his words, he could almost believe it himself, that he wanted Genna, to marry her.

'She comes with a handsome dowry, my boy. Very respectable amount. I made certain of that.'

Ross rubbed his chin. 'About the dowry, sir.'

'Is it not enough?' Tinmore looked anxious. 'We can negotiate the amount. Might be fitting for me to increase it for marrying the heir to a dukedom.'

'I do not wish an increase,' Ross said. 'I do not want it at all.'

'Do not want it?' Tinmore's voice rose.

'I have no need for it,' Ross responded. 'I am

wealthy in my own right and my wealth will increase when I inherit the title. Make some other use of the dowry. Gift it to the poor. God knows there are plenty of hungry people in England with these Corn Laws.' Very likely Tinmore voted for the Corn Laws that made bread so expensive that many people could no longer afford it. 'I can advise you on where the money might do the most good.'

'If you insist,' Tinmore said, like air leaking from a bellows. 'Give it to the poor.'

Ross raised his eyebrows. 'May I see Miss Summerfield now?'

'You want to speak with her?' Tinmore seemed completely rattled.

Ross straightened and looked down his nose as his father did when his father wanted to intimidate someone. 'It is my wish to speak with her now.' He made it sound like a command.

'Yes. Yes.' Tinmore's head bobbed up and down. 'I will make certain she sees you.'

Ross felt quite certain Genna would need no pressure from Tinmore to receive him.

'Now, if you please,' Ross mimicked his father.

Tinmore popped up from his chair so fast he needed to hop to get his balance. 'Dixon!' he cried. 'Dixon!'

The butler opened the door. 'My lord?'

Tinmore waved one hand. 'Escort Lord Rossdale to the drawing room, then find my wife's sister and send her to him.'

The butler bowed.

'Now, Dixon! Now,' Tinmore cried.

Ross followed the butler to the drawing room, but he wound up cooling his heels for several minutes before Genna entered the room.

She grinned at him. 'I waited ten minutes so I would not look too eager.' She took his hands and led him to the sofa. 'How was it? Did he faint away in shock?'

'He was gratifyingly surprised.' Ross would not tell her how Tinmore tried to talk him out of proposing to her.

'Did he bring up the dowry?' she asked eagerly.

He nodded. 'As you predicted.'

'And did you refuse it?' she pressed.

'I refused it and told him to give the money to the poor.'

Her eyes sparkled. 'Oh, that is famous! He won't do it, of course. It is not in his nature. Why waste good money on poor people?'

'Are you ready for me to propose to you now?' he asked.

Her fingers fluttered. 'You already did so yesterday.'

'I think I must repeat the event.' Ross glanced towards the door. 'Is there a crack between the door and the doorjamb?'

She looked startled. 'I have no idea. What does it matter?'

'Just in case there are curious eyes watching, I will

do this right.' He slid to the floor on one knee. 'Will you become betrothed to me, Miss Summerfield?' He lowered his voice. 'Now you must act surprised. Slap your hands on your face. Cry out. Act as if you are being proposed to by a duke's son.'

She giggled. 'I *am* being proposed to by a duke's son.' But she slapped her cheeks and squealed with pleasure. 'Oh, Lord Rossdale,' she said louder. 'This is so sudden.'

'Do not keep me in suspense.' He put his fist to his heart. 'Let me know if I will be the happiest man in all of Mayfair, or cast me down into the depths of despair.'

'What should I do?' she cried, playing along with his joke. 'I cannot decide.'

'Why, say yes, of course.'

Her smile softened. 'I will accept your proposal, Lord Rossdale. I will become betrothed to you.'

Chapter Fourteen

After Ross left, Genna danced around the drawing room, the way she'd danced in her bedchamber the day before. No one would guess that her happiness was not in anticipation of marriage to a duke's heir. It was because he'd set her free to be herself for the whole Season and more.

It would be impossible to keep her happiness a secret. It burst from her every pore. The source of it might need to be kept secret, but the emotion could not be held in. Still, it felt so precious to her she wanted to keep it to herself a little while longer, savour it alone in all its aspects. Unfortunately Tinmore would tell Lorene soon enough. Genna would rather her sister hear the news from her.

She smoothed her skirt and tidied her hair and took a deep breath. She could pretend to be composed, at least for a little while. She left the room with her head held high and her step unhurried, when she really felt like skipping and taking the stairs two at a time.

Lorene would probably be in her sitting room

where she spent a great deal of her time practising on the pianoforte there. It was not as grand as the pianoforte in the drawing room, but it was the one she preferred.

As she neared the room's door, though, she did not hear music—except the joyous refrain inside her.

Genna knocked anyway and heard Lorene say, 'Come in.'

Genna opened the door.

Lorene stood. 'Genna, I was just about to send for you. Look who is here.'

Her sister Tess came up to her and bussed her cheek. 'I thought I would call upon my sisters. I have not seen you since the opera. Lorene has been telling me all about the musicale you attended and the Duchess of Archester's ball. Did you enjoy yourself?'

Ross had engineered those invitations, Genna was sure. 'I did.'

She could hardly keep from hopping from one foot to the other. How fortunate that both of her sisters were here. She could tell them both at once.

'I am glad you are here, Tess,' she said, 'because I have some news.'

'That Lord Rossdale called upon Tinmore?' Lorene broke in. 'I told her of it.'

Genna hesitated. Had Lorene been told why he called? Did they already know?

Lorene turned to Tess. 'Tinmore has lately become better acquainted with Rossdale's father, the Duke of Kessington.'

'Did you tell Tess that Rossdale took me for a ride in Hyde Park yesterday?' she asked instead.

Tess looked surprised. 'He did?'

'That is not all,' Genna said. 'He called upon me today after seeing Tinmore.'

'He has been attentive to Genna, that is true.' Lorene made it sound as if she'd forgotten such an unimportant event.

'He had a reason for calling upon me,' she said.

Genna looked from one sister to the other. 'I am betrothed to him.' The words sounded awkward to her ears, but she could not make herself say he'd asked her to marry him. He had not done that. The proposal was for a betrothal, not marriage.

'What?' Lorene cried.

Tess gave a surprised laugh, but immediately seized Genna's hands. 'Do not say so! He asked you to marry him? Just now?'

Genna nodded. 'First he spoke to Lord Tinmore and then to me.' She glanced at Lorene. 'Yesterday he spoke to me about it a little. To see if I might be willing.'

Lorene looked dazed. 'I did not expect this—I—I feared his intentions were dishonourable.'

'Dishonourable?' Genna retorted. 'Rossdale is an honourable man.'

If you did not count his willingness to engage in a scandalous secret, that was.

Tess pulled back and peered at Genna. 'One moment—was this another of Tinmore's machinations? Did he put pressure on Rossdale?'

Tinmore had forced Tess and Marc to marry. Marc rescued Tess from a storm and the two were forced to take refuge overnight in a deserted cabin. Tinmore insisted Marc had compromised Tess.

'No,' Genna told her. 'Rossdale really asked me. There was no pressure or any such thing. I believe he merely sought Tinmore's approval before asking me.'

'Not that you would want Tinmore's approval,' Lorene said sarcastically.

Genna met her gaze. 'You have the right of it, Lorene. I do not care a fig whether your husband approves or not, but it was a respectful thing for Rossdale to do.'

Tess sat down on a sofa near Lorene. Genna was too excited to sit.

'A duke's son,' Tess said breathlessly. Her voice changed to shock. 'Oh, my stars. He is the heir, is he not? You will be a duchess some day!'

No, I will not, Genna said to herself. But her sisters could not know that. Genna felt her insides squirm with guilt.

'It makes no sense, does it?' Lorene said. 'A duke's son and a penniless baronet's daughter.'

'We get on well together,' Genna said defensively.

'Of course you do,' Tess said soothingly.

'We must do something for a formal announcement.' Lorene frowned. 'A ball or something.'

'I do not know—' Genna plopped down next to Tess. This was becoming too big. A formal announcement seemed wrong when the betrothal was not real.

'Of course you must do something,' Tess agreed. 'If not a ball, *something*. You will be marrying a man who will be a duke. You cannot go higher than that unless you married one of the royal princes.'

Genna was as likely to marry one of them as to marry Ross.

A small pang of disappointment struck her at that thought, but she pushed it away immediately. She did not wish to marry a duke. She did not wish to marry anyone and be trapped the way Lorene was trapped.

'A ball.' Lorene sounded stressed. 'I do not know how to host a ball.'

Genna had not thought that she would distress her sister. She felt as small as a bug. 'A ball is too much fuss! I do not see why you should even think of it.'

'Oh, it must be done,' Tess said with decision. 'It would cause more talk not to have some sort of event to announce your engagement.' She laughed. 'Do you realise this will be the only wedding in the family that adheres to propriety?'

'The wedding,' Lorene groaned. 'What is proper for a future duke's wedding?'

This was all going too far. Genna felt miserable. 'Do not talk of wedding plans. It will not be before next autumn at the earliest.'

'So long a wait?' Tess looked surprised. 'Whatever for?'

How could she explain? 'Because that is what we've decided.'

'Oh, but never mind that.' Tess took Genna's hands

in hers again. 'Tell us about Rossdale! He is very handsome, is he not?'

Genna had to agree. 'He is handsome.' But that was not the half of it. They could laugh together. But he did not laugh at her plans or her ambitions.

Lorene and Tess would never understand how important both those things were to her.

Lorene leaned towards her. 'Genna, do you have a genuine regard for him? Or do you feel obligated to marry him? Because you do not have to accept the first offer you receive. I will support you in waiting for a love match. It is all I've ever wanted for you.'

Now Genna felt even worse. Lorene wanted her to be happy so much she'd defy her husband for it. And all Genna was doing was deceiving her.

Genna softened her tone. 'I do have a great regard for Rossdale. What is more, I believe he feels the same towards me.'

They *liked* each other and that was the truth.

'Oh!' Tess had tears streaming down her cheeks. She hugged Genna. 'You have found the dream! A husband you love who loves you!'

Genna stiffened. 'You found it as well, Tess.'

'Yes, but mine was hard won. Luck was a big factor in it, too.' She shuddered. 'If I had been rescued by some wretched man my life would be a misery.'

Like Lorene's, Genna thought.

'I care only that my sisters are happy,' Lorene said, her voice catching.

Tess gestured for her to join them on the sofa and

the three sisters wrapped their arms around each other. Genna was filled with love for them.

And consumed with guilt for deceiving them.

Dell sat at a desk in the bedchamber he used in the Kessington town house. He tried to make sense of a line of figures representing crop yields and estimates of the effect of allowing foreign grain and produce to undercut prices. He tried to make his own calculations based on the figures provided, but his results did not match the author of the material he'd been studying.

He sat back and pinched his nose.

A knock sounded at the door and a familiar face peeked in. 'Do you need an interruption?'

Dell glanced up and smiled. 'Ross! An interruption would be most welcome.'

Ross approached the desk and sat in a nearby chair. 'What are you reading?'

'Writings about grain prices. This author seems to have fabricated his results, however. I don't know how one ever knows who to believe.' Dell set the papers aside. 'What do you wish to see me about?'

Ross looked defensive. 'What? I cannot simply knock on your door?'

'I think you have a reason,' Dell said. It was written all over Ross's face.

Ross stood again and paced. 'I do have a reason. Something I want to talk over with you. Something I want to tell you.'

Dell watched him and waited.

Ross finally faced him. 'I've become betrothed to Genna Summerfield.'

Dell could not believe his ears. 'What? You don't want to marry. You've always said.'

'I don't want to marry,' Ross agreed. 'At least, not yet.'

Dell felt alarmed. 'Do not tell me you are being forced into this.'

Ross held up his hand. 'No. Not at all. Hear me out. I'll explain the whole thing.'

Dell crossed his arms over his chest.

'It is not a real betrothal—' Ross looked uncomfortable. 'Genna does not wish to be married any more than I do. We are merely pretending to be betrothed so that my father will take the pressure off me and Tinmore will no longer plague her. I'll take her all the places she wishes to go, to see what she wishes to see. We will have an enjoyable Season instead of one spent dodging suitors or matchmaking mamas.'

Dell looked sceptical. 'You never had difficulty resisting your father's pressure before or dodging matchmaking mamas. Why take such an extreme step? It makes no sense.'

Ross sat again. 'You are correct. It is not for me, but for her. I want to help her.'

'Help her resist pressure from Tinmore?' Dell scoffed. 'Genna seems strong-willed and self-assured. I'd wager she knows just how to resist whatever Tinmore wants her to do.'

'That may be so, Dell.' Ross rose again. 'But why should we have to fight everyone when there is enjoyment to be had instead?'

Dell frowned. 'Enjoyment?' Surely Ross did not intend to trifle with the young woman?

'Nothing untoward, I assure you,' Ross said.

'You've told me over and over that you find no pleasure in a frivolous life any more. So do not tell me you do this for enjoyment.'

'I like her company, Dell.' He paced. 'There are places to show her here in London that I could not show her unless we are betrothed.'

Dell peered at him. 'You will pretend to be betrothed so she can see the sights of London?'

'It is more than that,' Ross insisted. 'I cannot explain. I cannot see the harm.'

Dell raised his brows. 'Can you not? I can think of all kinds of harm. People will be hurt over this; you mark my words.'

'It is only for a few months,' Ross added. 'Next autumn she'll cry off and that will be the end of it.'

'Oh, yes.' Dell spoke with sarcasm. 'That will not cause harm. Nor gossip. Nor scandal.'

Ross leaned across Dell's desk. 'It will not be that bad.'

'I disagree,' Dell said. 'This is a mistake.'

'I'll prove you wrong,' Ross challenged.

'We'll see,' Dell said.

They glared at each other, as they had done when they were boys and argued about something or another.

Ross backed away. 'No matter. It is done. I simply wanted you to know the truth of it all.'

So he was burdened with the secret as well? He wouldn't mention that bit to Ross, though.

'Just take care,' Dell said. 'I'd not like to see either of you hurt.'

Ross met Dell's eyes again. 'May I have your word you will keep this in confidence?'

Dell nodded. 'You have my word. I will keep your secret.'

'Even if you believe it is a mistake?' Ross pressed.

'Even so,' Dell said.

Ross left Dell's bedchamber with some of his high spirits dampened. He supposed he harboured the hope that Dell would understand his reasons for this betrothal, not that he could tell him the whole of it.

He had an idea of how to make certain Genna's plans worked out just as she wished, even though he had more to work on how to make that happen. To help her live the life of her own choosing was all he desired. He might be destined for duty, but he'd make certain Genna could be free, like he, his mother and father had been free in the days before duty took over.

Ross's next task was to inform his father and the Duchess. He dreaded it.

It was nearing time to dress for dinner. With luck he'd catch his father and the Duchess alone for a few minutes before guests arrived. There were always guests for dinner, it seemed. Dinner was one of the venues where his father could influence others to agree with his views.

He had his valet dress him hurriedly and he was the first to enter the drawing room where they would wait for dinner to be announced. A decanter of claret was on the table. Ross poured himself a glass and sipped it while he waited for his father and the Duchess.

They walked in the room, discussing the impending marriage of the Princess Charlotte to Prince Leopold of Saxe-Coburg-Saalfeld and the various monies and property Parliament would vote to bestow upon the young woman who might some day become Queen.

'Ross!' his father exclaimed upon seeing him there.

Ross was rarely early.

'Do you stay for dinner, Ross?' the Duchess asked. 'I do hope so. It will even out our numbers. I already told the butler you would dine with us.'

'I will stay, then,' he said. 'When do the guests arrive?'

'Not for a half-hour,' she said. 'Unless they are late, which they usually are.'

He poured them each a glass of claret. His father took a long sip of his.

No reason to delay, Ross thought. 'There is something I wish to tell you.'

Interest was lacking in both their eyes. His father considered most of what Ross talked about to be of no consequence, usually about some poverty or injustice he'd discovered. His father thought only in terms of the fate of the country, not individuals. The Duchess merely regarded Ross as the heir and not as a person who could further the Duke's influence and power.

'I have done something you have begged me to do—' he began.

They both glanced at him then.

'I have become betrothed.'

'What?' cried the Duchess.

'This is excellent!' His father's face lit with excitement. 'Who is the lady?'

'As long as she is suitable,' the Duchess said warily.

Ross met her eyes. 'She suits me very well.'

The Duchess blanched. 'Please do not say it is that woman—'

Ross knew that his father and the Duchess would not approve. That was part of what would make the scheme work, but it angered him, nonetheless.

'Miss Summerfield, do you mean?' He did not want the Duchess to say her name first. 'Yes. I have made Miss Summerfield an offer and she has accepted.' Which was the truth.

'Summerfield?' His father raised his voice. 'That chit connected to Tinmore?'

'Ross, she is a nobody,' the Duchess said quickly. 'Worse than that, look at her family. There is not a one of them who has not been the subject of gossip. Her mother and father—bad blood, indeed.'

'Has Miss Summerfield done anything objectionable?' Ross challenged.

The Duchess's lips thinned. 'Not as yet.'

In that she was correct. In a few months, Genna would cry off and that would certainly cause gossip. Not to mention what people would say when she became an artist and lived as an independent woman.

'Will you not reconsider?' his father pleaded. 'I'll never get Tinmore off my neck if you are married to his wife's sister.'

Of course, his father would think of himself. 'Miss Summerfield will have no difficulty distancing herself from Lord Tinmore, if that is your only objection.'

'Not my only objection,' his father snapped. 'She's not spent any time in town. She knows nobody of importance. What does she know of entertaining? Of managing houses as grand as our family's?'

'She has a quick intelligence,' Ross said. 'These matters can be learned.'

His father's eyes turned pained. 'Some women cannot learn.'

Like Ross's mother. She'd never adapted to the strains of being a duchess.

Ross's anger at his father melted a little.

'You are in your prime, Father,' he said softly. 'There will be time for Genna to learn how to be a duchess.'

But it would never get that far. He'd forgotten that for a moment.

His father's wife broke in. 'Why could you not court Lady Alice? She is a sweet girl. And her father is a marquess. It would be much wiser for you to court the daughter of a marquess and bring some advantage to the union.'

'It is done, Constance.' There was no use arguing over what would never come to pass. 'I am betrothed to Miss Summerfield.'

'But we could induce her to cry off even before word gets out,' she persisted. 'It is not too late.'

'I do not want to break this engagement. I have a high regard for Miss Summerfield.' Which was very true. 'And I intend to honour my promise to her.'

Both the Duchess and his father's faces were pinched in disappointment.

For no reason. The marriage would never take place.

'Regard this,' he told them. 'I have done as you wished, as you have begged me to do for years now. I have become betrothed. We will marry in the autumn, probably.'

The Duchess lifted a shoulder as if to say that was not concession enough.

'Well, if you say it is done, it is done and we will have to devise the best way to approach this.' His father poured himself another glass of claret. 'I beg you not to speak of it at dinner. Let us think upon how to have this announcement made.'

'As you wish.' Ross finished his claret.

Chapter Fifteen

For the next week Ross called upon Genna every day, taking her to all the places she'd desired. They'd battled the crowds to see Napoleon's carriage at the Egyptian Museum, gaped at the beasts kept at the Tower, and sat in choice seats at Astley's Amphitheatre. Every day brought new delights and new ideas and Genna could not have been happier.

She had almost been able to forget that Lord Tinmore had invited the Duke and Duchess of Kessington and Ross to dinner to discuss the announcement of the betrothal.

She wished the announcement could be made in the newspapers, rather than for her to face the stares and whispers of those who wouldn't think a duke's son would actually wish to marry her. It made it worse knowing she and Ross were deceiving everyone about their true intent.

The dinner with the Duke and Duchess was the only entertainment for Tinmore and Lorene this week. It had taken that many days to find an evening the Duke and Duchess could attend. Ross requested that Lord Penford be invited, to which Tinmore readily agreed, but about whom Genna and Lorene heard Tinmore's endless complaints that the table would be uneven.

Lorene had little to do with the planning of the dinner. Nothing would do but for Tinmore to see to every detail, in consultation with Mr Filkins, his secretary, and Dixon, the butler. She knew nothing of planning important dinners, Tinmore had said, so Lorene spent long hours practising her new music instead. Genna regretted leaving her for the pleasures Ross's outings provided, but she shoved her feelings aside. She must learn to see to her own well-being and leave Lorene to cope with the life she'd chosen.

Even though Lorene had chosen this dismal life for Genna's sake.

When the evening of the dinner came, Genna's mood darkened. She did not need Ross to tell her that the Duke and Duchess would disapprove of the betrothal. No one would approve such an unbalanced pairing. Besides facing them, she would also be seeing Lord Penford for the first time since he'd learned the truth of the betrothal. And she would have to endure Lord Tinmore, who took credit for the match.

In a way, Tinmore deserved credit. If he were the least bit tolerable, she might never have decided to pursue a career as an artist. Truth be told, she was nowhere near being able to do that. She'd solved one problem by agreeing to this pretend betrothal, but she still needed to learn so much more before she could begin to support herself with painting and she'd not painted for days.

Before her maid came in to help her dress, she sat down with her crayon and sketched some of the images she'd seen over the week. A lion from the African continent. Dancing horses from Astley's. The crowd gaping at Napoleon's carriage. She forgot everything else and lost herself in her drawings.

When the maid entered the room carrying her dress, Genna jumped in surprise.

'Is it time already?' She closed her sketchbook and walked over to her pitcher and basin and washed the chalk from her fingers.

'I'll dress your hair first,' the maid said.

Genna missed the camaraderie she'd had with Anna, her maid at Summerfield House. She did not dare confide in this woman even in simple ways. Tinmore's servants had a habit of reporting back to Tinmore everything Genna or Lorene said or did. So she merely told her how she wished to wear her hair and what dress she desired.

This night she was donning a pale rose dinner dress, a nice complement to the deeper red Lorene had chosen. She wanted to take some care with her appearance for Ross's sake, so the Duke and Duchess would not find fault with her looks.

The maid seemed to be moving particularly slowly this evening. Genna feared she would be late in presenting herself in the drawing room where they would all have a drink of wine before dinner.

Before the line of buttons down the back of her dress were fastened, Genna heard a carriage arrive. 'Please hurry, Hallie. I believe they have arrived.'

'Yes, miss,' the maid said, but she went no faster.

When the maid finally finished, Genna dashed down the stairs to the drawing room. She forced herself to stop at the door and compose herself. Why did she worry? The more the Duke and Duchess disliked her, the less dust they would kick up when she broke the sham betrothal.

She lifted her chin, put a smile on her face and walked in.

'About time, girl,' Tinmore snapped.

He stood near the fireplace with the Duke and Ross. The Duchess sat on the sofa with Lorene and Penford stood apart from them all.

Ross was the only one to smile at her entrance. 'Genna!' He walked up to her and took her hand.

She curtsied to the Duke. 'Good evening, Your Grace.' And to the Duchess. 'Your Grace. Forgive my tardiness.' She decided to give no excuse.

'We have been discussing how to make an announcement of this betrothal,' the Duchess said, making it sound like it was something loathsome. 'We have decided that it should be done at the ball we are already scheduled to give in two weeks' time.'

Tinmore spoke up. 'I would be honoured to host

the entertainment where the announcement is made. I think it only appropriate—'

The Duchess held up a hand. 'No. We've settled it. It will be at our ball.'

Genna glanced at Lorene, but her face was blank and she could not tell how Lorene felt about this.

'I should most like to do what my sister wishes to do,' Genna said. 'If you have her approval, then I am happy to have the announcement at your ball. I do wish for my whole family to be included. Our brother will not come, of course. He and his wife are too far away, but I insist my sister Tess and her husband be included. And his parents, of course.'

'Lord and Lady Northdon?' the Duchess said through a sneer.

Lord and Lady Northdon were practically shunned by the *ton*, because Lady Northdon was a French commoner by birth and the daughter of French Jacobins.

'Yes.' Genna kept her gaze steady. 'I consider them part of my family.'

The Duchess glanced away. 'If we must.'

'Certainly we must,' added Ross. He turned to Genna. 'Would you like some Madeira?'

'I would.' Lots of it, in fact.

It was Penford who poured her the wine and handed it to her.

'How are you, sir?' she asked him.

He met her eyes. 'Very well.'

His expression was as blank as Lorene's, but

not hostile. Genna supposed she must be content with that.

He turned to Lorene. 'More wine?'

'Thank you,' she murmured, handing him her glass.

The dinner was a stilted affair. What troubled Genna the most was her sister, who seemed even more unassuming than usual. It was as if all the life had been sucked out of her. Genna had caused it, she knew, and it ate at her. But what could she do about it now? She could not blurt out to them all that the betrothal was a sham and they should not take it all so seriously.

Her saving grace was having Ross seated across from her. When Lord Tinmore and the Duke's conversation became particularly tedious, Ross needed only to look at her and she could smile inside.

After dinner when the ladies left the gentlemen to their brandy, the Duchess spent the time lecturing Genna and Lorene in proper behaviour at this upcoming ball, as if they did not know how to behave. She also discussed the politics of the day, to which Lorene and Genna agreed to her every word merely to be polite.

When the men returned to the drawing room, Ross rolled his eyes at Genna, making her smile again. Dell looked bleak. Lord Tinmore and the Duke continued to discuss Princess Charlotte's impending wedding and the Duchess joined in.

Dell looked down on Lorene. 'Do you play for us this evening, ma'am?'

Her gaze rose to his. 'If you wish it.'

Dell extended his hand to Lorene to help her rise. She sat at the pianoforte in the corner of the room and played softly the Mozart piece that had been performed at the musicale.

While Tinmore, the Duke and Duchess discussed politics and Lorene played Mozart, Ross gestured for Genna to come with him. They sneaked out of the room and into the hallway. Genna pulled him into the library, which was dark. She could hardly see his face.

'Has it been too ghastly for you?' he asked.

She smiled. 'Perhaps a bit more than dinners here usually are.'

He stood close. 'The Duchess is intent on having her own way. I apologise for that.'

She felt the warmth of his body even though they were not touching, such an odd but pleasant sensation. 'I wish we did not have to make a formal announcement.'

'Do not put too much on it,' he responded. 'No one else will. We will be stared at for a while, whispered about and then they will forget us. They will be talking of Princess Charlotte and no one else.'

The wedding of the Princess was a welcome distraction. As the only child of the Prince Regent, she would be Queen one day.

'I hope you are right,' she said.

He held her hands. 'I will call upon you early tomorrow. Are you able to spend the day with me?'

She smiled. 'I would be delighted.'

He gave her a kiss on the cheek, then stepped away. 'We should go back.'

She put her fingers where his lips had touched and where she still felt the sensation of the kiss. 'Yes. Let us go back.'

The next day Genna stopped by Lorene's sitting room before leaving for her outing with Ross.

Lorene was playing the pianoforte when Genna knocked and entered the room. 'I'm off with Ross in a few minutes. I just wanted to let you know.'

Lorene made an attempt at a smile. 'Where do you go this time?'

Genna sat in a chair near the pianoforte. 'I do not know. It is to be a surprise.'

'A surprise? How nice.'

Genna had not had a chance to speak with Lorene after the Duke and Duchess left after dinner. 'I wanted to see if you are all right.'

'All right?' Lorene blinked. 'Of course I am. Why ever would I not be all right?'

'You—you seemed different last night,' Genna said. 'So very subdued. I worried about you.'

Lorene turned back to the keyboard. 'Oh, there is nothing to worry about. I—I merely had little to say. The Duke and Duchess and Tinmore had so many strong opinions on what should be done, I merely let them sort it out.'

Genna rose and leaned over to give her sister a hug from behind. 'I am certain I would have been happier with whatever plan you could come up with.'

Lorene covered Genna's hand with her own and squeezed it. 'A very small dinner party with family and close friends?'

'Perfect!' Genna said. Especially if the betrothal were real.

Lorene turned to her again. 'I cannot tell you how delighted I am that you are going to marry Rossdale. The two of you are so fond of each other. Your happiness shows.' She still held Genna's hand and squeezed it again. 'It is what I dreamed of for you.'

Genna felt her guilt like a dagger twisting in her chest. How shameful to deceive such a loving sister! Still, she had to steel herself. She needed to find her own way.

'I am happy,' she said and realised there was truth in those words. When she was with Ross, she could push aside all the other feelings that swirled around inside her.

A footman came to the door. 'Lord Rossdale has arrived, miss.'

She hugged Lorene again. 'I'll stop in when I return and let you know where it is he has taken me.'

'Yes,' Lorene gave her that forced smile again. 'Do enjoy yourself.'

Genna always enjoyed herself when in Ross's company.

She raced to her room and had the maid help her into her pale pink pelisse and bright blue bonnet. She hung her reticule over her arm and pulled on her gloves as she hurried down the stairs.

When she entered the drawing room, Ross stood with another man.

'Look who will accompany us today,' Ross said, gesturing to the man standing next to him.

'Mr Vespery!' She smiled at the artist who'd been so kind to her at the Duchess of Archester's ball. 'How lovely to see you.'

The artist blew a kiss over her hand. 'Miss Summerfield, it is my pleasure to be in your company.'

She turned to Ross, even more excited than before. 'Where are we going?'

Instead of answering her directly, he said, 'Somewhere you will like. But first I have a gift.'

He handed her a package wrapped in brown paper. She looked at him, puzzled.

'Open it,' he said.

She removed the paper. It was a beautifully bound book. She opened it and found the title page. '*A Treatise on Painting* by Leonardo da Vinci,' she read aloud, then words failed her.

'It is the only book on art I could find,' he said apologetically.

'It is wonderful,' she finally managed, leafing through the book and glancing at da Vinci's words.

'A classic work,' Vespery added.

'And a hint about where we are bound today,' Ross said. 'We are going to look at art.'

Genna looked up and grinned. To be with Ross gazing at art and learning from Vespery. This day was going to be wonderful.

* * *

Ross had come with one of the Duke's carriages so they all sat comfortably for the short ride to their destination. When the carriage stopped and Ross helped her out, she was even more puzzled. They were in front of Carlton House, the residence of the Prince Regent.

'Here we are,' Ross said.

'But this is—'

He threaded her arm through his. 'This is our destination.'

The palace of the Prince Regent.

As they walked through the portico and up to the door, he explained, 'With His Royal Highness's permission, we will meet one of his art advisors, Sir Charles Long, who will take us on a tour of His Royal Highness's collection.'

Before Genna could form a coherent thought, the door opened and they were greeted by a line of four footmen and a nattily dressed gentleman.

'Ah, you must be Lord Rossdale. Welcome.' He bowed to Ross and turned to Vespery. 'Good to see you again, sir.'

Vespery bowed.

The gentleman then regarded Genna. 'And you must be the young lady who Rossdale insisted be shown the collection.'

Ross stepped forward. 'Miss Summerfield, may I present Sir Charles Long, one of His Royal Highness's art advisors.'

Genna curtsied. 'Sir Charles, I am in awe already!'

They stood in the entrance hall, which was as bright as daylight with its white marble floors, white walls and domed ceiling accented with yellow-gold columns and statues in alcoves.

The footmen took their coats.

'His Royal Highness is quite a collector of fine art. There are one hundred thirty-six paintings in the principal rooms and another sixty-seven in the attics and bedrooms. We will not see those, of course. We will not intrude on His Royal Highness's private rooms,' Sir Charles said. He gestured for them to follow him. 'Come.'

Genna lost track of time as they walked from one spectacular room to another. The architecture and decor rivalled the paintings on the walls. So opulent. So beautiful. So much like pieces of art in themselves. The grand staircase deserved its name as it rose in graceful, symmetrical curves. Gilt was prominent in almost every room. Light from the candles and the fireplaces reflected in the gold, making them seem to glow from within. There were rooms of all colours and styles. Round rooms. Blue rooms. French rooms. Gothic rooms. She wished she had a sketchbook with her to record the unique beauty of each.

Then there was the art. Almost every wall displayed a painting or several. Vespery and Sir Charles pointed out the different styles and time periods and artists. There were old paintings, many of them by the Dutch masters—Rembrandt, Rubens, Van Dyck,

Jan Steen. And newer ones like Reynolds, Gainsborough and Stubbs. And countless others. Genna tried to keep everything they said in memory, but she knew she would forget half of it. She listened as intently as her excitement allowed her.

When it was possible, Vespery had Genna look closely at the brushwork of the paintings. He explained how the artists created the effects, some of which were so real looking that Genna thought the people would come alive and join them on the tour. Sir Charles spoke of how the Prince Regent was able to purchase so many paintings so quickly. In the aftermath of the French Revolution, a glut of paintings came on the market, paintings once owned by aristocrats.

Genna gasped. 'The owners must have died on the guillotine!'

'Indeed,' agreed Sir Charles, his expression sombre. 'Or drowned at Nantes.'

'At least the Prince Regent rescued the art,' Vespery said.

'Because one could not save the people,' added Ross.

Snatches of memory came back to Ross, memories of the Terror—or what he'd heard of it from his parents or other adults who seemed to have spoken of little else during that time. What he remembered was mostly feeling their fear and anguish. His mother had known some of the aristocrats who'd been executed. A cousin had been killed. That whole time was fraught with upheaval and tension. His grandfather had just died and his father disappeared into his new role as Duke. His mother, so carefree and gay, turned fearful of an uprising in England such as had happened in France. She feared she, his father and even Ross would be targets if the people rose against aristocrats, high aristocrats especially, like dukes and duchesses.

His mother never recovered from that time, Ross realised later. She tried to fulfil her duties as duchess, but without any pleasure whatever. His father did not help, always too busy with Parliament and running the estates. Ross had been sent to school by that time. On holidays, his mother seemed even more anxious and withdrawn.

When she became ill, she simply gave up.

He was at school, his father in town and she in the country at Kessington Hall when the last fever took her away for ever.

He'd vowed then to live as his mother had once lived, for adventure and enjoyment, like his family used to do. He'd succeeded, too, until he realised men like Dell and other friends were putting their lives at risk fighting in Spain. Then he tried to do his part, meagre as it was, transporting men across the Channel.

He'd been thinking more about his mother lately. Since meeting Genna, actually. Like his mother, Genna embraced new experiences and was not afraid to let her enjoyment of them show. He liked that about her.

Genna, though, was brave. She was unafraid of a very uncertain future.

He was perhaps a bit more realistic about what she would face trying to support herself as an artist, but he was determined to help her succeed.

Vespery, Genna and Sir Charles continued to discuss the paintings in these rooms while Ross stood nearby. Afterward Sir Charles returned them to the entrance hall where the footmen were waiting with their things.

'I do not know how to thank you, Sir Charles,' Genna said, her voice still ebullient. 'And please convey my thanks to His Royal Highness. Tell him you have made a lady artist very happy.'

'I will do so at my first opportunity,' Sir Charles said.

Vespery also bade him goodbye.

Ross extended his hand to Sir Charles. 'Thank you, sir, and convey my regards to His Royal Highness.'

When they went out the door, their carriage was waiting for them.

Genna clasped Ross's arm as they walked to the carriage through the portico with its Corinthian columns. 'I do not know how to thank you, Ross. Nothing could duplicate that experience!' She reached one arm out to touch Mr Vespery's hand. 'And to you, sir. I learned so much by listening to you.'

When they were seated in the carriage, Ross

said, 'There is more planned, Genna. Not for today, though.'

'Good.' She sighed. 'I do not think I could endure any more today. I am already bursting with new knowledge.'

The carriage first took Mr Vespery to his rooms in Covent Garden.

When he left the carriage, Genna said, 'Thank you again, Mr Vespery.'

His eyes twinkled. 'I will see you again soon, my dear.'

'I hope so, sir.'

When the carriage pulled away she turned to Ross. 'What did he mean by "I will see you soon"? Do you have another outing planned?'

He grinned. 'Perhaps.'

She leaned against his shoulder. 'You could not possibly please me more than you have done today.'

He could try, though. He could try.

Chapter Sixteen

The next day, Genna eagerly watched out the window for Ross's arrival. This time he drove up in his curricle with his tiger seated on the back. She rushed down the stairs and was in hat and gloves by the time he was admitted to the hall.

'I am ready!' she cried.

His ready smile cheered her. 'Then we shall be off.'

The footman held open the door as Ross escorted her out of the house. He helped her on to the curricle and climbed up beside her. The tiger jumped into his seat.

When they pulled away, Genna could not resist asking, 'Where are we bound?'

Ross grinned at her. 'Do you actually think I would tell you?'

She pretended to be petulant. 'I had hoped you would not be so cruel as to leave me in suspense.'

'But that is my delight,' he countered.

She spent the rest of the time guessing where they might be bound.

He turned down Park Lane to Piccadilly. 'Are we to visit the shops?'

'No.' He looked smug.

'Westminster Abbey!' she cried. 'Are we headed there? I've always wanted to see Westminster Abbey.'

'Another time, perhaps,' he said.

He turned on Haymarket.

She had a sudden thought, one that made her heart beat faster. 'Somerset House?'

Somerset House was the home of the Royal Academy of Art.

'Not today,' he said.

She gave up and felt guilty for being disappointed, but her hopes grew again when they turned down Vespery's street. 'Will Vespery accompany us again?' If so, where would he sit? This curricle sat two comfortably; three would be a crush.

'No,' he said.

He pulled up in front of the building where Vespery had his rooms. The tiger jumped down and held the horses. Ross climbed down and reached up to help Genna. He held her by her waist and she put her hands on his shoulders. She felt the strength of his arms as he lifted her from the curricle. When her feet hit the ground she lurched forward, winding up into his arms. Her senses flared at being embraced by him and she did not wish to move away. Ever.

It was he who released her. 'We are calling upon Mr Vespery.'

That was the surprise? She'd enjoy spending time

with Vespery, especially because he was so filled with helpful information, but her mind had created something grander. How nonsensical was that? To be disappointed in whatever nice thing Ross created for her. What an ungrateful wretch she was.

'Calling upon Vespery will top Carlton House?' she said in good humour.

'Oh, indeed it will,' he assured her in a serious tone.

He must be making a jest. What could top Carlton House?

The housekeeper answered the door. 'He is in his studio.' She turned and started walking. 'This way.'

Genna's interest was piqued. 'I've never been in an artist's studio before.'

His studio was in the back of the building with a wall of large windows facing a small garden patch. As they entered, he turned from his canvas to greet them. 'Ah, Miss Summerfield. Lord Rossdale. Welcome to my studio.'

The housekeeper left.

In the corner of the room was a chair behind which was draped red velvet fabric. Obviously this was where his clients sat for him. Facing that area was a large wooden easel with a canvas on it large enough for a life-sized figure to be painted upon it. The painting in progress, Genna noticed right away, was of the Duchess of Kessington.

She approached the painting. 'Oh! Am I to have the honour of watching you work?'

Next to the easel was a table stained with paint of all colours. Vespery's palette was equally as colourful. Several brushes of all sizes stood in a large jug.

'You will watch me work, my dear,' Vespery said. 'And you will paint, as well. Lord Rossdale has asked me to give you lessons in oil painting.'

She swivelled around to Ross. 'Painting lessons?'

'As many as you need,' Ross said. 'You said you had much to learn.'

She ran to him and clasped his hand, lifting it to her lips. 'Ross! How can I thank you?'

He covered her hand with his. 'When you are ready, paint my portrait.'

She stood on tiptoe and kissed his cheek. 'It will be my honour.'

'Come,' Vespery said. 'I have a smock to cover your dress. Let us begin.'

Ross found a wooden chair in the studio and sat in it, stretching out his legs in front of him. He watched as Vespery showed Genna the easel, palette, brushes, paints, canvas, and other necessities Ross had purchased for her at Vespery's direction.

Vespery started by teaching Genna about the paint. How the colours were made. How they could be mixed to create any colour she wished. She seemed to pick up the concepts quickly from her knowledge of watercolours and Ross learned more than he'd ever known before about this basic element of oil painting. She practised mixing the colours and then she practised putting them on a canvas stretched on a wooden frame. Vespery showed her how to draw on the canvas, either with paint or with a pencil. It seemed that artists did not make detailed drawings on the canvas, but rather bare outlines.

Next Vespery taught her about the different brushes and the effects produced by each and she practised with each one.

'You are quick enough to begin a painting,' Vespery told her. He wiped the paint off her canvas, though an imprint of the colours remained. 'With the oil paints, you are able to paint over them. You can scrape off your mistakes and start again. You can change what you don't like in the painting.' He set a plain bowl on a table covered with a dark cloth. 'Try painting this.'

Ross watched her with pride. She painted a credible likeness of the bowl, although she was not satisfied with it. She scraped it off with a palette knife and started over.

The time passed with impressive speed. From a distant room, Ross heard a clock chime. 'By God, we've been at this for three hours. I believe I must return you to your home and leave Vespery to finish the Duchess's portrait.'

'Oh!' She dipped her brush in the turpentine and cleaned it off with a nearby rag. 'I had no idea we were here that long! I hope I did not take you too long from your work, Mr Vespery.'

'The light is always better in the morning,' the artist said. 'That makes the afternoon perfect for your lessons.' He took her palette and covered it with a cloth. 'That should keep your paint moist until tomorrow. Let me show you how to clean your brushes.'

When Vespery finished instructing her how to clean up at the end of a session, they retrieved their hats and gloves and overcoats. Vespery walked them to the door.

'Thank you, Mr Vespery,' Genna said, shaking the man's hand.

'My pleasure, Miss Summerfield,' he responded.

Ross said his goodbyes, as well.

When he and Genna stepped outside, the curricle was not there.

'We are at least a half-hour later than when Jem was told to bring the carriage here,' Ross explained. 'He will be walking the horses around the streets, I expect.'

'I do not mind waiting,' She met his gaze. 'That was—' She paused as if searching for words. 'That was—marvellous.'

'I am glad you thought so,' he responded. 'You will have as many lessons as you need.'

She blinked. 'I should not accept this. I am certain it is costing you dear.'

'I have wealth enough to afford it.' He wanted to spend it on her. 'Think of it as a betrothal gift.'

She gave a nervous laugh. 'But we are not really betrothed.'

'Then think of me as being a patron of the arts. That is a long tradition, is it not?'

She smiled up at him. 'Then I accept.'

His tiger appeared at the end of the street. 'Ah, here is Jem now.'

During the drive back to Mayfair, Genna kept hold of his arm and sat close to him. He found it a very comfortable way to ride.

'Where do you go after you drop me off?' she asked.

He paused, uncertain of what to say. 'Somewhere I cannot take a lady.'

'Oh.' She let go of his arm.

He glanced at her, but she turned her head away.

'I am sorry.' Her voice was strained. 'I did not mean to pry into your—your affairs.'

Did she think he was going carousing? He certainly did not wish to give her that impression. 'I—I do not make a habit of speaking of this,' he began. 'I am driving to a workhouse. There are some soldiers there. I am paying their debts so they can be released.'

She turned back to him. 'You are paying their debts?'

He glanced away. 'It is a trifle to me, but will mean a great deal to them and to their families.'

She took his arm again. 'How did you find out they were in the workhouse? Did they tell you? Or did someone else tell you.'

He turned the curricle on to the next street. 'Someone told me. One of the other soldiers I help.'

'Other soldiers? What other soldiers?'

The soldiers should thank Dell for this. If Dell had not taken Ross to the hospital to see those wounded men from his regiment, he never would have sent baskets of food to their families. He never would have created a system where several needy families received food from him on a regular basis. Enough to keep them, their wives and children in good health.

'There are several soldiers and their families who I help.'

He lifted a shoulder. 'I simply went to the workhouse and asked if there were any soldiers there. I gathered their names and the amounts of their debts and today I return to pay them and secure their release.'

She lay her head against his shoulder. 'How good of you, Ross. How very good of you.'

After Ross brought her home, Genna could not get out of her mind how wonderful this man was. To her and to others. He was giving her the best chance for her to achieve her desire to support herself with her art. How could she ever repay him?

'Lady Tinmore wishes to see you,' the footman attending the hall told her.

How could she repay her sister? Look what Lorene had done for her, misguided as it was. She must become a success. What other choice did she have than to give them what they desired for her?

'Will I find her in her sitting room?' she asked him.

'I believe so, miss.'

Genna hurried up to her bedchamber where she removed her hat, gloves and redingote. She looked at her fingers. All the paint had not washed off them. She scrubbed them some more at her basin without complete success, gave up and hurried to Lorene's sitting room.

She knocked and entered without waiting for an invitation. 'I am back. You wanted to see me?'

Lorene sat at her pianoforte, but Genna had not heard her playing. She looked up at Genna with an expression of disapproval. 'We had a fitting scheduled this afternoon. Did you not remember?'

Genna placed her hand over her mouth. 'I completely forgot.' She had been so enthralled with painting that everything else dropped out of her mind. 'Lorene, I am so sorry.'

The fitting was for their new ball gowns, the ones they were to wear to the Duke and Duchess of Kessington's ball.

'I sent word that we would come tomorrow.'

'What time?' Genna asked.

'Morning.'

Excellent! She would not have to miss her art lesson.

She did not want to tell Lorene about her lessons, afraid Lorene would somehow stop them.

'I promise I will be ready tomorrow,' she said. 'Will Tess come?'

'Tess and Lady Northdon,' Lorene responded.

Nancy, Tess's former maid turned modiste, had come up with an idea for their gowns to complement one another, so when they stood together, they would make one pretty picture.

'I will not fail you tomorrow,' Genna vowed.

She turned to go, but Lorene stopped her.

'Will you attend the rout with me tonight?' There was an edge to Lorene's voice that made Genna pause.

'Is Tess not going?' Genna asked over her shoulder.

'No,' Lorene said. 'They did not receive an invitation.'

It was shameful how often Tess's husband's family was shunned by the *ton*. If Tess was not attending this rout, then who would Lorene talk to? Tinmore would leave her for the card room.

Genna turned back to her sister and gave her a reassuring smile. 'Of course I will attend with you. It should be very enjoyable.'

Dell walked through the crush of guests at the rout and kicked himself for attending. Why had he come?

He knew why. He suspected Lord Tinmore would receive an invitation and Dell wanted a moment with Lorene to see how she was faring.

The last time he'd seen her—at that ghastly dinner party with the Duke and Duchess—she'd looked even more beaten down than usual. Not that he'd believed Tinmore beat her—God knew what he would do if he discovered her husband was beating her. It was bad enough to witness Tinmore slashing at her spirit.

He was concerned because they were cousins— was that not so? Distant cousins, though. They shared a great-great-grandfather. That made them family and he had no one else but the Summerfield sisters.

If only he'd known their plight perhaps he could have convinced his father to allow them to stay at Summerfield House. Then Lorene would not have needed to marry Tinmore for his money. His father might have helped them instead.

Foolish notion. His father would never have listened to his younger son. Had his brother Reginald spoken it would have been a different matter, but Dell could not see either his father or his brother taking pity on the scandalous Summerfield sisters.

He heard a grating voice. 'Duke! How good to see you!' It was Tinmore greeting Ross's father. 'Do you play cards tonight?'

Tinmore was abandoning her again. Did the man not realise he left her adrift like a ship without a rudder? Someone must guide her, protect her from those pirates who delighted in attacking the vulnerable.

He found her in the crowd. Standing with her was her sister, a young woman made of sterner stuff than Lorene.

'Good evening, ladies.' Dell bowed.

Lorene lowered her gaze. 'Good evening, sir.'

'Lord Penford!' Genna responded. 'At last we see a friendly face. I was beginning to think that no one would know us here.'

Though he suspected several of the guests had been introduced to these two ladies before. 'I am happy to be of service. Would you like some refreshment?'

'Would you get us whatever is in those wine glasses we keep seeing the servants carry?' she asked.

'My pleasure.' He bowed and went in search of a footman carrying a tray.

When he returned, Lorene was conversing with the Duchess of Archester, but she accepted the wine with a fleeting smile. He bowed to her again.

Genna stood close to him. 'I hope you are speaking to me, Lord Penford.'

'Why should I not?' he asked.

She gave him a knowing look. 'Because of the betrothal.'

He met her gaze. 'I am not fond of keeping secrets. No good comes of it.'

She lowered her gaze for a moment, then raised her chin. 'Have you no secrets?' she asked.

He resisted the impulse to glance at her sister. 'I have your secret,' he said. 'I gave my word to keep it.'

She placed her hand on his wrist. 'I thank you for it, I really do. I know you do not approve.'

He lifted one shoulder. 'It is between you and Ross, ultimately.'

She glanced over to her sister. 'I know it will affect others, but Ross will make certain everything concludes well.'

'I hope so.' But he could not keep the scepticism from his voice.

She glanced around the room. 'I never know what to do in these entertainments. Everyone seems to stand around and talk and take some refreshment.'

'One is supposed to mingle,' he said.

She laughed. 'You make it sound very easy, but there are few people who wish to mingle with Lorene and me. That is why I am here. To be certain she is not alone.'

Lorene was one of the most alone people Dell had ever known. 'That is kind of you.'

She sighed and tapped her foot. 'She will never know what a sacrifice it is! I have yet to devise a way to make a rout enjoyable.' She watched a young man approach. 'But I shall try.'

It was Baron Holdsworth's younger son. 'Good evening, Lord Penford.' He tossed a shy glance to Genna. 'Miss Summerfield.'

She gave the young man a big smile. 'Hello, Mr Holdsworth! How good to see you. I was just trying to make Lord Penford explain to me how one should act at a rout. Do you know?'

He looked stricken. 'Why—why—you merely talk to people.'

'Ah.' She shot a mischievous glance to Dell. 'How lucky I am, then. I will talk to you.'

Dell took a step back, intending to leave Genna

with Holdsworth, an obvious admirer. He slid a glance to Lorene, who was still conversing with the Duchess of Archester. He slipped away.

Better not to be seen paying too much attention to the Summerfield sisters. All he needed—all *Lorene* needed—was to be talked about because he paid too much attention to her.

He had just found another footman with a tray of wine, when the Duchess of Kessington, Ross's step-mother, sidled up to him.

'I see *she* is here with her sister,' the Duchess said in scathing tones.

Dell knew precisely whom she was talking about. 'Who with what sister?'

'You know who I mean. Those odious Summer-fields.' She glanced towards Genna.

Dell took a sip of his wine. 'You forget, Duchess, that I am a Summerfield.'

'But you are not one of *those* Summerfields,' she protested. 'You have a title and property.'

He'd trade it all to have his family back.

She leaned towards his ear. 'What are we to do about this betrothal?'

'What can be done of it?' he countered. 'Ross made his decision.'

'He cannot marry her!' she said in an agitated whisper. 'She is entirely unsuitable. Why, her mother is still living in Brussels with the man she ran away with years ago. And her father—'

He held up a hand. 'I have heard the gossip.'

'Even Lord Tinmore cannot put enough shine on her,' the Duchess went on. 'Why, the girl received no offers last Season. She was not even admitted to Almack's, you know.'

'Many young ladies have Seasons without offers. Many do not attend Almack's.'

She sniffed. 'Obviously she was waiting for a duke's son.' She placed a hand on his arm. 'I hope I can rely on you to do what you can.'

He faced her. 'Duchess, recall the lady you are discussing is my relation.'

She lifted her nose. 'A distant relation. You cannot credit it.'

But he did credit it. He held on to that distant family connection much more firmly than he would have imagined he could. 'In any event, the matter is between Ross and Miss Summerfield. I will not interfere.'

Her eyes flashed. 'I see I cannot rely on you. I must act alone to prevent this ghastly mistake.'

She turned with a swish of her skirts and strode away, joining another group with a cordial smile and ingratiating manners.

Chapter Seventeen

During the next week, Genna had lessons with Vespery almost every day and when she was not at the easel in Vespery's studio, she snatched time to read the da Vinci book Ross gave her. Vespery said she was progressing very quickly, but not quickly enough for her. She had only half a year to prepare to be a working artist. Painting still life—vases of flowers, food, cloth of various textures—like Vespery had her doing was not going to earn her money. She needed to paint portraits and she needed to be good at it.

She sighed. Patience was not one of her virtues!

Genna paced the floor of her bedchamber. There would be no lesson today, no outing with Ross. She sat at the desk in her room and pulled out her latest sketchbook from the drawer.

If she could not paint, she could at least draw.

The pencil in her hand made some sweeping curves on the page, but, before she knew it, she was making a sketch of Ross, how he appeared when his face was in repose. For practice, she told herself. For when she would paint his portrait.

She had to admit, she missed Ross as much as the painting lessons. He stayed during most of her lessons, always ready to assist, to bring them food, to shop for supplies. He professed to find the process interesting, but he must become bored some of the time. When Vespery left her to paint, Ross talked with her. Or rather she talked with him, telling him all the inconsequential details of her unvaried life at Summerfield House. She told him about the governess who'd taught her to draw and paint in watercolours. What a talented woman that governess was, nurturing Lorene's love of piano, as well.

Until their father, who'd stopped paying the woman, forced her to find employment elsewhere. She was their last governess. After that, Tess and Lorene took over teaching Genna mathematics, and French and history and such. Genna and Lorene tended to their talents on their own.

Ross listened to her tell all this nonsense. She wished he would tell more about himself, but he did not. There was so much she wished to know about him.

Tonight was the night of the Kessington ball, the night their betrothal would be announced and more people deceived by the secret they kept. The announcement would not be applauded, she suspected. Who would think it a good idea for a duke's heir to marry one of the scandalous Summerfields?

Tinmore had insisted she stay home this day, to be rested and ready for the ball. Her maid would be coming in at any time to help her dress. She'd refused a hairdresser this time, setting off a tirade from Tinmore, but his tirades had become a mere annoyance now that he had no power over her.

Her maid Hallie entered the room, carrying her ball gown. 'Are you ready to dress, miss?'

'I am indeed.' She closed her sketchbook and put it away.

She promised herself she would not worry about her appearance. She would wear her hair in her favourite way, high on her head with curls cascading. Her dress was lovely, a blush so pale it was almost white. It matched Lorene's and Tess's and even Lady Northdon's, Tess's mother-in-law. Genna's was designed to shine the brightest. She was eager for the scandalous Summerfield sisters and the notorious Lady Northdon to be seen together as the very height of fashion.

While Hattie was putting the last pins in her hair, there was a knock at the door.

A footman handed Hattie a package. She brought it to Genna. 'This came for you.'

First she read the card. 'It is from Lord Rossdale.'

Genna unwrapped the paper to discover a velvet-covered box. She opened it.

'Oh, my!' she exclaimed.

It was a pendant and earrings. The pendant was a lovely opal surrounded by diamonds set in gold and on a gold chain. The earrings were matching opals.

It would go perfectly with her gown.

'But how did he know?' she said aloud.

'Do you wear them tonight?' Hattie asked without enthusiasm.

'Of course I will!' Genna cried.

With a gift such as this, who could ever guess their betrothal was a sham? She must remember, though, that such a gift must be returned when their charade was over.

When Lord Tinmore's carriage pulled up to the Kessington town house, Tess, her husband and his parents were waiting for them on the pavement.

Tess hurried up to Genna and Lorene as they were assisted from the carriage. 'We saw you coming and Lady Northdon said we should wait. We can be announced at the same time and walk in together!'

Genna gave her sister a buss on the cheek. She said hello to Lady Northdon. 'It is a wonderful idea.'

'Let us give them a spectacle, no?' Lady Northdon said in her French accent.

Lord Tinmore grimaced when he greeted Lord Northdon, who looked no happier, but Lord Northdon's expression changed to completely besotted when his wife took his arm. Lord and Lady Northdon might defy Genna's disbelief in happy marriages, except for the fact that the Northdons had been miserable together until very recently. Who knew how long this period of marital bliss would last?

They all walked into the house and were attended

by footmen in the magnificent marbled hall whose vaulted ceiling rose over two floors high. Other guests were queued on the double stairway of white marble with its gilt-and-crystal bannisters. It struck Genna that the design of this stairway mimicked the one at Carlton House. Or was it the other way around? Surely this house had been built first. It was a majestic sight, one Genna tried to commit to memory. What a lovely painting it would make with all the ladies in their colourful finery gracing the stairs like scattered jewels.

'Come. Hurry,' Tinmore snapped. 'There are enough people ahead of us as it is.'

They hurried to their place on the stairs. Genna looked down and noticed that each step was made of one complete piece of marble.

Her sister Tess stood beside her. 'Do you realise that all this will be yours some day?'

'I cannot think that,' Genna said honestly.

A quarter of an hour later they reached the ball-room door.

The butler announced, 'Lord and Lady Tinmore and Miss Summerfield.'

Tinmore marched ahead, but Genna and Lorene held back until Lord and Lady Northdon and Mr and Mrs Glenville were announced. The four ladies crossed over the wide threshold together as heads turned towards them and a murmur went through the crowd already assembled in the ball room, a room even bigger than the ones they had been before.

A *frisson* of excitement rushed up Genna's spine. They presented a lovely picture, each dressed in a shade of pink, Genna's the palest, Lady Northdon's the richest. Their gowns were not identically styled, but the fabric was the same, net over fine muslin so that their skirts floated around them.

Genna leaned to Tess. 'Tell Nancy her styles have triumphed.'

'How gratifying it is,' Tess responded. 'Because you know half these guests were certain we would not come off so well.'

Genna glanced at the receiving line, where Lorene had hurried to catch up with Lord Tinmore. Ross shook the hand of the gentleman who'd been announced before them, but when the man moved on, Ross glanced up and smiled at Genna.

Suddenly all that mattered was that he like her gown.

She touched the opal pendant and stepped forward to greet the Duke and Duchess.

The Duchess greeted her with a fixed smile. 'Don't you look sweet, my dear.'

She curtsied to the Duke.

'Good. Good. You are here.' He made it sound as if he wished she wasn't.

'I am honoured to be here, Your Grace,' she responded.

Then she came to Ross who clasped her hand and leaned close to her ear. 'You look beautiful.'

Her spirits soared.

She touched her opal. 'Thank you, Ross. It is lovely.'

'Save me the first dance,' he added.

She smiled at him. 'With pleasure.'

Lady Northdon waited behind her. 'There are guests behind us,' she reminded Genna.

Genna stepped away from Ross, but waited for Lady Northdon and Tess to be finished. Together they walked across the ball room to where Lorene stood with Tinmore.

As soon as they reached her, Tinmore glanced from Lorene to Tess. 'I am off to the game room, but I will return for the announcement. In the meantime, behave with decorum. I'll not have the Tinmore title besmirched by hoydenish antics.'

As if Lorene could ever be hoydenish. Genna felt like creating a fuss just to upset him.

'Look at this room!' Tess said in awed tones.

The walls were papered in red damask, but were covered with huge paintings depicting scenes from Greek mythology. Genna wished she could get up close to examine the brushwork, the use of colour. She knew so much more now than when she first met Vespery.

'Look at the ceiling!' Tess said.

The ceiling had intricate plasterwork dividing the ceiling into octagons and squares, each of which were painted. It made the ceiling of the drawing room where they had been the night of the musicale look plain in comparison.

Her husband came to her side. 'This is a magnificent room, is it not?'

Lorene said, 'There is Lord Penford standing alone. I believe I will walk over to him and say hello.'

Ross joined Genna as soon as he could leave the receiving line. He danced with her, with each of her sisters and even with Lady Northdon, whom he'd never met before but liked immediately. He noticed plenty of disapproving stares, which angered him. Why should the Summerfields and Lord and Lady Northdon be judged so negatively? Nothing they had done deserved this denigration. Except maybe for Lady Tinmore, who did marry for money, but after five minutes seeing her with Lord Tinmore, one could feel nothing but pity for her.

One of the footmen approached him. 'Her Grace says you should come now.'

Time for the announcement. 'Thank you, Stocker.' Ross turned to Genna, who was laughing at something Lady Northdon said. 'It is time,' he told her.

Her face fell, but she nodded and said to her sisters, 'I think they are ready for the announcement.'

'Oh,' cried Tess. 'Let us all go up front where we can see you better.'

Ross and Genna led the way and the rest of their party followed. In their wake were audible murmurs from the other guests.

Ross's father and the Duchess stood at the far end of the ballroom where, on an elevated platform, the orchestra still played quietly. The Duchess looked crestfallen; his father, grim.

'Are you ready?' his father asked.

Ross smiled down on Genna. 'Indeed we are.'

She straightened her back, lifted her chin and smiled back at him. Brave girl.

His father and the Duchess, all smiles now, climbed on to the orchestra's platform. The musicians sounded a loud chord and went silent.

Ross's father raised his hands. 'May I have your attention? Attention!'

The guests turned towards him and fell silent.

'We have an announcement to make,' his father said. 'A happy announcement.' He gestured to Ross. 'As you know, the Duchess and I have long desired to see my son Rossdale settled and tonight I am delighted to report that he has done as we wished.'

The crowd murmured.

Ross's father went on. 'My son, the Marquess of Rossdale, has proposed marriage to Miss Summerfield, daughter of the late Sir Hollis Summerfield of Yardney and ward of Lord Tinmore—'

Tinmore waved and bobbed from nearby.

The Duke continued, 'And I am happy to report that Miss Summerfield has accepted him.'

'No!' a lone female voice cried from the back of the room amidst other shocked sounds from other guests. The Duchess's smile faltered.

Ross stepped on to the platform and helped Genna up to stand beside the Duke and Duchess. 'Thank you, Father.' He turned to the crowd. 'Miss Summerfield is not well known to many of you, but I am confident you will soon see all the fine qualities she possesses. I could not be a happier man.'

He put his arm around Genna, who smiled at him with much admiration in her face. Her family beamed from below them, but only a few others in the crowd looked pleased.

Ross knew this world, where birth and titles and wealth mattered more than character. He and Genna knew the disapproval they would face. So why should he feel so angry at these people and so protective of Genna?

He lifted her off the platform. 'There. It is done.'

She grinned at him. 'And I am still standing!'

Her sisters, Glenville and his parents clustered around her with hugs and happy tears of congratulations. Lord Tinmore disappeared into the card room again. Several others offered congratulations, a few genuinely meant, others so as not to offend the Duke of Kessington.

Dell approached them just as the music for the supper dance began. 'I thought I should congratulate you as well, or it might look odd.'

'I appreciate it.' Ross kept a smile on his face as he shook Dell's hand. 'I'm glad this part is over. Now we can simply enjoy the rest of the Season.'

Dell turned to Genna. 'How are you faring?'

She smiled, too, as if accepting good wishes. 'I

am actually surprised that some people with whom I have no connection seemed happy for me.'

It had surprised Ross, too. He planned to make a note of those people.

'Are you dancing the supper dance?' Genna asked Dell.

'With your sister,' he responded. 'As it is likely Lord Tinmore will not escort her in to supper.'

'So good of you,' Genna said.

His face turned stony. 'My duty to my cousin.' Dell bowed and presumably went in search of Lady Tinmore.

Ross took Genna's hand. 'Let us skip the supper dance. There is someone here I should like you to meet.'

'As you wish,' Genna said in exaggerated tones. 'I am a biddable fiancée.'

He laughed. 'Biddable?'

He brought her to a pleasant-looking woman in her forties who sat among other ladies not dancing.

'Lady Long.' He bowed. 'Allow me to present to you my fiancée—'

'Your very biddable fiancée,' Genna broke in.

'My *biddable* fiancée,' he corrected. 'Miss Summerfield.'

'How do you do, ma'am.' Genna curtsied.

'Not as well as you, young lady,' the woman said in good humour. 'Landing yourself a future duke.'

Genna made a nervous laugh.

Ross quickly spoke. 'Your husband was gracious

enough to give Miss Summerfield and me a tour of the artwork at Carlton House.'

'You are Sir Charles's wife?' Genna exclaimed. 'I am so delighted to meet you. Your husband was too generous to take the time for that wonderful tour. I learned so much!'

Ross continued. 'Lady Long is an accomplished artist, Genna. She has exhibited at the Royal Academy.'

Genna's eyes grew wide. 'You have?'

Ross turned to Lady Long. 'Miss Summerfield is also an artist.'

'It is my abiding passion,' Genna said. 'What do you paint? Portraits?'

'Landscapes,' Lady Long responded. 'I suppose you could say that gardens and landscapes are my abiding passion.'

'Landscapes,' Genna repeated in awed tones.

'And what do you paint, my dear?' Mrs Long asked.

'I am hoping to learn to paint portraits, but most of what I've done before are landscapes.'

Like the one she'd painted of Summerfield House with the purple and pink sky and blue grass.

'What medium do you use?' Genna asked.

'Watercolours,' the lady said.

'I love to paint landscapes in watercolours.' Genna sighed. 'Tell me, Lady Long, do your watercolours sell for a good price?'

'Sell?' Mrs Long scoffed. 'Goodness me, no. I do not *sell* my paintings, my dear. I enjoy painting and am lucky enough to have my skill recognised, but I enjoy many pastimes. I adore designing my garden, but I would never hire myself out to design anyone else's.'

Ross saw disappointment in Genna's eyes, but she kept a pleasant expression on her face for the older woman. 'Do you design your own garden, then?'

Ross suspected Genna was not very interested in moving trees and shrubbery about.

'Sir Charles and I are creating our garden. We've been inspired by Repton and Capability Brown, but the ideas are our very own,' she answered proudly.

'That is an art as well, is it not?' Genna added diplomatically.

The lady smiled. 'It is, indeed, my dear. You must call upon me some time and I will show you my garden—in my sketchbook, that is. Our house is some distance away. We are staying in town while Parliament sits.'

'That would be lovely,' Genna said. 'I would love to see your sketchbook.'

Genna curtsied and Ross bowed and they walked away.

'I am ever so much more interested in the sketch-book than actually seeing the gardens,' she told him in a conspiratorial tone.

'I would have surmised that,' he responded.

She drew closer to him. 'Thank you for introducing me to her. Imagine. She has exhibited at the Royal Academy!'

'I thought you would like to meet a fellow lady artist,' he said.

'I should like to meet one who earns enough to live on from her art. Someone like Vigée-LeBrun.'

'Who?'

'Madame Vigée-LeBrun. She was Marie Antoinette's portraitist.' She peered at him. 'You really know very little about art, do you not?'

'Only what I have learned from you, Sir Charles and Vespery,' he told her. 'Before that I either liked a work of art, disliked it, or noticed it not at all.'

Her eyes looked puzzled. 'Then why become an artist's patron?'

He raised his brows. 'Because of you, of course.'

She gave him a puzzled look. 'I do not understand.'

The music was loud and the guests who were not dancing tried to talk above it. He did not fancy shouting at her to be heard.

'Let us go somewhere quiet.' He escorted her out the ballroom door and down a hallway to a small parlour.

The room was lit by a crystal chandelier. Most of the rooms were lit in case the guests should wander in. The Duke refused to appear as if he needed to economise about such things as the cost of candles.

As soon as they entered, though, Genna was distracted by the decor. 'Oh, more plasterwork and gilt. Is every room in the house so beautiful?'

Her attention was caught by a painting in the room, a long painting depicting some Classical battle scene, with overturned chariots, rearing horses and fighting soldiers in gleaming helmets, swords and shields.

'Who painted this?' she asked.

'I have no idea,' he responded. 'I grew up with these paintings, but I knew nothing of them. I liked this one when I was a boy, because it was a battle scene—not that I saw it often when my grandfather was alive. He would not allow children in the public rooms, in most of the rooms, actually, but sometimes my mother would sneak me out of the nursery and take me on a tour of the house.'

She turned from the painting to him. 'I think I would have liked your mother.'

He gestured to a sofa in a part of the room set up as a seating area.

She sat on the sofa and he sat next to her.

'I think I understand why you are helping me,' she said. 'It is like your soldiers, is it not? When you discover someone in need, you help them.'

His reasons for helping her were a great deal more personal than that. 'Genna—' he began.

From the hallway they heard a loud voice making an announcement.

She grimaced. 'It must be time for supper.'

He extended his hand to help her up, but pulled too hard. She wound up in his arms, her body flush against his.

She laughed and looked up into his eyes. 'If anyone saw us now, they would think we truly were betrothed.'

The blood surged through his veins, as powerful an arousal of his senses as he could remember experiencing.

'Let us convince them even more.' He lowered his head and took possession of her lips, suddenly ravenous for her.

An eager sound escaped her lips. She put her arms around his neck and pressed her mouth against his. Her lips parted, giving his tongue access. He backed her up until she was against the wall and he could hold her tighter against him. His lips left hers and tasted the tender skin of her neck. She writhed beneath him, her hands holding his head as if she feared he would stop kissing her.

From the hallway, the butler's voice rose again.

Ross froze. Good God. 'We must stop,' he managed, releasing her and stepping away.

Her chest rose and fell, her breath rapid. 'Oh, my!'

He filled with shame. 'Genna, I—'

She expelled one more deep breath before smiling up at him. 'That was quite wonderful, Ross! Last Season a fellow or two pecked at my cheek, but now I feel I have been truly kissed!'

He'd resisted such impulses so many times when they'd been together. Why had he weakened now? 'It was poorly done of me.'

She laughed and threw her arms around his neck again, giving his mouth a quick kiss. 'I would say your kiss was rather skilfully done.'

He held her cheeks in his palms. 'You are outrageous, Genna Summerfield.' He released her again. With difficulty.

She straightened the bodice of her dress and smoothed her skirt. 'Me? You are the one who kissed me.'

He checked his own clothing and made certain he was together. With any luck the visible evidence of his arousal would disappear by the time they reached the dining room.

Chapter Eighteen

Genna hardly knew what to think as Ross escorted her to the dining room. Such a kiss! She'd never imagined a kiss could be so sublime. Could leave one so… wanting.

She should have been furious at Ross. She should have slapped his face.

Instead, when he'd pulled away from her, she'd wanted to pull him back and start the kiss all over again. Was this the sort of physical thing that made men and women desire to marry? Or, like her unhappily married mother and father, was this what made them seek other lovers?

If a mere kiss could be so powerful, what, then, would marital coupling be like? For the first time, she wanted to know. If Ross's kiss could bring such breathless pleasure, what could his lovemaking bring?

The supper was set out in three separate rooms, the dining room and two others set up with tables and chairs. Unlike the musicale, the food would be served at the table. She and Ross were expected in the dining room where the guests of highest rank were to be seated. When they entered the dining room, most of the guests had already taken their seats. The Duke at the head of the table, the Duchess at the other end, but, beyond that, precedence was abandoned. One supped with one's recent dance partner.

From across the room, the Duke stood and called, 'Ross!' He gestured for them to come to him. Two empty chairs next to the Duke had obviously been intended for them.

A footman held Genna's chair for her. To her dismay, Lord Tinmore procured a place almost directly across from her. She glanced down the table and spied Lorene seated with Lord Penford.

The room was another grand exhibition of opulence. Walls of green damask, two marble pillars at each end of the room, another intricate plasterwork ceiling, its designs outlined in gilt. The paintings on the walls were huge and awe-inspiring, depicting scenes from ancient history.

'You are late,' the Duke chastised.

'A bit late,' Ross responded without a hint of apology.

'You disappeared from the ballroom.' The Duke's tone did not change.

'Only briefly,' Ross said.

A gentleman on the Duke's other side asked him a question and he turned away.

The white soup was served, but the guests selected

other fare from the dishes set before them on the table. Because a hot meal would never have stayed hot for so many guests, the dinner consisted of cold meats and fish, jellies, pastries, sweetmeats and ices, among a myriad of other dishes. The room was soon filled with the noise of conversation, and silver knives and forks clanking against dinner plates of fine porcelain china.

The Duke and the other gentleman began a heated exchange about the rash of violence occurring lately, of several break-ins, thefts and murders by gangs of men.

The Duke half-stood, his face red. 'We cannot ignore that people are hungry, sir!'

Genna wanted to tell him that Ross fed hungry people. Perhaps the others should do the same. But she did not dare.

The Duke sat down again, drained the contents of his wineglass and suddenly clasped his hand to his chest, with a cry of pain. He collapsed on to the table, scattering dishes and food and spilling wine.

One of the guests screamed in alarm.

'Father!' Ross was first to his feet and first to reach his father. He sat his father back in the chair. 'Wake up, wake up,' he cried.

His father moaned.

Ross turned to the butler. 'Fetch the doctor immediately.'

The butler rushed from the room.

Penford ran up from where he had been sitting. 'Shall we carry him to his bedchamber?'

'Yes,' Ross immediately agreed.

The two men picked up the Duke and carried him out of the room.

The Duchess stood and tried to make herself heard above the rumblings of the guests. 'He's merely had a spell. He will recover soon. Please let us continue with supper.'

Finish supper? Genna could not finish supper. She left the room to see if she could help in some way. Out in the hallway, she looked for Ross and Dell, but they were out of sight.

She found a footman. 'Show me where Rossdale took his father.'

There was no reason the footman should do what she demanded, but he did. She caught up with them right as they reached the Duke's bedchamber door.

'May I help?' she asked.

Both men looked surprised to see her.

At that moment, though, the Duke made a sound and struggled to get out of Ross's and Penford's arms. 'What? What happened?'

'You lost consciousness, Papa,' Ross told him. 'We're bringing you to your room.'

'Nonsense. Must be—we are giving a ball. Perfectly fine.' He stumbled and Ross caught him before he lost his balance.

Genna spoke up. 'Your butler has sent for your physician. You should lie down until he comes.'

The Duke peered at her as if never having seen

her before, then the puzzlement on his face cleared. 'Oh, I remember you.'

'See?' She smiled at the Duke. 'That is a good sign. You remember me. But you continue to be unsteady on your feet. Best to wait for your physician.

'Come on.' She stepped forward and took his arm. 'If you feel dizzy you may simply hang on to me.'

'I do feel dizzy,' he murmured.

He was inside the door of his room when his valet appeared. 'They said below stairs that His Grace took ill.'

'A little spell, that is all,' His Grace said.

The valet lost no time in getting him in the room and over to his bed. Ross remained with him.

Genna walked back to the hall.

'I was amazed he would follow your orders,' Penford said.

She slid him a smile. 'So was I. Sometimes people do, though.' She peeked in the room where the valet and Ross were convincing his father to lie down. 'I hope he is not seriously ill.'

'Indeed.' Penford closed the door all but a crack. His voice turned low. 'We should not like to lose him.'

Another death for Penford to endure? How hard for him. 'You must know the Duke well.'

He shrugged. 'I know Ross well. The Duke is too busy and too steeped in politics to be known well. I do not believe he ever spoke to me until I inherited my title.'

'Ross is so unlike that,' she said.

He nodded in agreement. 'According to Ross, his father was never like that.'

'What do you mean?' she asked.

He peeked through the crack in the door. 'They are dressing him for bed,' he said before answering her question. 'According to Ross, his father was light-hearted before he inherited the title. He and Ross's mother were always taking Ross to some new place for some new adventure. His father was game for anything, apparently. His mother, too.'

'Did you know Ross's mother?' she asked.

Penford shook his head. 'I met her once, but by then she was ill and much altered, Ross said.'

She glanced away. She had no memory of her own mother and her father had never bothered with her at all.

'Let us hope he does not lose his father as well,' she murmured.

Penford's face was grim.

Ross came out the door. 'He is in bed resting. His valet will stay until the physician arrives. I should return to the guests. Apprise them of his condition.'

'And the Duchess. She will be worried,' Genna said.

Ross frowned.

'What does that frown mean?' she asked.

'She should be here,' he said bitterly. 'Not trying to salvage her social event.'

Another less-than-ideal marriage? Genna was not surprised.

'Everyone will still be at supper,' she said. 'While

you go to the Duchess, shall I tell the guests in the other rooms what occurred and of your father's present status?'

Ross did not answer right away.

'I'll do it,' Penford said.

Ross threaded her arm though his. 'Come with me. Stay by my side.'

At this moment, if they were truly betrothed, she would be expected to stay by his side. Oddly enough, at this moment, it was also where she most wanted to be.

Although the Duchess had wanted the ball to go on in spite of her husband's sudden malaise, no one wished to dance and pretend to enjoy themselves while the host of the party had taken to his bed.

So Ross stood where his father would have stood, at the Duchess's side, while one after the other, the guests approached to say goodbye and to extend their good wishes to the Duke.

In the midst of all this, the doctor arrived and, since the Duchess showed no inclination to accompany the physician to her husband's room, Ross accepted that duty, as well. He managed only the briefest goodnight to Genna, a mere glance as he hurried behind the doctor.

After examining him, the doctor told his father, 'It is your heart. We have talked of this before. You must curtail your activity. Now it is imperative that you rest. For at least a month.'

'A month!' the Duke cried. 'I cannot rest. There

is much to do in Parliament. And my duties to the wedding of Princess Charlotte—I will be expected to participate.'

The doctor was unfazed by these excuses. 'If you fail to rest, another episode like this one could put a period to your existence.'

Ross's father crossed his arms over his chest and pursed his lips like a sulking child.

The doctor stepped away from the bed. 'I will stop in to see how you are faring tomorrow, but now I am very desirous of returning to my bed.'

'We are grateful you came,' Ross said, extending his hand.

The doctor shook it. 'I'll see myself out.'

Ross walked him to the door. Ross was also eager to get some sleep.

His father called to him. 'Ross?'

He turned. 'Yes, Father?'

'You must take over for me.'

Ross knew this even before the doctor gave his diagnosis. 'Yes, whatever you require, but sleep now. I'll come in the morning. Tell me then what you need me to do.'

The next day instead of Ross coming to pick up Genna for her painting lesson, he sent a message and a carriage, explaining why he could not go with her. She understood. Goodness! His father was ill; what else could he do? He promised to call upon her in the afternoon.

When she arrived at the studio, Vespery was disappointed that Ross was not there. 'I was going to have him pose for you. You are ready to try a portrait.'

The portrait seemed suddenly much less important to her than before.

'I could paint you,' she said.

'No, *you*. Paint you.' He brought over a mirror and set it up where she could look at herself and her canvas.

Genna began as he'd taught her to begin on other paintings. Make a few lines as a guide, a rough idea of the shape of her head, where to place her eyes, nose and mouth. At each step, he stopped his own work and taught her what she needed to know next. What colours to mix for skin pigment, what colours for shadow and highlights. How to block in the colours, then how to refine them. By the end of the day she had a portrait of herself in a rough, unpolished form.

'This is a very good effort,' Vespery said. 'A very good effort, indeed.'

She wondered if Ross would be pleased.

'I am becoming used to the paints,' she said to Vespery.

When the carriage came to take her home that day, all she could think of was seeing Ross that afternoon.

She entered Tinmore's town house more subdued than at any other time when returning from her art lessons. She'd barely stepped into the hall when Lorene came down the stairs.

'Where were you?' Lorene's voice was angry. 'You were not with Rossdale. I saw you leave. You were alone.'

'He sent a carriage for me,' she stalled.

'You did not meet him, though, did you?' Lorene accused. 'Lord Tinmore said it was Rossdale, not the Duke, who met with some of the other lords to discuss the changes in coinage.'

Parliament would vote on changing the currency to a fixed gold standard. She'd heard gentlemen talking about it at the ball last night.

Lorene glared at her. 'If Rossdale was there, he was not with you.'

'No, he was not with me,' Genna admitted. Her art lessons were another secret she kept from her sister.

'Then where did you go alone in Rossdale's carriage?' Lorene demanded.

Genna glanced around her. The footman who had opened the door for her was standing stony-faced, but in hearing distance. 'May we go up to your sitting room? I will explain everything there.'

Lorene answered her by simply turning and climbing the stairs again. When they reached the sitting room, Lorene remained standing.

'Explain, then,' Lorene said.

'I have been taking lessons in oil painting,' Genna said.

Lorene's brows rose. 'Oil painting?'

'From Mr Vespery. Do you remember him? He

was at Her Grace's musicale. He is painting portraits of the Duke and Duchess.'

Lorene shook her head in disbelief. 'Lessons? With a man? Unchaperoned?'

'Well, Ross was with me until today, but, I assure you, Mr Vespery is merely my art teacher, not my paramour.'

Lorene's eyes scolded. 'Genna! Honestly! You are much too free-speaking.'

Genna lowered her gaze. 'I am sorry, Lorene. I should not have been so sharp.'

Lorene waved a hand. 'Never mind that. Whatever possessed you?'

'To get art lessons?' How much could she explain without telling all of it? 'We've been surrounded by astounding paintings in this house, at Tinmore Hall, in every house we've visited. I want to paint like that.'

'Genna, those paintings were done by masters. You cannot expect to paint like them.'

Lorene's words stung, but Genna wanted her to understand. She took her sister's hand and pulled her over to the chairs. 'I love it, Lorene. And I am progressing very quickly at it. Please do not make it so I cannot continue.' In other words, tell Lord Tinmore.

'But why? How did you even start it?' Lorene asked.

'One day I mentioned to Ross that I would like to learn to paint in oils and the next day he took me to Mr Vespery's studio. Ross bought me all the supplies and paid for the lessons.'

Lorene looked shocked. 'You cannot accept that!'

'Why not?' Genna countered. 'He is my fiancé. If he gave me a diamond bracelet, you would think that a fine thing.' If he were really her fiancé, she should say.

Lorene's eyebrows knitted. 'I do not know. In some ways Lord Rossdale seems the perfect husband for you, but it is difficult to see you as a duchess.'

On that Genna could agree. She would make a horrible duchess.

Genna leaned forward. 'Please do not spoil this for me, Lorene. I am doing no harm and I do love it so.'

Lorene glanced away. 'I suppose…'

Genna sprang from her chair and kissed her sister on the cheek. 'You do understand! It is like your music.'

'Like my music,' Lorene said wistfully. 'Like if I could take lessons…'

'You could!' Genna seized her sister's hands. 'London is the perfect place to find a wonderful piano master. We can ask if anyone knows of one. I'll ask Ross. Or Lord Penford.'

'No!' Lorene said sharply. 'It is a lovely idea, but I cannot do it.'

'You could.' Genna sat again, but kept hold of Lorene's hands. 'Ask Lord Tinmore. He likes to do things for you.' But not for anyone else. She shook her sister's hands. 'Think of it! You already play beautifully, but you were mostly self-taught. There might be all sorts of things you could learn.'

'Perhaps…' Lorene glanced away.

* * *

When Ross called that afternoon Genna met him in the drawing room. Seeing him standing, waiting for her, she had an impulse to rush into his arms. It stunned her. The events of the previous night, seeing Ross so distressed, it had changed something in her.

'Ross,' she managed.

He walked towards her and took her hand. 'Forgive the message this morning. I hope you got to your lesson with no difficulties.'

'None at all.' She led him to the sofa and they sat. 'But, tell me, how is your father?'

His brow furrowed. 'Weaker than he will admit. The doctor said he must rest for at least a month. The only way I could get him to agree to do that was to take over whatever of his duties I am able to perform.'

'Of course you must.' But she felt sad for him. It must be a great deal of responsibility thrust upon him so suddenly.

'I must renege on my promise to take you wherever you wished to go,' he said.

She put her hand on his. 'Do not fret over that.'

'Tell me.' He gave a wan smile. 'What did you paint today?'

The stress on his face put all thoughts of painting out of her mind. She did not wish to cause him worry so she exclaimed, 'It was the very best day! Vespery started teaching me to paint portraits. At last!'

'Who did you paint?' he asked.

She'd not mention that he was supposed to have been her first model. 'I painted myself. Vespery gave me a mirror.'

'I would like to see that,' he said.

She laughed. 'No, you would not. It is rather awful at the moment, but I will improve it.' She took a breath. 'I can master this, Ross. I can paint portraits. Thanks to you, I will be able to earn money.'

'And that is what you desire more than anything,' he stated as if finishing her sentence.

She sobered. 'But how are you faring?'

He smiled sadly. 'I can manage. I suppose I absorbed more of my father's thinking than I guessed. I still hope to break away one of these days and come and visit Vespery's studio.'

'Whenever you are able,' she said. 'I would welcome you.'

Chapter Nineteen

Ross returned to the Kessington town house after calling upon Genna. The footman attending the hall told him his father wished him to come to his bedchamber.

Ross knocked and was admitted.

He walked to his father's bedside. 'How do you fare today, Father?'

His father, always so strong and commanding by nature, looked shrunken and pale against the bed linens. 'I'm tired, is all. Merely need a little rest.'

'The doctor listened to your heart. You need to heed him,' Ross countered.

His father made a dismissive gesture. 'I know. I know. I am doing as he says.'

His father's valet, who was in the room folding clothes, spoke up. 'Your Grace, I dare say the physician would not have approved of your getting up and working at your desk for over an hour.' His father's desk was in his study attached to the library on the floor below.

'You may leave us, Stone,' his father snapped.

The valet bowed and left the room.

'Gossips worse than an old woman,' Ross's father muttered.

'He is concerned about you.' Ross's brows knitted. 'You must rest, Father. It has only been a day since your spell.'

'Sitting at my desk did not seem such an exertion,' his father said.

'But walking there. Climbing stairs. Stay in this room. Please. I can take care of what you cannot.' What other choice did Ross have?

'Very well. Very well,' His father gestured to a chair by his bedside. 'Sit, my son.'

Ross sat.

His father glanced away as if uncertain what he wished to say. Finally he spoke. 'This spell has alarmed me, if you must know. Your grandfather died of such a spell. He was about my age.'

Yes. Everything changed when his grandfather died.

'It is time for you to settle down, my son,' he said.

Ross's brows rose. 'I am. I am betrothed—'

His father interrupted. 'But you plan to marry in autumn! I may not be here in autumn. I do not know how long I will be here. I would like to know if there will be an heir to the title before I die.' He leaned forward in the bed. 'Get on with it! Get a special licence and marry right away. What is this waiting?'

This deception of his and Genna's suddenly felt like a foolish mistake.

His father's voice rose. 'It is nonsensical to wait. Are you wishing to get out of it? Believe me, Constance and I would be delighted to see you look elsewhere. But if it must be this Summerfield chit, marry her now, even though I doubt she is up to the rigours of becoming a duchess!'

Ross disagreed. Genna would make a duchess unlike any other. The problem was, if he truly wished to make her his wife, he would kill her dreams. His mother's dreams had been dashed; Ross would not see the same for Genna.

She'd become that important to him.

Ross answered the Duke defensively. 'Stop trying to control when I marry and what I do.' He rose from the chair. 'I will take over whatever duties you need me for. I will do that for your sake and for the sake of the title and all the people dependent upon us, but allow me my own choice of who to marry and when.'

'You are a disappointment to me!' his father shouted. He pressed a hand to his chest and sank back against the pillows.

'Calm yourself, Papa!' Ross cried in alarm. He softened his tone. 'Just rest. Trust me. You will get well. All will work out as it should.'

His father turned his face away.

Ross stepped back. Curse his idea of this false betrothal!

'Rest, Papa,' he said again. 'I'll come see you later.'

His father continued to ignore him. Ross turned and strode out of the bedchamber.

The Duchess stood right outside the door. She joined him as he walked away.

'I am not in favour of your marrying right away,' she said.

He did not look at her. 'Eavesdropping, Constance?

She huffed. 'I was walking by. Your voices were raised. I could not help but hear.'

Ross did not believe her.

'You can change your mind about marrying Miss Summerfield,' the Duchess went on. 'I am certain she can be persuaded to cry off. She has not the vaguest notion of what it will take to be a duchess. She is entirely unsuitable.'

'It is none of your affair, ma'am,' he warned.

She continued anyway. 'Now that your father is ill, you can see how important it is to marry well, to have a dignified, capable woman for a wife, not a frivolous girl with a scandalous upbringing.'

What had his father ever seen in this woman? Ross wondered. She was all calculation and no heart.

He stopped and faced her. 'Take care, Constance. If my father's health fails completely—if he dies— you will want to be in my good graces. I will be Duke then.'

He left her and did not look behind.

For the next three weeks, Ross barely had time to think about his father's wishes and the Duchess's mean-spiritedness. He was too busy going from one task to another. There always seemed to be problems on the estates, decisions to make about finances, Parliamentary bills to advocate for, or Court functions to attend.

There were more Court functions than a typical Season. All to celebrate the upcoming wedding of Princess Charlotte. To these functions he was required to escort the Duchess. They were dreary affairs.

When he could Ross included Genna in his attendance to other parties, but those were infrequent. There were one or two functions which she attended with Lord Tinmore and her sister.

All in all, though, he saw very little of her.

He missed her.

He stopped in at Vespery's studio a few times. It was clear she was thriving there. Her portraiture was remarkably skilled, he thought. He coveted the self-portrait she painted. Perhaps he could own it, to remember her by.

He found himself dreading the day they must part. Too often he wished their betrothal to be real.

But it was time for him to face truth. She did not want to marry. Even if she did want it, marrying him would rob her of everything she desired—to be an artist. To answer to no one but herself. To live free of constraints.

Life with him would be nothing but constraints.

His father gained strength, enough that the doctor allowed him to participate in Princess Charlotte's wedding, but afterwards Ross must continue to assume the lion's share of his father's burdens.

On the day of the wedding, his father seemed his old robust self. Perhaps the excitement over this event would carry him through.

Ross had not been included in the wedding invitation, but ladies and gentlemen were allowed to stand in the entrance hall of Buckingham House to greet the Princess and other royal personages as they came out to their carriages. Ross took the opportunity to escort Genna and Lady Tinmore to the event. Also in their party were their other sister, her husband and his parents. And Dell. To everyone's delight, Tinmore begged off, unable to bear the exertion of the event.

When the royals emerged, Genna's excitement burst from her and spilled over all of them.

'Look! There is the Queen! I never thought to see the Queen!' She jumped up and down.

Princess Charlotte appeared.

'Tess! Look!' Genna cried. 'Look at the Princess's gown. It shimmers!'

She commented on all of the Royal Princesses, as well. Ross was surprised she recognised them.

'I've seen engravings of their portraits in magazines,' she explained.

Afterwards they all walked to the Northdons' town house for a breakfast.

'It is said that Charlotte's choice of a husband is a love match,' Tess remarked over the meal.

'Yes, but what about Prince Leopold?' Genna retorted. 'Surely the prospect of becoming the Queen's consort had much to do with his agreeing to the marriage. Much higher status than the prospect of ruling a duchy.' Leopold was one of the German princes of a duchy that had been taken over by Napoleon. 'Did he fall in love with the Princess or with the idea of being the husband of an extremely wealthy queen?'

'One can fall in love even if a marriage has political advantages, can one not?' Tess asked. 'Look at you and Rossdale. People will say you marry him because of his rank.'

Genna reddened. 'I assure you, Ross's rank is of no consequence to me.'

Again, their deception reared its ugly head. These good people thought them to be in love, thought they would marry. Ross could now admit to himself that he loved Genna, but he would never marry her.

After leaving the Northdons' breakfast, Genna walked with Ross through the streets of Mayfair to Tinmore's town house on Curzon Street. Lorene had left earlier, escorted home by Lord Penford. It was already dusk and the streets were a lovely shade of lavender against a pink sky.

The exhilaration of the day had settled into melancholy and Genna fought an urge to simply burst into tears. To see the royal family had been thrilling, but now sadness swept over her. How could she explain it to Ross when she did not understand it herself?

She forced herself not to dwell on it. 'I rather hope they will be happy.'

'Who?' Ross asked.

She held his arm. 'Princess Charlotte and Prince Leopold. They have little chance, of course, but it would be nice if they could be happy. Goodness knows, Princess Charlotte's parents were not happy with each other.'

It was well known that the Prince Regent and his wife, Caroline of Brunswick, detested each other from first sight.

'You cannot judge every marriage after that of the Prince Regent. Think of the King and Queen. Theirs has been a long and, by all reports, a happy marriage.'

He was right, of course, but she resisted any evidence contrary to what she believed. 'Well, he turned insane. That can't be happy.'

'You won't hear of a happy marriage, will you?' His voice turned low.

'There are far more unhappy ones, you must agree,' she said. 'Better to be like my mother and take a lover.'

He said nothing for several steps. 'Is that what you plan to do? Take a lover?'

'I suppose,' she said without enthusiasm, although what other man could she possibly want for a lover besides Ross? 'It seemed to be what made my mother happy.' Even at the expense of her children's happiness, but Genna would turn into a watering pot if she thought about that too much. 'What about your parents? Were they happy?'

He frowned. 'For a long time, very happy. Until my father inherited the title.' He paused. 'The revolution in France, becoming a duchess, it was all too much for my mother, not to mention my father's complete preoccupation with the role. It killed her.'

'Oh, Ross!' She leaned against him in sympathy. 'Could unhappiness truly kill her?'

He shrugged. 'She contracted a fever, but I believe she could have fought harder to live if she'd wanted to.'

'Both our mothers left us,' she murmured, blinking away tears, but it was not losing her mother that most pained her now. It was knowing she and Ross would have to part. In many ways, she'd already lost him.

Like his mother, she realised. She'd lost Ross to his new duties just as his mother had lost the Duke.

She continued to hold on to him tightly, as if that would keep him with her for ever.

They walked for half a street before he spoke again. 'We should talk—' he began.

That sounded ominous.

'My father's illness has changed things. He is pressing for us to marry right away. He wants to know the succession is secured in case his heart gives way completely. You might say he wants us to get on with it.'

With creating an heir, he meant.

He went on. 'Father doesn't know, of course, that we will not marry—'

'Do you want me to cry off sooner?' She tried to keep her voice from cracking.

He'd be free to marry someone else, then.

'No,' he said quickly. 'I tell you this only so you will be prepared if he speaks to you. I want us to continue as we planned. To make certain you are ready to become the artist you wish to be.'

To ultimately part in the autumn, when everyone expected they would marry. Would he marry someone else then? He must, she thought. What other choice did he have?

She made herself speak brightly. 'Yes! Let us enjoy the rest of the Season. You will have more time, will you not, now that your father is more recovered? You must let me paint you.'

'I would be honoured,' he said, but his eyes looked as sad as she felt inside.

The next morning Ross called upon Vespery before Genna was expected. His housekeeper sent him to Vespery's studio where the artist was at work on a portrait.

'Ross, my boy, how good to see you.' Vespery put down his brushes and palette and greeted him. 'To what do I owe the pleasure of this visit? Without Miss Summerfield?' He gestured to the seating area where Ross used to sit to watch Genna paint.

'I am here about Miss Summerfield,' Ross said, taking a chair. 'How is she faring?'

'She progresses very rapidly, Ross.' He motioned for Ross to rise again. 'Come. I'll show you.' He walked over to several canvases leaning against the wall. He turned one of thcm, Genna's self-portrait.

'Here is her first effort at portraiture. It is compe-
tent, is it not?'

Ross thought it looked very much like Genna. It
even captured some of her irrepressible personality.

'I am no judge of competence,' Ross admitted. 'It
is very like her, though.'

'Yes. And that was her first effort.' He walked over
to another canvas still on an easel and removed the
cloth covering it. 'Here is another.'

It was the housekeeper and even Ross could tell
Genna had improved her technique.

'The woman's personality shows, does it not?' said
Vespery.

'Indeed.'

'I believe there is nothing she could not paint if
she wished to.' Vespery covered the painting again
and walked back to the chairs.

Ross sat with him. 'Painting is what Miss Summerfield wishes to do and I want to make certain she
can do it. So I have a proposition.'

Vespery's brows rose. 'Yes?'

'I will continue to pay you to take her on, but as an
assistant, not a student.' He paused to gauge the artist's reaction. The man still looked interested. 'I will
pay her salary, too, but she mustn't know it comes
from me. It must seem as if you are paying her. I want
this plan to continue until she has enough commis-
sions to set up her own studio.'

Vespery looked puzzled. 'But you are to marry
her, are you not?'

Ross stopped to think. Could he trust Vespery with the whole truth?

The artist's expression turned to alarm. 'Do not tell me you are planning to renege on your promise!'

'No,' Ross said. 'Not me. But lately I have thought perhaps—perhaps Miss Summerfield would like to cry off. The painting makes her much happier than being a duchess would do. I think that is beginning to dawn on her. When—if—she decides to end our engagement, I want her to have what she most desires—to support herself as an artist.'

'An artist's assistant makes a pittance,' Vespery cried. 'She cannot support herself on it!'

Ross lifted a stilling hand. 'You and I might know what an artist's assistant would make in salary, but she does not. I will pay enough for her to live comfortably.'

Vespery stared at him for a long time before answering. 'I will do it, of course. I would be a fool not to. I can double my output, be paid and have a skilled paid assistant at no cost to myself.' He leaned towards Ross. 'Are you certain, my lord, that Miss Summerfield would prefer art over marriage to you? I am not convinced.'

'I am certain,' Ross answered.

And he was also certain he wanted it for her.

Chapter Twenty

Three days later Genna put on her gloves, ready to be transported to Vespery's studio. It was time for the carriage to come and pick her up and she waited in the anteroom.

A knock sounded at the door. The footman announced, 'Your carriage, miss.'

She hurried out to the hall and was happily surprised. Ross stood there, hat in hand, looking magnificent in his perfectly tailored black coat, white neckcloth and buff-coloured pantaloons.

'Ross!' she cried, stilling an impulse to rush into his arms. Instead she approached him with her hands extended.

He clasped them and gave her a peck on the cheek. No doubt she would feel the sensation of his lips against her skin for the rest of the day.

'I was able to take the time.' There was only the hint of a smile on his face. 'Much has slowed down now that the Princess's wedding is over and my father is feeling better.'

'I'm glad.' She filled with hope. 'Will I see more of you, then?'

'As often as I can manage,' he responded, as she took his arm and they walked to the door.

The footman opened it and they stepped outside.

'You have your curricle!' she cried. 'It has been weeks since we were out in your curricle.'

He helped her up into the seat. 'I warn you, it is chilly today. I am regretting leaving my topcoat at home.'

'I do not care.' She cared about nothing else except that he was with her.

He took the ribbons and his tiger jumped on the back.

As soon as they started, Genna turned to him. 'Oh, Ross! I have some wonderful news!'

He glanced from the road to her. 'What is it?'

She could hardly get the words out. 'Vespery wishes to hire me to be his assistant. He will pay me a handsome amount, enough for me to live on.'

'That is wonderful news.' His voice did not sound as enthusiastic as she'd anticipated.

But, then, she did not feel as excited as she'd sounded.

She went on. 'I must tell him when I am ready, he said, but I am able to take as little or as much time as I wish.'

'That is good, is it not?' he responded.

'Yes. Very good.' She swallowed. 'It—it means we can break the betrothal whenever we wish.'

'I suppose it does.' His voice turned low. 'When do you wish it?'

'Never!' she cried, threading her arm through his and leaning her head against his shoulder. 'I wish everything could remain exactly as it is this minute.'

'Riding in a chilly curricle, you mean?' he quipped, but his throat was thick.

She tried to smile. 'You know what I mean.'

He turned on to Piccadilly. 'I was hoping you would want a break from the studio. A little outing. Two outings, actually.'

'Will you have that much time?' She hoped.

'I will.'

'I still want you to sit for a portrait for me,' she said.

He turned to gaze at her. 'I will make the time.'

When they reached Vespery's studio, Ross handed the ribbons to his tiger who would take the curricle back to the stable until it came time to pick them up again. Ross knocked at the door and the housekeeper admitted them.

The housekeeper broke into a smile when she saw Genna. 'Good afternoon, miss,' the woman said brightly. 'And to you, sir.'

'Good afternoon, Mrs Shaw!' Genna turned to him. 'I painted a portrait of Mrs Shaw. She was my second one.'

'Did you?' He knew it, of course, having called upon Vespery the day he made his bargain with him. Ross glanced at Mrs Shaw. 'And have you seen it?'

'Oh, yes, my lord.' The housekeeper beamed. 'Miss Summerfield made me look so very nice.'

'I merely paint what I see,' Genna said. 'Lord Rossdale has agreed to sit for me next. Is that not brave of him?'

Brave because it would put them in each other's company for an extended period. They'd not been together so much since he'd kissed her, since he'd realised how much he wanted her.

The housekeeper patted Genna's arm. 'You will do a fine job of it, miss.'

They left Mrs Shaw to her duties and walked to the back of the house to the studio.

Genna burst into the light-filled room. 'Look who I have brought with me!'

Vespery put down his brush. 'Lord Rossdale. Good to see you,' he said, a bit stilted.

'Ross will be able to stay the afternoon, too,' Genna added. 'Is that not grand?'

Ross nodded to the artist and placed his hat and gloves on a table by the door. 'It seems I am to be Miss Summerfield's next model.'

He helped her off with her redingote.

'I can hardly wait to get started.' She glanced around the room. 'Do we have a canvas already stretched that I can use?'

Vespery pointed to several stacked against the wall. 'Pick whatever size you wish.'

He gave Ross a conspiratorial look while she selected her canvas and carried it to her easel.

'Ross knows of your kind offer, Mr Vespery,' she said.

Vespery jumped and his voice turned high. 'He does?'

She gestured for Ross to sit in the chair in the corner. 'I told Ross today.'

Genna looked at home in the studio, comfortable around the canvases and paints. More so, she looked relaxed and happy. He had no doubt she would ultimately be as big a success as Vespery himself, but, in the meantime, he would watch and make certain she wanted for nothing.

She positioned him, stepped back and surveyed him, then positioned him again. 'You must remember to sit this way tomorrow, too,' she said. 'You can come tomorrow, can you not?'

'I had planned one of those outings for tomorrow,' he said, trying to remain still.

'The next day, then.'

Vespery spoke up from his side of the room. 'As of tomorrow I will not be here. I will be away for a week on a commission out of town.'

'But we can come in, can we not?' she asked. 'Mrs Shaw can let us in.'

'Mrs Shaw will be away, too,' Vespery said. 'She will be visiting her sister.'

'Then might we have a key?' Genna pressed. 'If I am to be your assistant, surely you would trust me with a key.'

Vespery shrugged. 'I suppose.'

She ran over and gave him a hug. 'Thank you!'

The clock Vespery kept in the room chimed two o'clock.

'Two o'clock?' the artist said. 'I must be off. I am delivering the portraits to your father and the Duchess.'

'Would you prefer I take them?' Ross asked, though it would necessitate explaining to them why he'd been at Vespery's studio.

Vespery hurriedly cleaned his brushes. 'No. The Duchess will want me to bring them. I must ensure they are acceptable.' He wiped his hands and bid them good day.

Ross attempted to remain still.

'It has been a long time since you and I were alone together,' Genna remarked.

'Since the ball.' He remembered that moment. He'd kissed her.

And then everything changed.

She paused, brush in the air, and gazed at him. 'I liked being alone with you that night,' she murmured.

'As did I,' he responded.

She met his gaze.

It was a good thing he needed to remain in the chair, in that pose. Otherwise he might have crossed the room and kissed her again. God knew he wished to do so.

She turned back to her painting, making quick big strokes with the brush. Soon he could tell she was lost in the work, the concentration on her face enhancing her beauty. The pose he needed to keep gave him a great advantage. He needed to look in her direction. He could indulge in watching her all he liked.

The next day Ross picked up Genna earlier than the usual time. They would have nearly the whole day together, plenty of time for what he had planned for her.

When she sat next to him in his curricle, she smiled happily. 'It has been so long since we've had an outing. I cannot imagine where you are taking me.'

He felt happy, too, happier than he'd been since his father took ill. A whole day together, a day she was bound to enjoy. He turned on to Audley Street, heading north to turn right on Oxford Street.

As they left Mayfair, Genna looked around at everything. 'I have never been in this part of town,' she said, commenting on whatever caught her eye.

When they reached the end of Oxford Street, she asked, 'What part of town are we in now?'

'Bloomsbury.' He hated to give her too many hints.

'Oh.' She turned silent.

He pulled up to their destination, what once was the mansion of a wealthy duke who sold it to the British government when the Bloomsbury neighbourhood was no longer the fashionable place to live. The mansion had a large expanse of garden in the front so it took some time for the curricle to reach the doorway.

Genna finally spoke. 'I know where we are. I've seen this building in books. This is Montagu House, is it not?'

'That it is.'

Ross's tiger jumped off to hold the horses. Ross climbed down and turned to assist Genna.

'You've brought me to see the exhibits of the British Museum!' she cried in delight.

He held her by her waist as he helped her down. 'Even better,' he said.

She landed on her feet, but he did not immediately let go of her. She tipped her head up and looked directly in his eyes. Her eyes darkened and she leaned a little closer.

He released her then, before he forgot they were in a public place.

She took a breath and recovered her composure. 'What could be better than the British Museum?'

He knew this would please her. 'We will see the Elgin Marbles.'

Her eyes grew wide. 'Truly?'

He offered his arm. 'Truly.'

Genna's excitement grew as they approached the door of the museum. Ross knocked as if visiting someone's residence.

'The museum is closed?' Genna asked.

'Not to us,' he responded.

Obviously he had gone to some effort for this outing. For her.

The door was answered by a well-dressed gentleman. His brows rose. 'Lord Rossdale?'

Ross nodded. 'Mr Hutton, I presume.'

'Welcome to the British Museum.' Mr Hutton swept his arm in an arc and stepped aside for them to enter.

Ross turned to Genna. 'Miss Summerfield, may I present Mr Hutton, who has made this excursion possible.'

'My pleasure, Miss Summerfield.' Mr Hutton bowed.

'I am so grateful to you, sir.' And to Ross for making this possible.

Mr Hutton looked apologetic. 'You do understand you will not be able to tour the entire museum at this time. Let me escort you to the courtyard.'

They walked by a grand staircase and Genna spied huge giraffes at the top of the stairs, appearing as they might have been when alive. Other curiosities could be glimpsed as they made their way to the back of the mansion and out the door to the courtyard. Mr Hutton then led them to a huge wooden shed, which he unlocked, and opened the doors, filling the space inside with light.

'I will return in an hour,' Mr Hutton said. 'Obviously you may not move any of the sculptures, but I doubt you could. They are quite marvellous. I think you will agree.'

He left them in the doorway.

Huge slabs of marble lined the sides of the shed.

Scattered around were ghostly figures. Headless. Armless. Standing. Reclining.

Genna stepped inside reverently. 'Oh, Ross!'

She walked along the perimeter gazing at the long slabs of marble that used to decorate the frieze of the Parthenon. The sculpted figures depicted all sorts of figures: men on horseback, on foot or racing chariots, women carrying items—for sacrifice to the gods, perhaps? Everything seemed in motion. Rearing horses, figures interacting, no two the same.

'It must tell a story,' Genna said. 'I wish I knew what it was.' She dared to touch the sculpture, almost surprised the figures were not as warm as flesh they were so realistic.

'Here is a Centaur fighting a Lapith,' he said.

It was one segment, not a part of the long procession of figures that had been part of the frieze. Had there been more Centaurs? Did they tell a different story?

'Lord Tinmore criticises Elgin for removing these sculptures from the Parthenon,' Genna said. 'He likens it to theft.'

'I have heard that sentiment,' Ross responded. 'I have also heard Lord Elgin praised for saving the marbles. Apparently the Parthenon was a ruin and local builders thought nothing of using its sculptures as building blocks in their own buildings, some of which were ground down for cement.'

Genna shook her head. 'Can you imagine these

magnificent carvings ground down into nothing? It would be an abomination!'

She walked the length of a section of the frieze. Many of the men were naked, some riding horses, some on foot. Genna was not such a green girl that she'd never seen a naked man before, although her knowledge of such was confined to seeing other statuary or spying her brother, a boy then, swimming naked. These figures, though, were all well-formed, muscular, powerful beings.

She glanced at Ross, who was examining one of the pieces. His shoulders were broad, like the Greek figures on the marbles, his legs well formed. She remembered the feel of his body pressing against hers when he'd kissed her the night of the ball. His muscles were as firm as marble.

Her skin flashed with heat.

She resisted the impulse to fan herself and turned away to examine the other marbles. One was a horse's head from what must have been a huge statue. She ran her hand down the horse's forehead to its muzzle, but it only made her wonder what it would be like to run her hand over Ross's skin.

She walked further away from him, over to three headless statues, all women attired in lavishly draped cloth. For all three, it was easy to see the bodies underneath, as evident as if they were real.

Then she came to a naked reclining male, exuding raw masculine strength.

Like Ross.

'Here is another Centaur,' called Ross from across the room.

She crossed the shed to him and her insides fluttered at being so near. She forced herself to gaze at the marble.

A mistake.

The Lapith in this fragment had the better of the Centaur, even though the Lapith's head and feet were missing. His body, though, splayed across the marble, displayed the muscles of his abdomen, his ribs, his masculine parts.

Her cheeks burned, not from embarrassment, but from a sudden desire to see Ross without his clothes, to again experience the warmth of his mouth against hers. She wanted to experience that kiss again. And more.

Sensible, independent Genna wanted a man's kiss—no, not a man's kiss—*Ross's kiss*. Ross's lovemaking.

She finally understood. The sensations she experienced in Ross's presence were carnal ones. She desired him, the way her mother had desired many men.

Was she like her mother? She must be. Like her mother, she felt willing to abandon all propriety to make carnal love with a man. *With Ross.* At this moment she desired Ross more than anything. More than respectability.

More than…art.

Why not? She had no intention of living a conventional life. Artists were allowed their passions, were they not?

Ross jarred her from her thoughts. 'I seem to remember a legend about Centaurs fighting Lapiths.
Something we read in school.'

She turned to him, her whole body vibrating with
wanting him. 'Did you read Greek?'

He groaned. 'Not well, but it was part of my stud-
ies.'

She crossed her arms around herself and forced
herself to sound unaffected by desire. 'This is likely
as close as I may get to studying a man's body. Vespery told me that the Royal Academy barred women
from the classes with naked models.'

'You would want to take such a class?' He sounded
surprised.

'Yes. I would.' She turned to him. 'I would like to
study a man's naked body—' Ross's body. 'Does that
shock you?'

His gaze seemed to smoulder. 'Nothing about you
shocks me, Genna.'

Did she know she was arousing him? Ross wondered. Something was different.

A change had come over her, a change that made
him think of how it would be to touch her naked skin,
how it would feel to kiss her again. To make love to her.

He became more aware of her hint-of-jasmine
scent, more aware of how she moved, of how her
eyes slanted up when she smiled.

Good God. Was he going to be able to keep his
hands off her?

She gazed up at him and he caught her chin between his finger and thumb. He tilted her face so he was looking straight down at her.

'Genna,' he murmured.

She rose on tiptoe, bringing her face just a little closer.

No. Not again. Not here. He released her and stepped away.

Mr Hutton appeared at the door of the shed. 'I fear it is time, my lord, miss.'

Genna turned towards him. 'I am ready.'

They walked through Montagu House again and out the front door where Jem waited with the curricle, just as Ross had arranged.

'Where are we bound now?' Genna asked when they started off again.

'To Vespery's, if you like.'

'Yes,' she murmured. 'I would very much like that, if you are able to stay with me.' She paused. 'For the portrait, I mean.'

He also paused before responding. 'Yes. I am able to stay.'

Chapter Twenty-One

Ross and Genna entered Vespery's studio, which, Genna was acutely aware, they had all to themselves. She put on her smock and uncovered her palette. Ross sat in the chair and assumed the pose she'd placed him in before. They said little while she painted. She felt his eyes on her, though, and it made her hand tremble.

'I have another outing planned for you,' he told her after an hour had passed. 'Are you able to make a morning call with me tomorrow?'

'A morning call?' Her brows rose. 'To visit someone?'

'Precisely.'

'Am I to know to whom?' she asked, knowing he would not tell her, that he delighted in surprising her.

'No.' He smiled. She loved how his smile reached his eyes.

She turned back to her canvas. 'What time?'

'Eleven o'clock.'

She kept painting. 'Nothing grander than the Elgin Marbles, I am sure. Nothing could be.'

'Different' was all he said.

The marbles had been so magnificent, so detailed, so beautiful and real. If only she could bring those elements to her painting. Her portrait of Ross was flat. The statues gave the sensation of skin under drapes of clothing. Or muscles and veins under skin. Surely there was a way to convey the same impression in paint.

She closed her eyes and tried to imagine the naked statues.

It was not the same, though.

'Ross, unfold your arms' Maybe if he stood differently, she could see differently.

He unfolded his arm, stretching them as if to get the stiffness out.

Still they were covered with cloth—his coat, his waistcoat, his shirt.

She stepped away from the canvas and walked over to examine one of Vespery's nearly completed portraits set on his easel.

'What is amiss?' Ross asked her.

'Mine is too flat.' She pointed to Vespery's. 'See? His gentleman has shape to him. A sense of his physique.' She put her hands on her hips and stared at Vespery's painting. 'I begin to understand why artists take classes with naked models. For that sense of the body under the clothes.'

He gave a dry laugh. 'Do not tell me you wish me to take off my clothes.'

She turned to him. 'Would you? It would help so very much.'

'Genna, do not jest.'

She hurried over to him. 'I am not jesting. I need to know what you look like under your clothes. So—so the portrait is not flat.'

His return look was very sceptical.

'Please, Ross?'

'Do not be nonsensical,' he countered. 'You saw enough naked men in the Elgin Marbles. Think of those.'

'It is not the same. They were ideal images, not real men at all.' Although she suspected he might also be an ideal.

She faced him and stood so close she could touch him.

His eyes darkened as he held her gaze.

'It is for the art,' she protested. 'So I can paint a decent portrait of you.'

His gaze did not waver. 'You propose we act indecently so you might paint a decent portrait.'

Her face flushed. 'What harm would there be? No one would know.'

Still seated in the chair, he leaned forward. 'Do you know what I think?' His voice turned to silk.

It was difficult to take a breath. 'What?'

'I think this has nothing to do with art. You just wish to see me naked.'

Her heart pounded. How dare he say this wasn't for her art? 'What if I match you?'

His brows rose. 'Match me?'

She untied her smock. 'Tit for tat.'

She pulled it off and tossed it on to the floor.

It was a game. A dare.

Ross had no doubt at all that Genna wanted to see what a real man looked like beneath his clothes. No doubt she resented that women artists were barred from such experiences. But there was something more there as well, something she did not yet understand.

She did not know her powers of seduction, how easily she could draw men to her and how easily they could take advantage.

He ought to teach her. Arm her with that knowledge so she could protect herself when he could no longer be there keeping other gentlemen away.

'Tit for tat, then.' He unbuttoned his coat and removed it.

He thought he saw a flicker of anxiety in her eyes, but she quickly recovered and stared directly in his eyes.

She removed the fichu tucked into the neckline of her dress.

He untied his neckcloth and unwound it from his neck. 'Your turn.'

He had his waistcoat yet to take off and he'd still

be covered by his shirt. For Genna, her dress would be next.

She flashed a grin and kicked off her shoes.

'Coward,' he said, unbuttoning his waistcoat and shrugging out of it. He lifted his chin in a silent challenge.

'I cannot do it myself.' She turned her back to him.

He had not accounted for touching her. He unbuttoned the buttons at the back of her dress, too aware of her slender neck and her smooth skin. She pulled off her sleeves and let the dress slip to the floor.

Only her chemise and corset remained. She spun around again. 'Now you.'

He could not help his eyes sweeping over her. Her corset showed her slender waist and pushed her breasts up to their voluptuous fullness.

She twirled a finger at him, indicating he should remove his shirt.

He undid the button at his neck and pulled his white linen shirt over his head.

Genna took in a sharp, audible breath.

She reached out and touched him, very softly, her fingers cool against his suddenly heated skin. She traced the contours of his bare chest, like he'd seen her touch the Elgin marbles.

'Oh, Ross,' she whispered.

He, unlike the statues, was not made of stone. Her touch, the awed look on her face, set his senses on fire. He forgot this was a game or a lesson he was going to teach her. He was alone with her, protected from everything outside, cocooned in a world existing only for the two of them.

'Genna,' he groaned, lifting her on to his lap so her legs straddled him.

She leaned into him, pressing against his arousal, and twined her arms around his neck. She dipped her head to him and he strained to meet her, capturing her mouth with his ravenous lips. The kiss was long and lingering. Like their one other kiss, she opened to him and his tongue touched hers, soft, warm and wet. She dug her fingers into his hair and matched his lips' demand.

When finally they broke apart long enough to take a breath, Genna murmured, 'Make love to me, Ross. Please. I want you to show me. No one else.'

He longed to show her. He wanted no other man to possess her like this.

He lifted her and rose from the chair. Her chemise was bunched about her waist and her stockinged legs wrapped around him. He carried her out of the studio into a small drawing room. He sat her on a couch and unlaced her corset, slipping it off entirely. He ran his hands over her body, still covered by her chemise. He freed her breasts from the thin fabric of the undergarment and relished their soft flesh and the nipples that hardened under his touch.

'Mmm...' she hummed. 'You were right. Not the art. This. I wanted this. From you, Ross. Only you.'

He lay next to her on the couch and kissed her

again, still rubbing his palm against her nipples. It seemed so right for him to make love to Genna. He could not think of another time or another woman who felt this right. He wanted to show her pleasure, a fair exchange for the pleasure just being with her brought to him.

She placed her hands in his hair again and pulled him into another kiss. He felt her hunger, her yearning resonate within his whole body.

They were surely kindred spirits, two of a kind, and at this moment they were as free as ever they would be, without anyone nearby to see. Her kiss was eager and urgent and he knew he could satisfy her urges. Why not make love to her? Why not show her? Bring her pleasure?

His lips made a path down her neck to her breasts to her nipple. He relished the feel and taste of her against his tongue. She twisted and squirmed beneath him. He backed off for a moment and rubbed her in long, sweeping strokes. She calmed again.

His hand splayed over her abdomen. She seized his wrist and guided his hand downward over her bunched-up skirts. Her arousal must tell her where the greatest pleasure lay. He obliged her by sliding his hand lower and gently touching the soft moist skin around her most womanly place.

'Ross!' she rasped. 'Yes. Yes.'

She moved beneath his fingers and he could feel her pleasure building, building. He wanted to give her the pleasure, to feel her pleasure beneath his hand.

He found her tender spot and her voice became more urgent. 'Yes. More. More,' she cried.

He gave her more, able to feel the passion rising in her, higher and higher until her back arched and she cried out, writhing with the explosion of pleasure he'd released in her.

'Ross,' she cried as her spasm eased. 'Ross.'

Genna basked in the sensations he had created in her. She'd never dreamed lovemaking could feel so—so pleasurable and unsettling. His touch was so acutely pleasurable it very nearly was pain. Not hurting, but agonising her with wanting what she had not known would come, that—that explosion of pleasure.

She pressed herself against him on the narrow couch. 'I—I never knew a touch could feel like that, but that was not all, was it, Ross? That was a mere taste of lovemaking, was it not?'

She was not so green a girl, even if she was a maiden. She knew the barest of elements of lovemaking. She simply had not guessed such pleasure and need could be built by a touch.

She loved it. And wanted to feel it again. She wanted to feel everything about lovemaking. She tried to remember every part of this. How his lips felt against hers. How warm his tongue was. How it tasted of tea. She wanted her body to remember the feel of his hands against her skin. And how different it felt for his hands to touch her breasts, how that sensation touched off a veritable riot in her feminine parts. If she could paint this, what colours would she use?

All of them, she thought.

The cool, smooth blues blended into purple and gradually built from red to orange to a bright yellow, as bright as the sun. How would she paint such a feeling?

Like a rainbow that burst and turned into sunshine.

This very sort of sensation must have been what tempted her mother away from her father, she realised, more powerful and compelling than the mothering of children. Genna understood it a little. Right before Ross created that explosion of pleasure, Genna would have given up everything else for it.

Was she like her mother?

It must be so.

'Show me the rest of it, Ross,' she murmured. 'I want to do this with you. Make love to me.'

He kissed her, a demanding kiss, one she was delighted to accept. Who knew a kiss could radiate throughout one's whole body? Or a touch could set off such pleasurable pain? Who knew a kiss and touch could lead to a rainbow bursting? She could hardly wait to experience what lay ahead.

She unbuttoned the fall of his pantaloons, her heart racing with excitement. She would join with Ross.

Only Ross.

She thought she'd never want this attachment to a man, like her mother's attachment to her lover, so imperative she'd leave her children for it.

She gazed down and saw his male member, swollen and long and so unlike the ones on the marble statues. She wavered. Would there be pain? How could he possibly fit inside her?

His hands, so gentle now, reassured her. Ross would never hurt her. Never.

His hand did not linger this time, but it tantalised, igniting her need for that bursting of colour.

'Now, Ross,' she begged. 'Now. Please.'

He groaned and positioned himself on top of her. She felt his member touch the now-throbbing skin of her feminine parts. She parted her legs wider and he began to push in gently, gingerly.

She did not wish for him to be gentle. She wanted him to hurry. She wanted that pleasure to explode inside her again. Now.

'Please,' she begged, feeling that agonising need.

He pushed in a little more, and more, and pulled out again.

'Mmm...' she urged, ready for more, relishing the feel of him entering her. Joining with her.

He broke away and moved off her. Moved off the couch to stand a pace away.

'No, Genna,' he cried, raking a hand though his hair. He buttoned his pantaloons. 'I will not do this with you.' He sounded angry.

She felt bereft. Deserted. 'Why not, if I want it?' she asked.

'You did not think, did you? Of what could happen? We could make a child.' He strode out of the drawing room.

She sat up, stunned.

She'd not given one single thought to the idea that she might get with child from this. Even though she knew what had happened to her brother, why he had to hurry to get married. She'd acted as if this was only about feeling good.

She picked up her corset and put it on, tightening the laces as best she could. She returned to the studio.

He had already donned his shirt and waistcoat. He picked up his coat off the floor and glared at her.

She spoke. 'I thought only of you and me.'

'I could have ruined your life,' he said.

She lifted her chin. 'If I am to be an artist, it does not matter. I will not need to be proper.'

He wrapped his neckcloth around his neck and tied it in a terrible knot. 'And how many members of the *ton* will pay to have their portrait painted by a baronet's daughter who has a bastard child in tow? How many would let you paint their daughters?'

She turned away.

All the colour had been leached away. Only the black-and-white truth remained. She could not simply do as she wished. She could no longer act as if she and Ross were in their own fairy tale.

He moved closer to her, close enough to hand her her dress. 'Do not make me the one who will ruin you, Genna.'

He despised her now. Why not? She did not like herself very much.

She donned her dress.

'We should not be together,' he said as he buttoned it for her. 'Tidy your things. Jem will not be here with the curricle for another two hours. I'll get us a hackney cab now.' He walked out of the studio.

She did not want a hackney cab. She did not want to leave. She simply wanted to perish.

The brisk air did not do a great deal to cool Ross's senses. He was still burning with desire and blazing with anger at himself. He'd nearly ruined her! He'd taken far too many liberties with her even before this. What had he been thinking?

He wasn't thinking. Probably had not been thinking since he'd met her. He'd simply craved her—why pretend otherwise? He'd come up with the hare-brained idea of a pretend betrothal so he could be with her. Had he thought of where that would lead? To seduction? Ruin? Risk?

He felt as if a fog had cleared and he suddenly could see around him.

He could have killed her dreams of being an artist. He could have got her with child. What then? He'd have to marry her. She did not want that. If he didn't marry her, he'd embroil her in a scandal that would affect the rest of her life.

Perhaps he already had ruined her life by encouraging her, by coming up with this misguided betrothal. What were the chances of her—a woman—becoming a successful artist? Successful women artists were rare.

He found the corner where the hackney cabs waited and hired one.

When it pulled up in front of Vespery's door, Genna emerged, locking the door behind her. Ross jumped out of the carriage to help her inside.

She did not look at him.

When the coach starting moving, she asked, 'What happens now?' Her voice was so tiny he hardly heard her.

'I take you home,' he said.

'And, then?'

He did not understand. 'And then—nothing.'

She averted her face, then suddenly squared her shoulders and lifted her chin. 'It was not such an abominable request, you know. To make love to me. Is it not how men and women are meant to be with each other?'

'If they are married,' he shot back. 'If they are safe from the kind of scandal that will wreck a lady's life. Widows can manage it. Married women sometimes manage it. But not you, Genna. Not you.'

She went on. 'I am not going to marry. I will not be in society. Are not the rules looser for women such as me?'

'If you came from Italy, perhaps. Or France. Or anywhere besides the home of one of their own. You cannot fall from grace in the eyes of the *ton* and be acceptable to them. You know this, Genna.'

'I thought you would understand,' she accused. 'You, of all people. No one would know except you and me.'

'You and I have to face reality, Genna. Enough of these illusions.' He lowered his voice. 'Some things cannot be hidden, Genna.'

'It might not have happened,' she protested. 'I might not have got with child.'

He turned her face to him, like he had in the studio. 'What if we lost that gamble?'

She wrenched away.

They spent the last of the trip in silence.

When the coach pulled up to Tinmore's town house, Ross paid the driver and walked her to the door.

'This is goodbye, then?' she asked uncertainly.

'Yes. Goodbye,' he responded, sounding the knocker.

The door opened and she stepped over the threshold.

He called before the door closed again. 'Be ready tomorrow at eleven o'clock.'

She swivelled around to face him again. 'Tomorrow? You do not wish to cancel?'

'It is all arranged.'

She stared at him without speaking for several seconds. Finally she said, 'I will be ready.'

Chapter Twenty-Two

The next day Genna was ready early for Ross's outing. A bad idea. She had nothing to do while waiting except to think.

She'd deliberately sought to seduce him. That was the truth. She'd merely been deluding herself by saying she did it for her art. It had all been her fault and now he despised her for it.

Why he still wished to take her on this outing was a mystery to her. Their friendship was ruined now.

She had ruined it.

Consequences. The cost of keeping her head in the clouds. She'd liked him. More than liked him. He'd become the most important person in her life. Now she'd come crashing back to earth.

We should not be together, he'd said.

He'd leave her, too. After this outing, she supposed.

Her mother had left her. Her father never cared for her. Lorene and Tess and Edmund had left her, too, in their way when they married. She'd always known

Ross would leave her. That was part of their secret plan. She'd cry off and they would part.

So why did it hurt so much?

She groaned in pain and rested her head on the table in front of her. She was making herself sick with all this self-pity.

The only person she could depend upon was herself. She'd known that since a child. She still had her painting. She still would become Vespery's assistant. She could take care of herself.

Thanks to Ross. He'd given her the lessons with Vespery. He'd showed her so much more, as well.

A footman knocked at the door.

'Is Lord Rossdale here already?' she asked him. 'I'll be right down.'

'Not Lord Rossdale, miss.' He handed her a card.

The Duchess of Kessington, the card said. She glanced up at the footman. 'I will be down directly. Is she in the drawing room?'

'Yes, miss.' He bowed and left the room.

What on earth did the Duchess want with her?

She glanced in the mirror and smoothed her hair. She deliberately walked from the room at a normal pace. No good appearing before the Duchess out of breath from rushing.

When she entered the drawing room, the Duchess was examining a blue-and-white porcelain bowl. 'Chinese,' she stated.

'If you say so.' Genna did not smile. 'Good morning, Your Grace. Do have a seat. Shall I send for tea?'

'Do not bother.' The Duchess lowered herself into a chair. 'This will not take long.'

Genna sat nearby and folded her hands in her lap, trying to look calm. She certainly did not wish the Duchess to know her emotions were in turmoil.

She waited.

An annoyed look came over the Duchess's face, but she finally spoke. 'I came here to discuss something with you.'

Genna raised her brows.

The Duchess pressed her lips together before continuing. 'You cannot possibly marry Rossdale.'

'I cannot? I am betrothed to him.' Genna *would* not marry him, of course, but the Duchess did not know that.

'You are entirely unsuitable.' The Duchess leaned forward. 'I have learned that you spend your days unchaperoned, alone with a man. That is scandalous, young lady.'

Alone with Ross? No. That could not be what she meant.

'Alone with Mr Vespery? I am taking painting lessons from him, Your Grace.'

'I know that,' she snapped. 'But it is what else goes on when you are alone with him that concerns me.'

The inference was appalling. 'Ask his housekeeper. She is always nearby.'

'Hmmph!' The Duchess scowled. 'A servant doesn't matter. This has the appearance of scandal. That is all I need to know. It is not fitting for the wife of a future duke to be so shameless.'

Genna felt her cheeks heat. With anger. 'Rossdale knows of the painting lessons. He arranged them. He provides me transport to and from Vespery's studio. If he does not object to the lessons, why should I be concerned with what you or anyone else thinks of it?'

'Because of the title, Miss Summerfield! You must think of the title. Some day Rossdale will be the Duke of Kessington. For five generations that title has been unstained by scandal. I will not allow you to tarnish it.'

Genna straightened her spine. 'You insult me, Duchess.'

'I speak the truth!' the Duchess cried. 'I assure you, I am prepared to do anything possible to ensure that this marriage does not take place.'

'Does Ross know you have come to speak to me like this?' He would not have sent her. There would have been no need. He knew they would never marry.

'Ross is as foolish as you are,' the Duchess said. 'We thought he was coming to his senses and then he became betrothed to you. He needs a proper lady for a duchess, not the supposed daughter of an improvident baronet.'

Supposed daughter? How cruel to throw that particular rumour in her face.

'If the scandals in my family do not concern Rossdale, I see no reason they should concern you. You have no say in his affairs.'

She lifted her nose. 'I am the Duchess.'

'But no relation to Ross.' Genna stood. 'I will hear

no more of your insults, though, Your Grace. Please leave.'

The Duchess rose. 'I have one more thing to say.'

Genna held the woman's gaze and waited.

'If you break your engagement to Ross, I will pay you handsomely for it.'

'Pay me?' Genna could not believe her ears.

'I am prepared to pay very well. *Very* well.'

Genna glanced away.

Money would provide her security. It was not as if she didn't intend to cry off anyway. The joke would be on the Duchess, then.

'Do you not wish to know how much money I offer?' the Duchess asked smugly.

Genna paused a moment before facing her. 'I assure you, Duchess, no amount of money would induce me to break my engagement to Lord Rossdale.'

Because it was already broken.

Genna walked briskly to the door. 'You must now have nothing more to say.'

The Duchess huffed and strode towards the door. 'You will change your mind. I am certain of it. You will change your mind or suffer the scandal I can spread.'

Genna held the latch of the door, blocking the woman's way. 'That is an empty bluff. Any scandal you cause me will bring shame on the precious title. That is precisely what you profess to avoid.'

She opened the door and the Duchess swept out.

Genna sank into the nearest chair and put her head in her hands. She'd defended herself as if the betrothal were real, but it had never been. She and Ross had fooled everyone, but, in so doing, they'd affected everyone. They'd certainly put the Duchess in a panic.

But it had all been lies.

Ross pulled up to Tinmore's town house and spied his father's carriage pulling away from its door. Through the carriage window he glimpsed the Duchess.

That did not bode well.

He jumped down from his curricle and handed the ribbons to Jem.

Ross was admitted by a footman at the same moment Genna appeared in the hall.

'You are here.' Her voice was stiff—and sad.

He nodded, wanting to ask her about the Duchess, but not in front of the footman.

'Are you ready?' he asked.

'I need to fetch my hat and shawl.' She climbed the stairs and disappeared from view.

The footman spoke. 'Would you care to wait in the drawing room, my lord?'

'No. I'll wait here,' he responded.

When she returned, they walked out the door to the curricle. He helped her into the seat and climbed up beside her. His tiger jumped on the back and they started off.

He could finally speak. 'I saw the Duchess driving away from the town house. What did she want?'

'She wanted me to cry off,' Genna said with little animation in her voice. 'I am too scandalous, ap-

parently, because I take painting lessons from Mr
Vespery and am, at times, alone with him. That and
merely being a Summerfield with uncertain pater-
nity.'

His anger flared. 'She said those things to you?'

'Think if she knew how scandalous I truly am,'
she added sadly.

He did not know how to talk to her about that. 'I
am sorry you had to endure her venom.'

She shrugged. 'Her threats were empty ones.'

He could not lay all blame for Genna's bleak mood
on the Duchess. He was at fault.

He'd been foolish not to realise what could happen,
what could ruin her friendship with him.

Their destination was not far. A mere street north
of Cavendish Square, but she did not tease him to
tell her where they were going. When he pulled up
in front of the town house at 47 Queen Anne Street,
she still asked nothing.

He needed to prepare her, though. 'This is the
home of Mr Turner. He is an artist and also a lec-
turer at the Royal Academy. His work is quite renowned. It is said that Canova visited here last year
and pronounced Turner a great genius.'

Canova was an Italian sculptor famous throughout
Great Britain and the Continent.

'Canova,' she whispered, but without enthusiasm.

Ross knocked on the door. They were admitted
by a housekeeper and joined Mr Turner in his sitting room.

'It is an honour to meet you, sir,' Ross said. 'And a very great privilege to be shown your gallery.' Ross introduced Genna. 'Miss Summerfield is an artist herself, sir,' he explained. 'A student of Mr Vespery, but I wanted her to see your paintings. She has been living in the country and has not had an opportunity to see the works of artists such as yourself.'

Genna managed, 'How do you do, sir.'

'A pleasure to meet a fellow artist,' Turner kindly said. 'Let us go straight to the gallery, shall we?' As he led the way, he asked, 'What is your medium, Miss Summerfield?'

'Watercolour, mostly, sir,' she replied. 'But I am lately a student of Mr Vespery, learning to paint in oils.'

'I have done both.' He chuckled. 'I often do both at the same time.'

He opened the door to a room built on to the back of his house. The room was bright from a skylight in the roof.

Genna stepped inside and gasped.

'Landscapes!' she exclaimed.

Hung on all four walls, or sitting on the floor, everywhere she looked, were landscapes. Large ones. Beautiful landscapes unlike anything she'd seen before.

Ross had known. He'd known she loved painting landscapes most of all.

'They are not all landscapes,' Mr Turner said. 'Some are history paintings.' He took her arm and walked her over to one painting on another wall. 'Like this one. This one is called *Hannibal and His Army Crossing the Alps*.'

History paintings depicted the people involved in some event in history, but in this painting, the landscape dominated and Genna had to strain to see the people. The painting depicted a huge black storm cloud, black paint that looked like it had been dabbed on by mistake, but, somehow, the canvas conveyed the feeling of the storm and of how inconsequential even a strong warrior like Hannibal was when faced with the forces of nature.

She walked over to a sea scene. There were several sea scenes. Ships or fishing boats or men fighting a stormy seas. Each conveyed the power of the ocean and its danger.

Turner painted how it felt, just as she had in that first fanciful painting Ross had seen that day overlooking Summerfield House. He'd remembered and brought her here.

Each of Turner's paintings were emotional, each done in ways she'd never seen a landscape painted.

One pulled at her artistic soul.

'This is *Dewy Morning*,' Turner said.

It was a lake scene, pretty ordinary in its composition, but, oh, the colour! The sky was orange and purple, its reflection in the water almost pink. It wasn't real. Ross had found a renowned artist who painted landscapes that were not real, just as she had done.

And he'd wanted her to see. It made her want to weep, especially because she'd ruined everything with him.

After they bid Mr Turner good day and returned to the waiting curricle, Genna spoke, even though she could not yet look directly at Ross, 'I know why you brought me here.'

Ross flicked the ribbons and the horses pulled away from the curb. 'To see the landscapes,' he said. 'It is what you first painted. I thought you would like to meet an artist who made his name painting landscapes not unlike the first painting I saw of yours, the one with the purple sky and blue grass.'

Her heart lurched.

He knew—no matter how much she went on about portrait painting—somehow he knew what she loved most to paint. Who else knew her that well? Who else would have cared?

'Shall I drive you to Vespery's studio?' he asked. 'I will not be able to stay with you, though. I'm required to do an errand for my father.'

She suspected he no longer wanted to stay with her. She felt a pang of pain, like a sabre slashing into her chest.

What she really wanted to do was return to her bedchamber and weep into her pillows.

'Take me to Vespery's,' she said instead. 'I want to paint.'

She wanted to finish his portrait even though it felt like she'd already run out of time to do so.

Ross drove her to Vespery's and escorted her inside, despite her protest that it was unnecessary. She did not wish to be in his presence at the place of her greatest pleasure and worst mistake, but he insisted and she endured it, watching his gaze wander to the couch in the drawing room and quickly look away.

'Will you be all right here alone?' he asked.

'I am used to being alone,' she replied, although, in truth, there were usually people around her.

He glanced around the room again. 'I'll pick you up at the usual time, then?'

'Yes. Thank you, Ross.' Her voice was tight.

He nodded. 'Goodbye, then, Genna.'

'Goodbye, Ross.'

He walked towards the door.

'Ross?'

He turned back to her.

'Thank you for taking me to call upon Mr Turner.'

He stared directly into her eyes. 'It was my pleasure, Genna.'

When he left, she dropped her shawl on a chair and removed her gloves and hat. She donned her smock and uncovered the painting and palette. When she stood in front of the painting, it was like standing in front of him. Only the eyes in the painting did not look upon her with strain, but with something warmer.

Something she'd lost.

Chapter Twenty-Three

Ross finished his father's errand and returned to pick up Genna at Vespery's studio.

He found her ready to go, but as distant as she'd been with him the whole day. This chasm between them seemed impassable.

She spoke to him only if he spoke to her first and he struggled to think of things to say. Their trip back to Tinmore's town house was a nearly silent one.

'How fares the portrait?' he asked her.

'I've done all I can do,' she answered. 'I need Vespery's opinion.' Several streets passed before she spoke again. 'So I do not need to go to the studio until he returns.'

Ross would have no reason to see her, then, unless he invited her to the opera or some other entertainment. If so, would she even attend with him?

He pulled up to the town house and helped her out of the curricle, holding her by the waist like he'd done before. He caught her gaze, fleetingly, and saw, not her usual sparkle, but pain and regret. It pierced him like a shaft to the heart.

He walked her to the door. 'I will not see you tomorrow, then?'

Those pained eyes looked up at him. 'There is no reason.'

Before Ross could knock at the door, it opened and the Tinmore butler stood in the doorway.

'Goodbye, Ross,' Genna said.

The butler stepped aside so she could enter. Ross turned to go, but the butler called him back. 'Lord Tinmore wishes a moment with you, sir.'

Ross and Genna exchanged puzzled glances.

'Certainly,' Ross told the man. He called back to his tiger, 'I'll be a few minutes, Jem. Just walk the horses.'

Ross entered the house.

The butler said, 'Follow me, sir.' He led Ross to the library. 'I'll announce you.'

Tinmore dozed in a chair, but woke with a start when the butler spoke to him.

'Show him in, show him in,' Tinmore said.

Ross entered the room. The butler bowed and left.

'You wished to see me, Lord Tinmore?' Ross asked.

'Indeed. Indeed.' Tinmore gestured to a chair.

Ross sat.

'This betrothal,' Tinmore began. 'It won't do. Won't do at all.'

First the Duchess, now Tinmore?

'Sir?' Ross said in a gruff tone.

Tinmore leaned forward. 'The way the two of you

are carrying on, you cannot afford a long engagement.'

Ross straightened. 'Carrying on?'

'Come now,' the old man said. 'The two of you meeting every day. At this rate the girl's belly will be swollen with child by the time you say the vows.'

'Lord Tinmore—' Ross's voice rose.

Tinmore went on as if Ross had not spoken. 'I'll not have it. I demand you marry the girl straight away. None of this waiting.'

'Tinmore!' he said more loudly. 'Enough! I'll not have you speak about Miss Summerfield in that manner.'

Tinmore pursed his lips.

'We are waiting until autumn.' But not to marry.

'Not good. Not good at all.' Tinmore coughed. 'I want the matter settled now before everyone knows you are carrying on. I won't have scandal. Won't have it.'

Ross spoke through gritted teeth. 'There is no carrying on. Miss Summerfield is taking painting lessons.'

Tinmore gave him a leering look. 'Is that what you call it?' He leaned towards Ross. 'I do not want anything to spoil this marriage. I want it settled now. The longer you wait, the more I think you are not going to come up to the mark. You asked for her hand in marriage and, by God, you need to take it.'

'Certainly not under pressure from you,' Ross said.

'I've already told your father that I will vote with

him on every issue, every issue, if he makes you marry now. Get a special licence. You can be married within days.'

This man was mad. What a reason to make a vote.

Ross stood. 'We wait until autumn, Tinmore.'

Tinmore smirked. 'Then I will make the girl's life a misery. No more *painting* lessons. No more parties or balls. I'll banish her back to Lincolnshire. See how she likes that.'

Ross leaned close again. 'If you make her suffer, your life will be a misery.'

He turned and strode out.

Genna waited outside the door. 'What did he want?'

'For us to marry by special licence now.' He wouldn't tell her the rest of it, the part about *carrying on*. Why upset her even more?

She walked with him. 'What did you say?'

He wanted to say that he'd protected her dream, that she would be free to live the life she chose, that he wished more than life itself he could live it with her.

'I said no.'

Ross left her then. Again.

Genna hurried back to the library, but met Lorene along the way.

'Was that Rossdale?' her sister asked.

'Yes,' Genna replied. 'He has just talked to Tinmore.'

Lorene made a frustrated sound. 'I'd hoped to warn you. I could not convince Tinmore to leave you both alone.'

'You tried?' Genna was surprised.

'Yes, of course,' Lorene said. 'He would only make things worse for you and Rossdale to interfere like that.'

'I am going to speak with him,' Genna told her. 'You may come if you wish.'

She would stop this.

She entered the library without knocking. 'I would speak with you, sir!' she demanded.

'Not now, girl, I am busy.' He was seated in a chair, the same one, she suspected, where he'd sat with Ross. There were no papers or books around him.

'I'll not be put off,' Genna persisted. She stood in front of his chair. 'I want you to know where your attempts at manipulation and control have led me.'

'Now, see here—' he sputtered.

She did not stop. 'I am not going to marry Rossdale. Do you hear? I am going to cry off. Rossdale and I will not suit.'

'Cry off?' His brows shot up. 'Oh, no, you are not. He will be a duke. You will marry him now, without delay.'

'I tell you we will not suit.' The previous day had showed her how unsuitable she was. 'And I will not marry a man if we do not suit.'

'Genna! Do not be hasty,' her sister cried. 'Anyone can tell he loves you and you love him.'

He'd done so many loving things for her, but she'd ruined it. Now, at least, she could do something for him—get him out of this foolish plan they'd made.

She turned to Lorene. 'We will not suit, Ross and me,' she said. 'I am everything the Duchess and your husband think of me. Too inconsequential to be the wife of a duke's heir. Too scandalous.'

Tinmore rose from his chair and waved his cane at her. 'Now you listen to me, girl. You will marry that man. I do not give a fig whether he loves you or you love him. It is a better match than you deserve. If you cry off there will be no dowry. You will not get another chance.'

She stood her ground. 'I will not marry him.'

He hobbled closer to her. 'Then pack your things! I'll not see your face in this house, not with the fuss you are making. Crying off. A duke's heir, no less. I can hear the gossip now.'

'You cannot send her away!' Lorene cried. 'She has a right to cry off.'

'She's a fool. I do not suffer fools.' He shook his cane at Lorene. 'And I'll not have you contradicting me, Wife. Enough of that talk from you.'

Genna turned to leave, but Lorene stopped her. 'You could go to Tess. You should stay in town. Work things through with Rossdale. I am certain he will want to. You are not inconsequential to him, I am sure of it.'

She gave her sister a quick hug. 'You are a romantic, are you not? Do not fret, though, Lorene. I want to go.'

Lorene faced her husband again. 'You cannot simply toss her out. It—it will reflect poorly on you.'

He waved a hand and his cane pounded his way to the door. 'She can go to Tinmore Hall, but she needs to be out by the time we return there. I'm done with her.'

When he left the room, Lorene spoke again. 'Genna, do not do this. Give love a chance. It is all I've ever wanted for you.'

She touched her sister's arm. 'A person can have love and ruin it, Lorene. I must pen a letter and pack. It is better this way.'

The next morning at breakfast, a footman handed Ross a letter. 'This just came for you, sir,'

He opened it and read:

Dear Ross,
Recent events have convinced me it is better if we break the engagement now and that I leave town for a while. You deserve, at the very least, a peaceful Season without interference in your affairs. Who knows? Without me around, you might even meet a young lady worthy of you.

Please know that you have my sincerest gratitude. To you I owe my life and future livelihood, as well as treasured memories of all the wonderful places you took me. Carlton House. The Elgin Marbles. Mr Turner's gallery. Words cannot express what it meant to me to see those places. And to see them with you.

I realise we can never now be the friends we have been over these last several weeks. I am

*to blame, but please know you will always be
my very best friend in my heart.
With fondest regards,
G.*

He felt punched in the chest.

'What is it, Ross?' his father asked. 'Bad news?
Nothing to interfere with our meeting today, I hope.'

The estate manager of their Kessington estate was
in town expressly to meet with Ross, his father and
his father's man of business. Overseeing the Kessington estate was one of the responsibilities Ross was
assuming for his father.

'I'll be there,' he said.

With Genna gone, where else did he have to be?

Why did he feel as if a rug had been pulled out
from under him? This was what he had planned, after
all. He'd arranged it so she could become the artist
she wished to be. He'd pay Vespery to make certain
of it. He'd had a fine Season full of new experiences,
shared with her. And finally she would cry off. He
could search for what the Duchess would call a more
suitable match.

Although that idea made him faintly ill.

Very ill, actually.

He'd made a terrible mistake with this scheme he'd
talked her into. He'd been attracted to Genna right
from the first meeting. It was not enough that he liked
her; he'd also desired her. He thought he could keep
that side of him in check. He had no illusions any

more. She would have defied Tinmore's pressures, as she'd defied the Duchess's. She did not break the engagement because of Tinmore, she did it because he'd allowed his desire for her to go unchecked. He'd known the power of lovemaking; she had no way of knowing it. It was because of him she'd cried off.

Now he would likely never see her again.

That thought made it hard to breathe.

He fought to get it out of his head.

He glanced over at his father. 'Did you know the Duchess called upon Miss Summerfield yesterday?'

His father lowered the *Morning Post*. 'Did she? Glad she is coming around. We all have reservations about your choice of Miss Summerfield...'

By 'all' Ross assumed his father meant the Duchess and his cronies.

'But she is your choice, so we might as well become accustomed to her.'

Well, if that was not damning with faint praise, Ross did not know what was. 'Is that how Grandfather perceived my mother when you became betrothed to her?'

His father placed the newspaper on the table, a faraway look in his eyes. 'No, but, in those days, I would not have cared what he or anyone thought.' He picked up the newspaper again. 'I was a great deal younger than you, though. I must suppose yours is a more mature choice, even if I cannot see it.'

Ross had been living a fantasy, the fantasy that he and Genna could be together without consequences.

To others. To Genna. To him. He'd made everything worse.

'Do you regret marrying my mother?' Ross asked.

'No,' his father said wistfully, but his expression hardened suddenly. 'Yes. Yes, I regret it. If I had not married her, she might still be alive.'

Ross stared at him.

His father lifted his newspaper again and spoke from behind it. 'Your Miss Summerfield is made of sterner stuff, I hope.'

Genna had been honed by living under an umbrella of scandal. She'd forgone all expected roles for herself to embrace one that fed her soul. Yes, that pointed to sterner stuff.

His father put down the *Morning Post* and stood. 'Well, I have much to do today before our meeting—'

His father listed several things he had to do, but, as Ross listened, he realised most were not important. What, really, would be different if his father chose to use that time, say, to visit the Elgin Marbles? Ross suspected the Duchess's duties were like that, as well. Optional.

His father left the room. Ross opened Genna's letter again and reread it.

Chapter Twenty-Four

A week later, Genna sat on the hill overlooking Summerfield House, her wide-brimmed straw hat shading her face from the warm sun. What a contrast to the chill and snow of the last time she'd been in this same place.

She glanced down at her sketchbook. Painting Summerfield House in a snow storm was a challenge in itself, especially on this fine May day with the hills dotted with white cow parsley, blue forget-me-nots, and, like an exotic accent, purple snakes' heads.

Perhaps she should give up painting memories and commit to what was presently before her eyes. Paint what you have, not what is gone.

She turned the page of her sketchbook and started again.

It was time to stop dreaming and to face life as it was. Not as vibrant and exciting as her fanciful drawing of Summerfield House with its impossible sky and grass, but lovely enough nonetheless.

She added the colour she saw before her and a

peace descended upon her for the first time in days. There was beauty enough in the world as it was. Why had she not seen that?

She stepped back from the watercolour she'd produced and decided to add one more thing to finish it, something not really in the picture in front of her.

One tiny memory could not hurt, could it?

She added a grey horse and rider, galloping across the field. The horse's mane and tail were raised in the wind and the man's grey topcoat billowed out behind him, just like it had last December.

She'd been at this vantage point for over two hours and the sun was getting lower on the horizon. It was time to pack up, although returning to Tinmore Hall held no real appeal. She was barely tolerated by the servants there, who seemed to go out of their way to let her know they resented serving her. Perhaps she would write to Lord Penford and ask if she might stay the rest of the time at Summerfield Hall. She'd be content to use a room in the servants' quarters and she'd be happy to perform whatever useful service he might require.

As she rinsed her brushes in her jug of water, something caught her eye. A horse and rider galloping over the same space in the field where she'd painted them. A grey horse. Its rider wore no topcoat, though, and he was too far away to identify.

Could it be? It made no sense that it would be.

Hope could turn fanciful, apparently.

She dried her brushes with a clean cloth and

poured the water on to the ground. Packing up her paints and her rags and placing them in her large satchel, she remembered the last time she'd done this very thing. It had started to snow and he had been watching her.

She heard a rustle behind her and the sound of a horse blowing air from its snout. She spun around.

'I did not nearly run you over this time,' he said.

The breath left her body. 'Ross.'

He smiled at her. 'I came to see if you needed assistance. A creature of habit, I suppose.' He dismounted and his horse, Spirit, contently found some grass to nibble. 'I see you are a creature of habit, as well, drawing the same scene.' He walked over to her easel and examined it. 'You've captured it,' he said. 'With the real colours this time.' He did not mention the horse and rider, though, but he touched them lightly with his gloved finger.

'I still do not understand why you are here,' she said.

A gust of wind blew over the easel. Ross caught the sketchbook before it tumbled to the ground.

He did not answer her. 'Are you returning to Tinmore Hall?' he asked. 'If so, may I convey you there? There is a place I would like to see on the way back. We could talk there.'

She nodded and he helped her pack the rest of her things into her satchel. He helped her on to Spirit and climbed on behind her. She knew where he was heading.

To the folly.

This part of the estate was as overgrown as ever. Apparently Lord Penford's improvements had not yet reached here. The white wood anemone covering the barely visible path reminded her of the snow that dotted this same area last time they rode here. They came to the folly, now canopied with trees bright green with new leaves. It looked even more fanciful than it had in the snow.

Ross slid off Spirit and reached up to help her down, their eyes catching as he held her waist. She climbed the three steps of the folly and sat on the bench, dangling her feet as she had done before.

She looked up at him. 'So?'

He leaned against one of the columns. 'I missed you.'

The words were like needles. She'd missed him, too. 'That cannot be why you are here.'

He paced. 'Not entirely.' He stopped and looked down at her. 'You once were willing to take a very big chance and I would not let you. Are you willing to take another?'

'Am I willing to seduce you again?' She shook her head. 'No.'

'Not that—although I might not object this time, provided you are willing to take this other gamble.' His eyes were warm on her face and filled her with so many memories.

'Just tell me what it is, Ross.'

He sat next to her and took her hands in his. 'Marry me.'

'Marry you?'

'Take a chance on me.' His voice was low and earnest. 'I know you do not believe in love, but I do. I have felt it since I met you and it did not leave even when you did.'

She pulled her hands away. 'No, Ross. I am unsuited. The Duchess was right in that regard. I would make a terrible duchess.'

'You would make an unconventional one,' he corrected. 'And I've no objection to that. I've watched my father plan his day and discuss his activities afterwards. It struck me that most of what he does is unnecessary. I do not have to play politics all the time. I can be a duke differently than the one he is, than who my grandfather was. You can be who you wish to be, as well. God knows I do not wish you to be like the Duchess. You can paint portraits or landscapes or whatever you wish. I have no desire to limit you—'

Think of the good she and Ross could do! Perhaps they could help all the hungry people, all the out-of-work soldiers—

No. Ross, perhaps, but not her. The *ton* would never accept one of the scandalous Summerfields as the Duchess of Kessington.

'I'm happy to use my rank to open doors for you,' he went on. 'And I will not require anything of you that you do not wish to do. All I ask of you is to take the chance to believe me. Believe that I love you and want you with me.'

He loved her now. Would he love her later? Or would he leave her like everyone else she loved?

'Would you answer me, Genna? Say something.' His voice sounded anxious.

She should stay safe and refuse him, but if she refused him now, it would guarantee losing him, would it not?

'I am too scandalous,' she said. Would he resent that some day? 'I have already caused scandal by breaking our engagement. I cried off. Surely the *ton* is abuzz with that news. Think what they will say if we wind up betrothed again.'

He stood and paced again. 'Do I care about that? Not a whit.' He turned and stood before her again. 'Besides, no one knows you cried off besides you and me. In the eyes of the *ton*, we are still betrothed.'

She looked up at him. 'Truly?'

He smiled. 'Truly.'

She glanced away again. 'I'm afraid, Ross. I'm afraid you will stop loving me, that I will do something odd or something scandalous, or something wrong and you will despise me for it.'

'I cannot promise to never be angry,' he said. 'Only to love you and be faithful to you.'

She thought of all the things he'd done for her. He'd known her better than anyone, even her sisters.

'Take a chance on me, Genna,' he murmured.

She rose and faced him. 'There is no one more important to me than you, Ross. No one. You have never failed me. Not once.' She took a deep breath. 'Very well, Ross. I will take a chance on you.'

He opened his arms and she bounded into them, holding him tight.

'I shall try to never fail you.' His lips caressed her ear.

'I love you, Ross.' Now she knew. Her feelings of friendship. The carnal desires. The wish for his well-being and happiness even over hers. What she felt was love.

'And I love you, Genna.' His head dipped down to hers. Before his lips touched hers, he added. 'For always.'

Epilogue

Lincolnshire—Christmas Day 1816

Summerfield House was fragrant with evergreen, with the turkey roasting in the kitchen and the flames licking around the yule log. The host and his guests burst into the hall, back from Christmas church services. Their cheeks were pink, and white flakes of snow on their hats, lashes and shoulders rapidly melted. They'd walked back from the village church, the one Genna and her sisters had attended all through their childhood. It was glorious to sit next to Tess again in the pew reserved for the Summerfields.

Almost all the Summerfields would be together to celebrate Christmas Day. Tess and Marc were staying at Summerfield House with Dell, Ross and Genna. Lorene and Tinmore were expected for dinner. No one was eager for Tinmore's company, but he was the price they would gladly pay to have Lorene with them.

Only Edmund could not be with them, which was a shame, but it was for a very happy reason. His wife, Marc's sister, was about to deliver a child in two or three months.

Other than Edmund being gone, it would almost be like it used to be.

Only better.

Because Genna was married to Ross.

People actually called her the Marchioness of Rossdale. It made her giggle.

In the hall of Summerfield House this Christmas Day, Genna hugged Lord Penford—Dell—the man responsible for this lovely day. 'Have I thanked you for inviting us all for Christmas, Cousin?'

'A dozen or so times, Genna.' Dell extricated himself from her grasp and turned to the others, who were all divesting themselves of topcoats, hats and gloves. 'I've asked the servants to have some wassail for us in the drawing room and something to eat.'

'Excellent!' Marc offered Tess his arm.

Before they had a chance to leave the hall, though, there was a knock on the door. The two footmen were already laden with coats and such, so Ross opened it.

'Lady Tinmore!' he exclaimed.

'Lorene,' she corrected, stepping inside. 'I did not expect to see you attending the door.'

He leaned his head outside before closing it.

'Lorene!' Genna ran over to her and gave her a buss on the cheek. 'Let us get those wet things off you. How did you get so full of snow?'

'I walked,' she said.

'Walked?'

'You are alone?' Ross asked. 'Where is Tinmore?'
Dell helped her off with her cloak.

'Tinmore refused to attend,' she said. 'I do not
think he wished to be among my family. He tried to
keep me from coming. Refused me the carriage, so
I walked.'

'Goodness,' Tess said. 'Was he very angry that
you defied him?'

Lorene shrugged. 'Quite. But I wanted to spend
Christmas with my sisters. So I came anyway.'

'Good for you!' Genna said. 'You stood up to him.'

'We will see how good it is when I return home.'
Lorene laughed.

'I do not know about the rest of you, but I am in
great need of wassail,' Marc said.

'As am I,' Ross agreed.

The Summerfield sisters had a lovely afternoon
together and a lovely dinner with the men most important to them. Afterwards, they all sat around the
yule fire, exchanging gifts, Dell gave Lorene some
piano music. He gave Tess and Genna trinkets from
the house. Tess and Marc gave everyone books. Like
the previous year, Genna gave them paintings she'd
done. She'd painted scenes of Summerfield House,
parts of the house or estate that had been special to
each of her sisters. She gave a miniature of herself
to Ross and one of Tess to Marc. She'd done one of

Lorene for Tinmore, as well, as she had the year before. At least this one would not be thrown on the floor. Dell offered to hang it in Summerfield House instead. For Dell she framed an oil painting of the landscape around Summerfield House, showing the house in the distance.

'It is not a Turner,' Genna said, 'but I have improved since last year.'

'I do not know what the devil a Turner is,' Dell said, 'but this is quite good, I'd say.'

'It is very good,' Ross said. 'I may want to borrow it and get it accepted in the Royal Academy Exhibition.'

'I have a gift,' Tess spoke up excitedly. 'It is mostly a gift for Marc.' He took her hand and her gaze swept all of them. 'I am going to have a baby!'

'Another baby!' Genna cried. 'First Edmund, now you.'

'Lovely news,' Lorene said, rising to give her sister a kiss on the cheek.

Ross took a small wrapped box out of his pocket. 'I thought of giving Genna oil paints and watercolours, but those are her tools. She must always have what she needs. So I got this.'

He handed Genna the box and she opened it. It was a lovely diamond pendant. 'Oh, it is beautiful! I must wear it. Put it on me, Ross.'

He fastened the clasp. His fingers were warm against the tender skin of her neck and, as always, they made her body come alive. But she could wait, because she wanted to spend this precious time with her sisters and these wonderful men who had been so good to them. She could also wait, because she knew Ross would be there for her every night. She'd sleep in his arms tonight in the bed she'd slept in as a young girl vowing to make her own way in the world.

She could have done it, too. She could have made a living with her painting, but she'd found something she wanted even more.

Ross.

As it got later, Tess was yawning and Marc insisted on having her retire for the night. Dell ordered his carriage for Lorene and offered to accompany her back to Tinmore Hall. Genna and Ross were left alone in the drawing room.

'I suppose we ought to go to bed, too.' She fingered her pendant. 'I believe I shall sleep in my diamond. I do not wish to take it off.'

Ross put his arm around her and kissed the back of her neck. 'I am delighted it pleases you.'

She turned around and hugged him close. 'We should go.'

'One moment.' Ross stepped away and took a candle from one of the tables. He went to the hidden door and opened it. 'Let's take the hidden passage.'

She giggled. 'Of course.'

By the light of his sole candle she led him expertly to the hidden stairs and up to her bedchamber.

'The door is here.' She extended her hand to push the door open.

He seized her hand. 'Not so hasty.' He blew out the candle and the only light came through slits where the doors were. 'I want to do something I wished to do a year ago.'

'What did you wish to do?'

'This.' He pulled her into an embrace and placed his lips upon hers.

She could have stayed like this with him for ever.

* * * * *

If you enjoyed this story, make sure to pick up
these other great reads in Diane Gaston's
THE SCANDALOUS SUMMERFIELDS
miniseries
BOUND BY DUTY
BOUND BY ONE SCANDALOUS NIGHT

and don't miss her THE MASQUERADE CLUB
trilogy

A REPUTATION FOR NOTORIETY
A MARRIAGE OF NOTORIETY
A LADY OF NOTORIETY

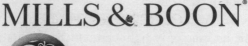

MILLS & BOON®

AWAKEN THE ROMANCE OF THE PAST

A sneak peek at next month's titles...

In stores from 29th December 2016:

- **The Wedding Game** – Christine Merrill
- **Secrets of the Marriage Bed** – Ann Lethbridge
- **Compromising the Duke's Daughter** – Mary Brenda
- **In Bed with the Viking Warrior** – Harper St. Georg
- **Married to Her Enemy** – Jenni Fletcher
- **Baby on the Oregon Trail** – Lynna Banning

Just can't wait?
Buy our books online a month before they hit the shops!
www.millsandboon.co.uk

Also available as eBooks.

MILLS & BOON®

EXCLUSIVE EXTRACT

Wealthy gentleman Benjamin Lovell has his
eyes on the prize of the season. First, though, he
must contend with her fiercely protective sister,
Lady Amelia Summoner!

Read on for a sneak preview of
THE WEDDING GAME
by Christine Merrill

'I merely think that you are ordinary. My sister will
require the extraordinary.'

The last word touched him like a finger drawn down
his spine. His mind argued that she was right. There was
nothing the least bit exceptional about him. If she learned
the truth, she would think him common as muck and
far beneath her notice. But then, he remembered just
how far a man could rise with diligence and the help of
a beautiful woman. He leaned in to her, offering his
most seductive smile. 'Then I shall simply have to be
extraordinary for you.'

For Arabella.

That was what he had meant to say. He was supposed
to be winning the princess, not flirting with the gate-
keeper. But he had looked into those eyes again and had
lost his way.

She showed no sign of noticing his mistake. Or had
her cheeks gone pink? It was not much of a blush, just

the barest hint of colour to imply that she might wish him to be as wonderful as he claimed.

In turn, he felt a growing need to impress her, to see the glow kindle into warm approval. Would her eyes soften when she smiled, or would they sparkle? And what would they do if he kissed her?

He blinked. It did not matter. His words had been a simple mistake and such thoughts were an even bigger one. They had not been discussing her at all. And now her dog was tugging on his trousers again, as if to remind him that he should not, even for an instant, forget the prize he had fixed his sights on from the first.

She shook her head, as if she, too, needed to remember the object of the conversation. 'If you must try to be extraordinary, Mr Lovell, then you have failed already. You either are, or you aren't.'

Don't miss
THE WEDDING GAME
by Christine Merrill

Available January 2017
www.millsandboon.co.uk

MILLS & BOON®

Why shop at millsandboon.co.uk?

Each year, thousands of romance readers find their perfect read at millsandboon.co.uk. That's because we're passionate about bringing you the very best romantic fiction. Here are some of the advantages of shopping at www.millsandboon.co.uk:

* **Get new books first**—you'll be able to buy your favourite books one month before they hit the shops

* **Get exclusive discounts**—you'll also be able to bu our specially created monthly collections, with up to 50% off the RRP

* **Find your favourite authors**—latest news, interviews and new releases for all your favourite authors and series on our website, plus ideas for what to try next

* **Join in**—once you've bought your favourite books, don't forget to register with us to rate, review and join in the discussions

Visit **www.millsandboon.co.uk**
for all this and more today!